"You could have catapulted yourself to the top of the charts. So what happened?"

"I don't want to talk about it."

"Why not? We've talked about me." Kelly watched him. While the light from the dashboard had made Sam handsome, the moonlight brought out something else. "You couldn't handle being in the spotlight?"

"You don't know anything."

No, she didn't, which was her point. "So explain it to me."

He looked down at her, opened and closed his mouth as if trying to figure out the words. Then he leaned in and kissed her soundly.

The pressure of his lips on hers made her heart soar, a feeling she hadn't had in a very long time. She let her eyes close, and she savored the kiss. For now.

Dear Reader,

Life has a way of turning upside down at a moment's notice. Last year for me was one of those years. I got divorced and fought breast cancer, two things that have a way of shedding perspective on what is important. For me, it was surrounding myself with family and friends as well as rediscovering my passion for books. I also discovered that I had reserves of strength and determination just waiting to be tapped.

In *Two-Part Harmony* Kelly Sweet experiences a life turned upside down when her grandmother dies. Losing her biggest fan and believer, she suddenly questions who she is and what she wants. As she struggles to find those answers, she discovers a passion for songwriting and reconnects with her sister. Sam Etchason is on the other end of that self-discovery journey. He's found what he loves to do after he lost everything, but the demons from his past come back to haunt him after Mrs. Sweet's death. He finds a way of mixing his past with his present to find a strength that was waiting inside him all along.

I hope you enjoy reading this book and going on the journey with Kelly and Sam.

Syndi

HEARTWARMING

Two-Part Harmony

—

Syndi Powell

Recycling programs
for this product may
not exist in your area.

ISBN-13: 978-0-373-36737-5

Two-Part Harmony

Copyright © 2015 by Cynthia Powell

Printed in U.S.A.

Syndi Powell started writing stories when she was young and has made it a lifelong pursuit. She's been reading Harlequin romance novels since she was in her teens and is thrilled to be on the Harlequin team. She loves to connect with readers on Twitter, @syndipowell, or on her Facebook author page, facebook.com/syndipowellauthor.

Books by Syndi Powell

Harlequin Heartwarming

The Reluctant Bachelor
Risk of Falling

Dedicated to my sisters and best friends,
Susan Skrzypczak and Sherrie Hartman.
I remember entire days playing with Barbies,
acting out music videos and movies when we were
younger. We even created an imaginary brother
and made Dad stop the car to let him in. As the
oldest sister, I used to think I was the boss, but
you were quick to remind me I'm not. Much like my
characters remind me that while I think I may be in
control, they are the ones who direct the story.
I love you both.

CHAPTER ONE

"SHE'S GONE, KEL."

Despite being in Nashville and more than five hundred miles from Michigan, Kelly Sweet could hear the sound of despair in her sister Megan's voice. She reached behind her neck and pulled her long blond hair forward, fighting the panic that started to gather there. "What do you mean she's gone? Who's gone?" She paused, fear now starting to spread from her belly to her chest. "Grammy?"

"This is her late morning at the bakery, but she didn't show up at all. I got worried, so I drove home and I found her still sleeping in her bedroom." Her sister's voice broke on the other end of the line. "But she wasn't sleeping. She's gone."

Kelly sunk to the edge of her bed, shoving a stack of pillows to the floor. Oh, Grammy. No, no, no. Kelly wiped at the tears streaming down her face. The woman who had raised her and her sister. Her biggest supporter and fan. Her rock, gone. It wasn't possible. Couldn't be. She'd lost her grandfather and dad, so now she had to lose her dad's mother, too? How was that fair? She rubbed the center of her chest, hoping to ease the ache that had lodged there. "How?"

"Doctor thinks it was an aneurysm." Megs sobbed for a moment. "She said it was probably quick and that she didn't suffer."

"It's how she wanted to go." Grammy had always said she'd wanted to go to bed one night and not wake up in the morning. Yet that thought brought little comfort now. She was gone, and Kelly hadn't had the chance to say goodbye. To tell Grammy one more time that she loved her, that she wouldn't be the woman she was today without her support and encouragement all these years. She put her free hand to her belly and rocked back and forth on the bed.

"I just can't believe she's gone."

Her sister continued to sob on the other end while Kelly tried to think of something comforting to say. But what could she offer that didn't sound trite even to her own ears? That Grammy was better off? That she wouldn't suffer anymore? Things like that didn't matter when Kelly would trade everything she had for just one more minute, one second with her grandmother. "It's going to be okay."

Megs sniffed. "I'm meeting with the funeral home director tomorrow. The entire town is going to show up, you know. They all love, loved Grammy."

Right. Planning the viewing and the funeral would give her something to do amid the chaos that was her heart. Planning would give her focus, a purpose. Decision made, she said, "I'm on my way."

"What about your job?"

From which she'd been fired and replaced already. Not that she'd told her sister about it for fear that she'd look like a loser. It was temporary. It always was until she found another waitress job to pay the bills while she auditioned and waited for her big break as a country singer. So instead, she evaded. "I've got vacation time." Like for the rest of her life if she didn't find another singing gig soon. She shook her head as if to shake that idea free from her brain. She would get another one. She always did, if at least for the short term.

There was a pause on the other end. "Thanks. I don't think I could do this on my own."

Sure she could. Her sister Megs was the strongest person Kelly knew. While she herself had broken down after their father died when she turned fifteen and their mother abandoned them shortly after, her sister had held her hand and offered tissues. She acted as if she was the older sister, rather than the other way around. Nope. Megs could do this with her eyes closed. "I'm coming home." Home, although it wasn't home anymore.

"I can pick you up at the airport."

"No." Kelly winced at the harshness, the desperation in her voice. She couldn't even afford to log on to the airline's website. "It's too expensive. I'll drive up." She glanced at her digital alarm clock. "I should be there before midnight if I can get packed and leave in the next half hour."

There was silence on the other end. Kelly checked to make sure her cell phone hadn't lost the signal. Then Megs sighed. "Let's meet at the bakery. I've got a ton of things to take care of in the meantime."

Kelly nodded, knowing her sister couldn't see her. "I'll see you soon." She paused, letting the words rattle in her mind before she said them aloud. "I love you, Megs."

More silence. "Love you, too. Drive safe, huh?"

Kelly hung up the cell phone and glanced around her studio apartment. She had stashed her battered lavender suitcase underneath the bed. After her last gig as a touring backup singer she'd promised herself she wouldn't bring it back out until she was leaving for her own headline concert.

But death had a way of changing things.

She opened the suitcase then walked to the clothes rack she'd bought for hanging up dresses and tops. Thank goodness she didn't have many things to pack. A benefit of being a twenty-nine-year-old struggling country singer meant that any money she did have went for necessities: rent, utilities and food. Gas for her truck, when she could afford it.

She thought of the lone five dollar bill in her wallet and sighed. Walking to the freezer in the kitchen, she brought out a chunk of ice and started to melt it under hot water in the sink. Time to get that credit card ready to use.

SAM ETCHASON PARKED his truck across
from the Sweetheart bakery. He got out and
slammed the door behind him, looked both
ways, then raced across Lincoln Street. The
bakery's unlocked door surprised him, but
made it easier for him to enter and find Megs.
She was sitting in the darkened front room at
one of the tables and was staring at nothing,
her chin resting on her fist.

He went over to where she sat and took
the chair across from her. He slipped her free
hand into his. "I'm so sorry, Megs."

She looked up at him as if confused to see
him there. "Sam, thanks for coming. They
won't fire you, will they?"

"Don't worry about it. I'm my own boss."
He noted how empty the place was, and yet
pastries already filled the display cases. He
didn't hear any of the employees moving in
the kitchen. "Did you send Tom and Gina
home? You shouldn't be alone right now."

"My sister Kelly's on her way. I'll be fine."

She didn't look fine. Her skin so pale. The
red-rimmed eyes and swollen nose. He put
his hand on her shoulder. "You don't have to
open today."

"It's what Grammy would have done. I

managed to get some of the baking finished, but I can't seem to find the strength to officially open today." She stared at the silent room then looked back at him. Her face crumpled. "What am I going to do without her?"

He rose from the chair and came to put his arms around her, pulling her in tight. "She was a fine woman. My first friend here in Lake Mildred when I arrived two years ago, you know?" He drew back and studied her watery eyes, wishing he could erase the pain there. "You're just like her. Compassionate and kind. And you have the need to feed people's souls as well as their bodies."

She gave him a soft smile. "You were a good friend to Grammy, Sam. And to me."

"Well, I think of you like my little sister." He took his seat, smiling. "People will understand if you don't open today, Megs. Why don't you take the day off?"

"I need to be here. In her bakery." Megs stood and straightened her pink apron with the bakery's logo printed on the bib. "I wanted to be alone, so I sent the employees home. I couldn't deal with all their questions. What'll happen now? What are you going to change?

Are we closing for good?" She gave a small shudder. "I hope not. This is all I know."

He knew there was time for her to deal with those questions later. Sam held up his cell phone. "If you need me, call."

She hugged him once more. "Thank you, Sam."

THE HIGHWAY FELT lonelier as she drove north on I-75 toward Michigan. It was giving her too much time to think, to grieve, to regret. Adelaide Sweet had been a formidable force in Kelly's life. Her biggest cheerleader and fan. No one could sing as well as Kelly according to Grammy. Never had, never will, she used to say.

Kelly had promised Grammy that she'd pursue her music career until she turned thirty. If Kelly didn't have her first recording contract by that point, she'd return to Lake Mildred and start a new path. Only three months until her birthday and deadline, and she was returning, anyway.

For now, or for good? Kelly wasn't sure. If it was up to her, this would be only temporary. She'd go home to Lake Mildred and bury her grandmother. Grieve. And then figure out what to do for the next three months until she blew out those candles.

The town sign welcomed her back before she reached Main Street. No parades or paparazzi. No adoring fans. Just the same sign that had greeted everyone since the town had been established in 1892. Or so it read.

She ignored the angry churning of her belly as she followed the curve into the downtown district. The neon sign for Rick's Diner didn't glow, nor did the department store display windows of Roxy's. The other businesses were shut, and probably had been since nine o'clock that evening. Kelly glanced at the clock on her dashboard. Not even midnight and the small northern Michigan town had rolled up its sidewalks already. Not like Nashville.

She shook her head and turned right at the next street then parked in the lot behind the Sweetheart bakery. Her sister's car was there, so Megs had to be inside. She got out of her car, walked to the back door of the bakery and tried the door handle. Unlocked, of course.

Okay, so this was a small town, but safety was safety even here.

The aromas of yeast and sugar greeted

Kelly as she pushed open the door and stepped inside. "Megan?" she called.

No answer but the soft sounds of singing from the kitchen beyond.

Kelly took a deep breath to steady her nerves and locked the back door. Her sister might be naïve about the people in this town, but experience had taught Kelly that she couldn't trust anyone.

She found her sister standing at the marble work table, kneading dough with her eyes closed and singing along with whatever song was on her iPod. She looked…peaceful. Content. Like she knew she was right where she was supposed to be. Kelly ignored the sour feeling again in her belly and put her hand on Megs's shoulder. "Hey."

Her sister's eyes flew open, and she jumped back. "Oh. Hi." She rushed forward and hugged Kelly. "You made it okay."

"Yep." When Megs released her, Kelly wiped at the flour that now dusted the front of her jean jacket. "I drove straight here after you called." Her eyes got hot and wet as she focused on her sister. "Oh, Megs. Grammy's gone."

Megs nodded, her lip quivering. "It was

quick. She complained last night that she had a headache before she went to bed. I gave her a couple of aspirin, hoping it would help. She never woke up." Her sister wiped her, eyes with the corner of her pink apron. "She looked so peaceful. Like she was ready, you know?"

"At least she's with Grandpa and Dad now." Kelly glanced around the kitchen and noticed the pans of cookies, pastries and several loaves of bread. She frowned at the bounty of sweet treats. "You're not planning on opening the Sweetheart tomorrow, are you?"

Megs looked surprised to see all the baked goods there. "Huh. Guess I got carried away. This is all for the funeral home. I figured people might want a little something sweet."

Kelly guessed with all the food her sister had baked, people could stuff themselves on dough and sugar for the next week and there would still be leftovers. She pointed toward the lump of kneaded dough on the table top. "More bread?"

Her sister patted the doughy mound. "This? It's a new recipe I'm trying." She nudged an old ledger book towards Kelly. "Grammy gave this to me about a week ago. She said they're family recipes that were handed down to Pop Pop from his mother and generations before him. Grammy called them special. That I'd know when I was ready for them." Her sister's eyes were watery as she opened the ledger and located a recipe near the front. "See? Her handwriting says this bread is good to comfort those in their grief." She shrugged. "I thought, why not? There's going to be a lot of people who'll need comforting the next few days."

Grammy had been a cornerstone of the community for so long that Kelly couldn't imagine the hole she was going to leave in everyone's lives. She'd already left one in her own chest, so why not the entire town's? Kelly paused. "Did you call everybody? Do you need me to do anything?"

"Everybody in town knew as soon as the ambulance arrived at the house. The small town grapevine still works." Megs gave a deep sigh. "And I called Aunt Lillian's daughters to let them know, too. Grammy didn't have much family left. We're what's left of her blood."

Kelly shuddered. Grammy's sister Lillian had two daughters who had terrorized their dad when he'd been young, if you could believe the stories he'd shared. Being the only child of two bakers, Dad had struggled with a weight issue most of his life. And Lillian's daughters had never let him forget it. Granted, they were forty years older now. And they had families of their own.

Megs rubbed the back of her neck. "Do you mind if we take a little break? I need to let the dough rise. I can go over with you what we still have to do for the funeral."

The sisters settled at one of the tables in the front room with a legal-sized notepad and one of the pink pens that advertised the bakery and its phone number. Kelly drew a couple of scribbles then looked up at her sister. "What about Mom? Did you call her yet?"

"Thought I'd leave that up to you. I can't deal with her right now. Besides, I don't know where she is at the moment."

Kelly checked the time. "Last I talked to her, Florida. So it's probably too late to phone tonight. I'll call her tomorrow. Think she'll come up for the funeral?" Megs gave her a nasty look. "You're probably right. They didn't exactly see eye to eye on things."

"Except about Daddy. They both thought

he hung the moon." Megs stared at her dough. "I keep picturing him and Pop Pop waiting for Grammy when she arrived at the pearly gates. Welcoming her home."

Kelly cleared her throat as tears threatened to clog it, making it difficult to take breathe. "Yeah. Me, too." She wrote funeral plans at the top of the notepad and underlined the words. "Did Grammy ever talk about what she wanted at her funeral?"

"You know she didn't like talking about things like that."

Grammy hadn't liked talking about anything uncomfortable or unpleasant. Death and what to do for her funeral topped that list. "I thought that maybe in her later years that—"

"Don't." Megs claimed the notepad from Kelly. "You don't get to pretend that you know what she'd been thinking or feeling these days. You weren't here."

Ouch, that hurt a little. But she swallowed the bitterness and nodded. "I know. But I'm here now." She held out the pen to her sister.

"A bit too late, don't you think?" Her sister snatched the pen and wrote down a few lines, but crossed them out. And then burst into tears.

Kelly rose from her chair and gently put one arm around her sister's shoulders. "It's okay, Megs. Shhh, it's going to be all right." With her free hand, she stroked her blond hair, so much like her own, if shorter. They were alike even if they didn't always admit it. "We can do this together."

Megs buried her face, crying into Kelly's jacket sleeve. "I can't believe she's gone. I miss her so much already."

Kelly knelt and pulled her sister into her arms. Maybe Megs wasn't as strong as she'd thought. She put her cheek on her sister's head and cooed softly to her. "I know. I miss her, too."

They clung to each other until the sobs subsided. Megs got up and retrieved a box of tissues. She held out the box, and Kelly took one and wiped at her eyes, then Megs returned to her seat and clutched several tissues in case she should need one again.

"Since you knew her best, I'll go along with whatever you want," Kelly told her.

Megs smiled. "She'd want you to sing, you know? Her favorite song."

"Of course."

Her sister wrote that down on the notepad.

"I know people we can ask to be her pallbearers. Rick, Sam, some of our other regulars." She wrote their names then looked up at Kelly. "Are you hungry? I didn't think to ask when you got here."

"I guess."

Megs left her alone for a minute and then came back with a mini chocolate cake as well as two forks. "Grammy always said food was medicine to cure a hurting heart. This is one of her favorite recipes from the ledger."

With an endorsement like that, Kelly couldn't refuse. The dessert looked fabulous. Dark chocolate enrobed the tiny cake, and when she took a forkful, it revealed four layers of chocolate cake divided by three layers of pink raspberry mousse. Kelly placed the fork in her mouth and closed her eyes at the taste. It was rich, smooth and enticing. She chewed and let the flavors play on her tongue. The sweet chocolate, the tangy raspberry. "Oh my. Now that's a cake."

Megs watched her, eyebrows raised. "That good?"

"It's better than good. What do you call it?"

"Grammy called it True Love's Torte."

Kelly took another bite. "Always the romantic. Probably believed you'd meet your soul mate within a day of eating it, huh?"

Megs nodded, and they both smiled faintly. The idea of Kelly meeting her soul mate in Lake Mildred was as likely as meeting the person who would make her dreams of a singing contract come true. She shook her head and took another bite of the cake. But it would be just like Grammy to make both of those things happen even from the grave.

They silently ate the cake, remembering the woman they both loved.

CHAPTER TWO

KELLY OPENED ONE eye then another and peered around the bedroom. Purple exploded from every corner, and it took her a moment to realize where she was.

She turned over and looked into the face of Mr. Wiggles, a worn teddy bear who had been her first friend when she was a child. Had she gone back in time? She sat up and fingered the crocheted afghan that lay over her, a gift from Grammy after her father had died. Yes, she'd been transported to being fifteen once again. She snuggled under the covers and brought the edge of the blanket to her nose and sniffed. It smelled faintly of, well, of Grammy.

She wiped her eyes with the afghan. She had to get through the day somehow. Had to be strong. Had to keep moving forward, not just for herself and Megs, but for Grammy.

She could almost hear her grandmother whispering, "You can do it."

If only Grammy really knew.

Her cell phone on the nightstand beside the bed started to buzz and sing a country song. She stopped the alarm, then sat up and swung her legs off the bed. She thought about finding her old bathrobe, to cover up the nightshirt she'd put on before climbing into bed, but figured there wasn't anything she had that her sister hadn't seen before. She opened her old bedroom door and sniffed appreciatively at the scent of coffee climbing up the stairs.

As Kelly stepped into the kitchen, the coffeemaker gurgled its last gasps. She took a deep breath and walked to it, but froze when a man beat her to it. She jumped back and grabbed the toaster to defend herself if she had to. He was taller than her, but then it didn't take much to tower over her own five foot two. And he was built, as in construction-guy built. The back of his flannel shirt strained across his shoulders. He turned and gave her a nod, then poured himself a mug of coffee. "Good morning."

"That's all you have to say after breaking into my grandmother's home?" She raised the toaster higher, ready to take whatever action would be necessary to defend herself and her sister. It might have helped if she'd unplugged it first, so she reached over to do so. She'd taken a self-defense class years ago, and the advice that had been drilled into her repeated in her mind now, just in case she needed it.

He raised one dark eyebrow over his gray green eyes. "I didn't break in."

"Are you saying you used a key?" The man was delusional. Hot, yes, but definitely certifiable.

"Yes. Mine." He dug into his front jean pocket and brought out a silver key ring with a familiar gold key hanging from it.

Grammy was giving out keys to strange men? She'd obviously missed a lot being gone all this time. He leaned on the counter, watching her as she put the toaster down. But she kept her eye on him as she poured her own cup of coffee and added cream and sugar to it. He grimaced. She looked down at the creamy color. "Problem?"

"Good coffee doesn't need all that stuff. And this is good." He saluted her with his mug.

She rolled her eyes and sipped from her

mug. Steps behind her alerted her that Megs had joined them. "Oh, good. You've met," her sister said.

She glared at Megs. "Who is this guy? He let himself in with his own key."

Megs put a tea bag into a mug and poured water into it before putting it in the microwave and pressing a few buttons. "Grammy told you she was having work done on the house. This is Sam."

The way Grammy had spoken about him, she'd think he walked on water as he fixed things at the bakery and at home and had maybe even repaired her grieving heart. She'd mentioned that this Sam was good looking, but Kelly had expected older. Much older. Like Grammy's age. And her grandmother hadn't mentioned the muscles. Or those gray-green eyes that reminded her of a river with sun sparkling off the surface. Or the smile that sent shivers down her spine. "Sam the Saint? You don't look like you're in your seventies."

He smiled at that. "Maybe because I'm not."

"Grammy said she had a new man in her life. But I didn't expect someone so…" Gorgeous. Mouth-watering. "Young." She put her mug down. "You're not what I expected."

"I could say the same about you, Kelly." He finished his coffee then placed his mug in the kitchen sink and ran water in the cup. "It's been fun, but I've got to get to the job site early." He nodded at Kelly, then pointed at Megs. "You'll let me know about tomorrow?"

Megs agreed and retrieved her steaming mug from the microwave. "I'll know more tonight. Dinner at Rick's tonight, say seven?"

"You bet." He winked at Kelly. "Nice to meet you."

Of all the nerve. And if he didn't make her stomach flop, she would swear she was coming down with the flu. She turned to her sister. "Does he come over every morning?" She narrowed her eyes. "Is there something going on with you two?"

Megs shook her head and walked to the refrigerator. She pulled out a carton of eggs and a tub of butter. "Sam is just a friend. And he lives in the apartment above the garage. When he runs out of coffee there, he comes over and uses Grammy's. It's no big deal."

Kelly took a seat and watched her sister crack eggs into a bowl and whisk them together. Next, her sister got out a frying pan and melted butter in it over the stove before pouring the beaten eggs into it. She retrieved a loaf of homemade sourdough and cut thick slices, then dropped them in the toaster, which she plugged back in.

"Seems like a big deal if you and Grammy couldn't tell me that he was living here," Kelly said. Her mouth watered as the eggs cooked golden yellow. "By the way Grammy talked about him, I thought she was half in love with him."

"Maybe she was. In a grandmotherly way." Megs took down two plates and brought them to the stove. "Sam is a great guy. Not that you gave him much of a chance this morning."

"He startled me."

"Mm-hmm." Megs placed a piece of toast on the plate then spooned the cooked eggs over it. She put another pat of butter on top, then handed it to Kelly. "Can we discuss this while we eat? I'm starving."

Kelly normally didn't eat breakfast but her stomach growled loudly at the sight of the eggs and toast. "Grammy made this for us the first night after Mom left."

"I know." Megs took a seat on a stool at the kitchen island. "Seemed appropriate."

Kelly took a seat across from her. She picked up her fork then laid it back down next to her plate. "I don't know what to do without her."

"I don't, either."

SAM STEERED HIS pickup truck into the driveway and followed the curve until he had almost reached the lake. His potential client hadn't arrived yet, so he got out of the vehicle and walked to the truck bed and got out his red tool box.

He took a deep breath, reveling in the scent of pine and water. When he'd first arrived in Lake Mildred, he hadn't expected to find this sense of home. He assumed he'd take on a few well-paying jobs then move on to the next town, always searching for something.

Home.

And he thought he might be able to find it here in this sleepy lakeside town. A big part of that had been Adelaide Sweet, and he swallowed at the lump in his throat the reminder brought. *Come on, Addy. What am I going to do?*

Memories of Addy brought the image to mind of meeting her granddaughter that morning. Her worn nightshirt with a cat on it, plus the long blond hair in braids and huge blue eyes gave her an air of innocence. The way she threatened him with a toaster only added to his impression of her. Petite and cute, she was also strong, independent. Definitely a young woman raised by Addy. But something remained, which he couldn't put his finger on, that made him want to get to know her a lot better.

The appearance of a silver pickup truck in the driveway broke Sam from his thoughts. The truck pulled up and parked behind his. He shielded his eyes then waved at Rick Allyn, the mayor and hopefully his next, future client. Rick hopped out of the pickup and approached him. "I got stuck in a budget meeting." He made a face, and Sam squelched a grin.

The men shook hands then strolled down to the dock. Sam sighed and put his tool box down. He tugged the small notebook out of his back pocket and nub of a pencil. "I had a look at the supports, and they're still good.

It seems to be the boards on top here that are causing problems."

Sam crouched and peered at the rotting boards of the dock. He could remove the old ones, replace them with solid planks and then treat them so that they'd last for years. He mentally calculated the cost of the materials. He stood and made some notes on his pad. "It'll take me about a week to do the work, and I can get started on the job in a day or two."

Rick nodded. "And the price?"

Sam gave him a figure to which the mayor whistled.

"More than I'd hoped, but still it's half of what another company quoted me."

So he had competition for the job? Not that he expected less from a man who ran the town with a fair, but frugal hand, despite his dislike of budget meetings. Sam shifted his weight on his feet. "I can guarantee my work. I'll give you references if you need them."

Rick held up one hand. "You forget that I've seen your work at the Stones' house. I'm convinced. You've got the job."

They shook hands to seal the deal. Sam made more notes. "I'll get the contract and itemized materials list to you by the end of the day." He looked up at Rick as they walked back to their trucks. "Megs mentioned that you and I are pallbearers tomorrow for the funeral."

"It's my honor." Rick stopped at his truck and rested a foot on the back tire. "It's a real blow to the town. Mrs. Sweet was the cornerstone to a lot of charities besides providing all the pastries and desserts for town celebrations. She'll be missed."

Sam nodded, but couldn't say anything. He'd breezed into town over two years ago, looking for a job and a place to stay. Mrs. Sweet had opened up her home to him as well as introduced him to people who had brought work his way. She had encouraged him to find his dreams when he'd been ready to walk away.

She'd given him the kick in the behind when he'd needed it, too. Said the words he hadn't wanted to hear, but ought to understand.

What was he going to do now? He cleared his throat. "An amazing woman. One of a kind."

"Megs said they're meeting with Gene this morning at the funeral home."

He knew they would make the right decisions for Addy. She'd had a lot of love and pride in her granddaughters, but he'd seen little of Kelly to know if Addy's belief in her granddaughter had been warranted. She'd spoken often of her amazing voice and how she was trying to pursue her singing career in Nashville. He knew firsthand what that could cost. He hoped she'd returned home before it had changed her.

The fear in her eyes this morning when she'd discovered him in the kitchen told him that it might be too late. He realized that was the difference between the sisters. Megs trusted everyone while it seemed her sister was wary of them.

Sam took a deep breath. "I need to get moving to the next job." He held out a hand to Rick who shook it. "I look forward to restoring the dock."

"Not as much as I do. Maybe my wife will finally scratch it off my honey do list."

Although it sounded like a complaint, the twinkle in the mayor's eye told Sam that he didn't seem to mind. In fact, that he enjoyed it.

Sam took his leave. He wouldn't mind having a woman in his life that put that kind of twinkle in his own eye. But he needed to focus on work instead of the absence of one woman and the appearance of another.

"JUST COME WITH US. It's only dinner."

Megs tried to hand Kelly her jean jacket, but she refused. "I'm not hungry. I'll stay here."

Megs folded her arms across her chest. "And mope and feel sorry for yourself? You've done enough of that already today."

That wasn't what Kelly had been feeling. She had missed her grandmother so much that the ache in her belly didn't make food appealing. "I'll be spending enough time with people over the next few days. I want to be left alone for a while. Is that too much to ask?"

Her sister opened her mouth, as if to say something, but shook her head. She tossed Kelly her jacket. "Fine. I'll be back later. Call me if you want me to bring anything home for you."

"I'll be all right." Kelly walked Megs to the door and glanced at Sam who sat in his pickup, staring at them. "You're sure you two aren't an item? He seems awfully attentive and concerned about you."

"It's called friendship." Megs walked out the front door and down the steps to the truck and got in on the passenger side. Kelly held up her hand before Sam put the truck in reverse and backed out of the driveway.

Kelly shut the front door and leaned against it. Closing her eyes she listened to the night sounds of the house. The tick of the grandfather clock in the living room. The hum of the refrigerator in the kitchen. She lingered for another moment, and trailed her fingers along the smooth wooden banister as she stole up the stairs to her old bedroom. Once there, she flopped on the bed and stared up at the ceiling.

Grammy. The deep blue eyes that twinkled as she spoke of her life with Pop Pop. The white hair that she kept long and pinned on top of her head. Her tiny body wearing T-shirts and jeans underneath a pink apron with ruffles and pockets. She had often smelled of honey.

Grammy had grown up in Lake Mildred, and her own father had built the house she'd lived in until now. She'd married Pop Pop right before he shipped out to the Pacific during World War II and waited for him to return. Once Pop Pop was stateside, they tried for over a decade to have a child. She'd told the girls that their father had been a miracle baby because Grammy had given up hoping when she found herself finally pregnant. As much as she loved the bakery, she loved her son more and doted on him. When he died, a light dimmed inside Grammy, though she kept telling the girls that she was fine. Kelly remembered the look on her face each holiday as she stared at the empty chairs around the table.

And now hers would stay vacant, too.

Kelly flipped over onto her belly and sank her head into the pillow. She gave in to the despair she'd felt all day and sobbed.

Then there was a hand on her back. She shrieked as she found Sam sitting on the bed next to her. His voice was low, meant to be comforting. "I don't mean to keep startling you."

She propped herself up on one elbow and observed him. He looked as if he'd showered and changed since their meeting that morning. She could smell the faint but enticing traces of soap coming from him. "What do you want?"

His serious green eyes bore into hers. "You need to come to dinner with us."

She shook her head. Didn't they get the hint? "No. I already told Megs that I'm not hungry."

"It's not about the food. It's not even about you, although I get it that you're hurting, too. It's about being there for your sister, who won't insist that you come with us, even though it's killing her not to." He eyed her from head to toe. "She needs you right now. And if that means you paste a smile on that pretty face and pretend that going out to dinner with us is the best idea you've ever heard, then you do it."

He thought she was pretty? She squelched the pride that compliment rose in her chest. "You're wrong. She doesn't need me."

He shook his head. "The woman she loved like a mother is gone, and no one can ever replace her. But you're a close second. So go wash your face and meet me downstairs in five minutes. And do it because you love your sister enough to be there for her. Understood?"

He made it sound so easy. But what did he know about losing the woman who had meant the world to her? He had been friends with her grandmother, sure. But Grammy had been her everything.

Just like she'd been for Megs.

Her refusal to go to dinner started to sound hollow in her ears now. Maybe she should go. Her sister appeared to be doing well, but what if she was as messed up as she was? What if the carefully constructed outside only covered up the grief and turmoil on the inside? She glared at him. "I may not have been around lately, but I love Megs."

He picked up her jacket from where she'd hung it over the back of her desk chair. "Prove it by coming to dinner with us."

She looked at the jacket, then snatched it from his hand. She stood. She thrust her arms into the sleeves. "Why does it matter to you, anyway?"

"Because I loved Addy, too. And tonight I want to be around people who loved her as much, if not more. I want to hear stories about her and remember the good times. I didn't get enough of them, and I want to hear your memories." Sam took a deep breath as she buttoned the jacket, then grabbed her purse. "Thank you."

"I'm coming to dinner for Megs, not you." She pulled her hair out from underneath the jacket.

"At least you're coming."

She followed him down the stairs and to the pickup truck. Megs sat staring out the passenger side window. When she saw Kelly joining them, she scooted towards the center of the seat. "I didn't think you were coming."

Kelly glanced at Sam's figure as he walked around the truck and got in on the driver's side. "Changed my mind."

She kept her gaze fixed on the passing landscape as they drove the five miles from the countryside into town. Sam parallel parked the truck on Main Street, then hurried around to give a hand down to both of them. They strode down the street to the diner and entered. The overwhelming scent of grease in the air made Kelly's knees buckle and wish she had more of an appetite. Instead, she followed Sam and Megs to a back booth and squeezed in next to her sister.

A waitress brought them menus, but Sam and Megs laid theirs aside. Obviously they knew what they wanted while she had no clue. A salad? Probably should, but it didn't appeal to her. A burger? She remembered that Rick made the best, but she wrinkled her nose at the idea. She thought of Grammy and the dinners that she used to make for them when she was growing up. Grammy's roast chicken with stuffing had been her favorite hands down, although her meatloaf was a close second. And real mashed potatoes.

She sighed. Comfort food wouldn't heal her hurting heart, but it wouldn't harm it, either. She skipped to the dinner section and settled on her choice. Meals ordered, Kelly sipped her ice water and tried to think of something to talk about. She glanced at Sam briefly, then settled her gaze on Megs. "Is anyone else feeling lost, or is it just me?"

Megs tried to smile. "I was thinking the same thing. We brought Grammy here every Tuesday night for their all you can eat spaghetti and meatball special." Megs's eyes misted. "Doesn't seem right that she's not here to tell the waitress to keep those plates coming."

Sam chuckled. "Or that the shaker of parmesan cheese better be on the table before the spaghetti arrived. And the garlic bread—"

"Better be fresh." Megs nodded and smiled. Her voice quavered. "She's really missing out."

Kelly tried to smile in return, but she felt at a distance from the conversation, like usual. With Grammy and Megs, she'd felt as if she was intruding on their cozy group of two. They were more alike than Kelly was and her grandmother, and she'd felt like an outsider watching a family, rather than being a part of it. And now Sam and Megs had a routine they followed, and she felt as if she had intruded on that, as well. She played with the wrapper from her straw, and wished Grammy could be here, too.

Sam cleared his throat and glanced her way. "I wish you could have been a part of it. We had some good times."

Right. Times she hadn't been a part of. Could never be now. Instead, she'd chosen to pursue a dream.

She'd left for Nashville the morning after her twenty-first birthday with a kiss from Grammy, five hundred bucks in her pocket and a promise that she'd make it big. But after years of rejection, she'd wanted to give up. So many times, she'd been close to packing her bags and heading home. But a call from Grammy would convince her to stay. Her grandmother believed in her, in her talent. And she hadn't wanted Kelly to give up on it. She shrugged. "I have my own memories of Grammy."

She sat back as the waitress set down their salads and the parmesan cheese. Megs picked up the cheese and stared at it. Her sister looked across the table at Sam and they shared a smile, then she bowed her head and cried. Kelly put her arm around her sister and rubbed her shoulder. Maybe coming here hadn't been a great idea.

Megs leaned into Kelly and took several breaths. "Thank you for coming out with us. I don't think I can get through these next few days without you."

Again, Kelly was struck with how little her sister could see her own strength. "It's me who can't get through this alone. I'm sorry I didn't come home sooner."

"Grammy would have packed your bags and sent you back to Nashville if you'd tried."

Megs sat up straighter and wiped her eyes with her paper napkin. "She really believed in you. She was determined that you make it as a singer."

"I was just as determined." Kelly glanced over at Sam as she picked up her fork. "And I guess I should thank you for insisting that I come tonight."

Sam didn't say anything as he speared a piece of tomato. Instead, he chewed and gave her a wink.

She attributed the flip in her belly to the food, rather than the man sitting across from her.

SAM STOOD AT the diner's cash register and paid for their meals, then turned and watched the sisters as they gathered their jackets and purses. He thanked their waitress and gave her a tip, then walked to the front of the diner and waited. Megs reached him first, but Kelly lingered behind. Glancing around the diner, seeing something in her mind that he could tell was related to Addy. The sadness in her eyes threatened to spill over on to her cheeks, so he approached her and put his arm around her shoulder. "It's okay, kid."

She looked up at him and sniffed, but nodded. On Main Street she glanced over at the department store. "What time does Roxy's close? I need a couple of things."

Why did any emotion bring out the shopping urge in some women? He gave a nod. "We have about a half hour."

Megs wrinkled her nose. "You two go ahead. I'll wait in the truck."

Sam used the key fob to unlock the door. He watched as Megs walked to the truck, but followed Kelly into the store. Bright lights and the scent of heavy perfume assaulted him. Kelly headed off to the right, and he trailed behind her as she approached the women's section. She frowned. "It's years since I've been in here. I have no idea where anything is anymore."

Not that he frequented Roxy's that often, but he knew the basic layout. "What are you looking for?"

"Grammy always said a lady wears panty hose with a dress, and I don't have any."

"Ah." He had no clue where they were kept since he didn't shop in that section. "We could ask someone."

Kelly shook her head and moved on. He

stayed behind her, noting how she kept her head up and her back straight. Addy had trained her well as she appeared confident and strong. Only he'd guess the inner mayhem she felt.

She found the right section, and he stood in the aisle as she flipped through her different choices. She peered up at him once. "I'm sorry that I almost attacked you with a toaster this morning."

"I think I would have been able to defend myself."

She looked him over slowly, and for a moment he hoped that she approved. "I'm sure you would have." She returned her gaze to the panty hose and pulled one out a package, turning it over to scan the back. "Got it." She pulled out a second to go with the first, then brushed past him toward the cash registers.

Again, he followed her, noting how petite and fit she was. He could probably lift her without a struggle. Not that he had plans to do so, but still he wondered. What would she feel like in his arms?

The cashier rang up Kelly's purchase as she pawed through her purse. When the cashier told her the total, Kelly sighed. "Never mind. I left my wallet on my dresser back at Grammy's."

Sam pulled out the wallet from his back pocket. "I got this."

"I can't ask you to do that. You already paid for dinner."

He handed the cashier a twenty-dollar bill. "It's no big deal. You can pay me back at the house."

"That's not the point. I don't need you to save me."

He put the change in his wallet then handed the plastic bag with the panty hose inside to Kelly. "Just say thank you, and we can go."

She thrust the bag back at him. "I pay my own way."

"Don't make a big deal out of this. You'll pay me back." Didn't she have anyone in her life down in Nashville who looked out for her? By her reaction, he doubted it. And that was a shame because Kelly looked like a woman he wanted to help and protect. The fact that he wanted to volunteer for the position made him pause. Something to think about later. To lighten the mood, he leaned down and nudged her shoulder with his. "Besides, I know where you live, remember."

She snatched the bag from his hand, but stood still, staring at him. He considered that he might have to pick her up after all and carry her out to the truck if she didn't start moving soon. She swallowed several times, and then gave a nod. "Thank you."

"You're welcome."

She turned on her heel and started walking quickly to the front of the store. He had to lengthen his stride to keep up with her.

CHAPTER THREE

PEOPLE EVERYWHERE. No matter which direction Kelly faced at the funeral home visitation the following evening, there were more people. Long-time customers. Friends. Grammy's fellow business owners. Kelly's cheeks felt as if they were going to crack if she had to keep the smile pasted on one more minute and thank another person for coming.

What she wanted was to be alone. To close all the doors and just sit in her own grief, not deal with everyone else's. She glanced over at Megs who stood next to her in a white silk blouse and black woolen skirt. She seemed so composed. Looked so serene. How did she do it? She glanced at Megs's black ballerina flats. Must be the shoes.

She wiggled her toes in the heels she was wearing and turned to the next woman in the receiving line, Aunt Lillian's daughter Beth. Short like all of the women in Grammy's family had been, a black wool dress swallowed her, and the matching black hat obscured her face. "You girls sure have grown up."

Kelly wasn't sure how to answer that. Thanks? Yes, it's called time passing? Instead, she gave the woman a dry kiss on her papery thin cheek. "Good to see you, Beth. It's been a long time."

She sniffed and looked her over from head to toe then eyed Megs. "You're all that's left of my aunt. I expect you to stay in touch."

Megs leaned down and gave the woman a quick hug and pat on the shoulder. "Yes, ma'am. Is your sister Amy here?"

"She'll arrive in time for the funeral tomorrow." Beth glanced around the funeral home. "I'm glad to see everyone paying tribute to Aunt Addy. You both did a fine job planning this."

And with that she moved on with a regal air of dismissal. Kelly whispered in Megs's ear, "I feel like curtsying and kissing her hand when we're around her."

Megs squelched a smile by coughing into her fist. "Be nice. She's the only family we have left now."

"You're all the family I need." Kelly reached

over and squeezed her hand. "No matter what, I'm going to be here for you."

"Even if you're in Nashville?"

Kelly didn't want to think about that just yet. It was nice being home for now. To get to know her sister better and make some decisions about her future.

But she didn't say any of that.

Instead, she tried a smile yet found it difficult to keep it in place. "Especially then."

Folks continued to join the receiving line, so Kelly shook hands with the next person who stepped forward. The young woman looked as if life had chewed her up a bit, but she was still standing. "Your grandmother was an amazing woman. She always made sure to drop off extra bread to my house. There were nights when that's all we had to eat. God bless her."

The woman moved toward Megs, and they embraced. Her sister gave the woman a smile. "It will be all right, Shelley. You know I can't stop baking at one or two loaves."

Kelly turned to the next person, a man who held a fedora in his hands. He shifted his weight from one foot to the other. "Shame about Addy. She was one fine woman."

"Thank you."

Megs took one of the man's hands in her own. "She thought the world of you, too, Walt."

"The bakery is business as usual?" he asked.

Megs nodded. "I'll make sure to deliver your order myself. You don't need to worry."

When Walt left, Kelly leaned closer to Megs. "These people are worried they won't get their bread and cookies?"

"It's more than that. You wouldn't understand. They're checking to make sure I'm going to honor Grammy's promises." Megs greeted the next visitor and hugged the tiny woman. "Eva, you're looking splendid."

"Cancer can't beat me. And I'm gonna be a grandma again. Can you believe it's almost time for Suzy to have that baby?" The woman wore a huge grin that even death couldn't dim. She turned to Kelly and said, "Addy always swore the best thing she ever did was raise you two girls."

Kelly nodded and bit her lip to keep from crying again. The fact that Grammy had taken in two teenagers after their father died and their mother ran off had changed her life forever. Again, the loss of her grandmother shook the foundation of Kelly's world. She'd told her reflection over and over that morning that she could get through the visitation without crying, but it seemed as if she was growing closer to breaking that promise. "We couldn't have asked for a better parent."

"They don't make them better than Adelaide Sweet." The woman reached up and kissed Kelly on both cheeks then did the same to Megs before moving across the room toward the casket.

Kelly addressed her sister. "And that was?"

"Eva Stone. If you're in town for much longer, you'll get to know her. She works with as many charities as Grammy used to. And we're making the cake for her daughter-in-law's baby shower this Sunday." Megs groaned softly and massaged the back of her neck. "How many more people do you think are coming today?"

Kelly scanned the room and guessed that almost the entire town must be there. After paying their respects to Addy, people moved in small groups to the table in the back where Megs had placed all the baked goods she'd made. But every time Kelly thought they had seen the last visitor, two more would walk in. She looked up at the door as Sam entered the room. His presence suddenly made her feel lighter inside.

He made a beeline to the sisters and gave a hug to Megs then nodded at Kelly. "Quite a turn out. Addy must be mad as all get-out to be missing it."

"Something tells me she isn't." Megs wrapped her arms around her waist and took a deep breath. "And this is the easy part. I can't even imagine the funeral." Her sister glanced around the room, then at the two of them. "I need some air."

Kelly nodded. "I'll go with you."

"No."

Kelly took a step back at the vehemence in her sister's voice. She shrugged. "Fine. I'll stay and greet anyone that comes in."

She watched as Megs nodded but ran out of the room. Frowning, she spoke to Sam. "Every time I think we're making headway, she runs. I can't seem to get her to open up to me."

"Do you blame her?" Sam kept his gaze on the door Megs had disappeared through. "You've been gone so much that you're practically a stranger to her. She doesn't know you. Not anymore."

Kelly's frown deepened. "You think you know so much about me, but you have no idea."

"You're right. I'm sure I don't." He peered at her closely, then shrugged. "Neither does your sister. So why don't you give her some time?" He reached up and adjusted his tie that was already lying perfectly. "Unless you're planning on leaving right away again."

Leave for what? She needed this time to figure things out. "I don't have anything to go back to right now. I thought everything I had left was here, but maybe I was wrong. I don't have anything at all if I don't have my sister." She hung her head and closed her eyes at the sting in them. Breathe in, breathe out.

She felt a hand on her back and knew it was Sam. Assured, solid, she put her arms around his neck and clung to him. "Hey, you do have Megs even if it isn't exactly what you expected." He paused, but kept moving his hand in slow circles between her shoulder blades. "I don't mean to be so hard on you for this, but you're not alone. And I'll be there for you, too, if you want."

But what was Sam? A neighbor? A friend? She let him hold her, not wanting to think about it too closely. Borrowing some of his strength, she used it to push her emotions down. She couldn't cry here. If she did, she wouldn't be able to stop. And she had to be strong. For Grammy. For Megs.

For herself.

SAM SHIFTED THE woman in his arms. Kelly tried to come across as tough, but he suspected that maybe it was a front. That she wanted to keep up a tough exterior so no one could get too close. That she let him hold her surprised even him. The fact that she felt so good there in his arms awakened feelings he would have to figure out later. This was Kelly. Addy's granddaughter. He should consider her off limits.

She let go of him, and he led Kelly over to a sofa and sat next to her. He grabbed a box of tissues from the table beside them, pulled one out and offered it to her. She took it, but worried it in her hands rather than dabbing her eyes. He glanced at the door, hoping to see Megs returning to them. He didn't know what to say to Kelly. He didn't know her. Not like her sister, who had become like family. He nudged her shoulder. "Do you want a glass of water?"

She stared at the tissue in her hand and shook her head, the blond strands of her hair catching on the silver necklace around her slender neck. She pulled her hair behind her with one hand and let the strands fall down her back in a golden waterfall. "I'm fine."

"You don't look good."

She lifted her eyes to stare at him. "You're not supposed to say that to a crying woman."

"Well, I never claimed to be good with women, especially crying ones." He put his arm around her. "I want to help you feel better."

"You're not doing a good job of that right now." She wiped at the smudges of black under her eyes and gave a low laugh that sounded false. And bitter. "You don't understand. Grammy was more than just a mother figure to me. She was my biggest fan." She hiccuped, and the next words came out soft. "My only fan."

"She believed in you."

A nod. "But she believed in everybody. She always said—" Her voice broke, but she managed to continue, "She said that everyone had a talent, but only the lucky ones found their passion." She gazed up at him, and he longed to wipe the pain away from those deep blue eyes. "Do you think that's true? Do you have a passion?"

If he didn't, he wouldn't be in Michigan using the skills he'd learned from his grandfather Sam. Thankfully his grandfather had taught him how to build things, use his hands, even fix up houses that were diamonds in the rough. Without that, he'd have been stuck following his dad's dream of stardom for him. He smiled. "I do."

"Singing means everything to Grammy. And to me, but I don't know." Her gaze drifted over his shoulder.

He turned and found Megs back in the room. Kelly moved an inch away from him as her sister approached them. He held up the tissue box to Megs. "Are you okay?"

Megs gave them a weak smile. "I know we're supposed to stay for another half hour, but I gotta go somewhere other than here." She put her hand on Kelly's shoulder. "You can come with me, unless you'd rather stay."

Kelly didn't hesitate as she stood. "Take me with you."

They both turned and looked at Sam. He shook his head. "Wouldn't want to come between you two girls. Besides, I'll make sure everything gets taken care of here before they close for the night. You want me to take the leftover pastries to your place?"

"Mark from the shelter said he'd bring them home to his guys. I left bakery boxes to pack everything in." Megs slipped her arm around his waist for a brief hug. "Thank you, Sam. You've been amazing."

He shrugged and ducked his head. "What are friends for? Get some rest tonight. I'll come over in the morning to drive you both to the church."

He faced Kelly. Did he hug her? Shake her hand? He still didn't know what their connection was just yet. She made the decision for him and gave him a nod before turning and following her sister out of the funeral home.

JUST BEFORE THEY reached Grammy's farmhouse, Megs made a left turn down a dirt road. Kelly shifted to look at her sister. "Where are we going?"

Megs kept her gaze straight ahead. "I can't go back to that house. Not yet." She slowed the car, steering farther to the left, then stopped in the middle of a clearing surrounded by pine trees and switched the ignition off. She left the headlights on and got out.

Kelly shook her head as she watched Megs stare out into the darkness. What in the world had gotten into her sister? She'd driven them into the middle of nowhere to do what?

Kelly got out of the car and leaned on the door frame while watching her sister follow the beams from the headlights down a dirt path to the edge of the water. "You brought us to Miller's Pond?"

Megs didn't answer but kicked off her flats and unbuttoned her blouse. She tossed the shirt aside and started to unzip her skirt and step out of it. She turned back to look at Kelly. "You coming or not?"

Had grief finally driven her sister off the deep end? "It's October and barely sixty degrees out, and you're going to go swimming? Do you know what Grammy would say?"

"To stop being foolish and get back in the car." Megs turned back to stare at the dark watery depths. "And that's exactly why I'm going to go in."

Who was this woman and what had she done with her sister? "You're crazy."

"Yep." Megs took a deep breath and dove headfirst into the pond.

Kelly shrieked and left the car. In the moonlight, she searched the edge of the bank and found her sister floating on her back. She shook her head and muttered under her breath about grief making people, who were normally sane, stark raving mad. But she took off her shoes and pulled the dress over her head. "You're nuts. Absolutely bonkers."

She walked the few feet to the edge of the pond and dipped her toe in the water. And quickly snatched it back out. "It's freezing."

"Just come in already."

Kelly closed her eyes and cautiously went forward until she was waist deep in very cold water. The shock from the low temperature made her teeth chatter and goose bumps rise on her skin. She took a deep breath and dropped under the water. In for a penny.

She sputtered as she stood and broke the water's surface. "This is insane. Why are we doing this again?"

Megs turned onto her belly and swam slowly toward Kelly. "Because we needed something to wake us up."

"Becoming an ice cube works."

"You won't feel as cold if you only keep your head above water."

Kelly crouched down, but didn't feel any warmer. "I never figured you to do something like this. I thought I was the reckless one. The one who did things first and thought about the consequences later."

Megs swam a circle around her. "Maybe I do stuff like this all the time. How would you know?"

Her little sister a rebel? Please. She'd done exactly as Grammy had told her since they'd moved into the farmhouse as teenagers. Kelly was the one who disobeyed the rules, pushed the limits. Megs kept her head down and her nose clean. Kelly peered at her sister, wishing she could see better in the dark. "Do you really go swimming like this all the time?"

Megs rose and walked out of the pond. She gathered her clothes and shoes then headed to the car. "I didn't eat anything at the funeral home, and I'm starving. Let's go home."

About time. She would morph into a popsicle if they stayed in that pond any longer.

Back at the farmhouse, they each took hot showers then put on flannel pajamas and thick bathrobes and slippers before reconvening in the kitchen. Casseroles and salads dropped off by well-meaning friends filled the refrigerator, so they set the containers on the island and ate with their fingers while perched on stools.

She couldn't remember being so hungry before. But like Megs said, Kelly hadn't eaten since breakfast, either. And she'd been afraid that anything she ate at the funeral home would get stuck in her throat. She took a green bean from the three-bean salad and popped it into her mouth. She watched Megs as her sister chewed before having a sip of water. "So what was that out there at the pond?"

Her sister shrugged and concentrated on her plate of cheesy potatoes. "Needed to do something different." Megs looked up and pointed at Kelly. "Ready for your solo tomorrow?"

Nice way to change the topic. "I think I know the words. We sang the song often enough in church as kids. And you're switching subjects. Why?"

"Don't like the focus on me. Never did." She pushed her plate away from her, then patted her belly. "If I eat any more, I'm going to have a coronary. Sally put enough cheese in there to clog my arteries four times over."

"That's what makes them so good." Kelly helped herself to some potatoes from Megan's plate. "I can't believe how much food there is. You won't have to cook for a month."

"It's Lake Mildred. It's what we do when someone dies. Feed the family that's left." She started to cover dishes and put things away. "But then maybe you've been gone so long that you've forgotten."

"You won't let that go, will you?"

Megs looked up from replacing the plastic wrap over the chicken and noodle casserole. "I guess I'm wondering how long you're planning on staying this time?"

The big question. "I don't know."

Megs pursed her lips but didn't say anything. She shoved the food back into the refrigerator, letting the plates and pans clink louder than necessary. Kelly left her stool and handed her sister the remaining bowl of salad.

"What do you want me to say, Megs? That I'm moving back for good? Because we both know that would be a lie."

Megs slammed shut the refrigerator door and glared at her. "What is so wrong with this place that you always have to leave? Why couldn't you stay?"

"Why couldn't you leave?"

They stared at each other for a moment, then Megs closed her eyes and took a deep breath. "I'm going to bed. You can clean up the rest of the kitchen." Her sister walked out, not looking back at her.

Kelly took their dirty plates to the sink and washed them by hand before putting them in the wooden rack that always sat out on the counter. Then she found a dishcloth and wiped down the counters. She snapped off the light and stared out the kitchen window to the backyard. To her left, she heard Sam's pickup pull into the driveway. She glanced out the side door and saw him get out and run up the stairs to his apartment above the garage.

She couldn't figure him out. He acted like a big brother to her own sister, but she doubted he felt the same toward her. It was something different. Like he didn't know what to do with her any more than she did with him. Like when he'd hugged Megs at the funeral home but stood looking at her, waiting for her to handle the situation between them. Was she like a sister? Friend? More? Kelly still wasn't sure.

The kitchen cleaned, she took the stairs up to her old bedroom, but hesitated when she was standing next to the bed. Over her shoulder, she glimpsed the open doorway. She snatched her pillow and walked down the hall to the closed door of her sister's bedroom. Knocked once. Twice. Then she opened the door. "Can I sleep in here with you? I don't want to be alone tonight."

Her sister didn't answer out loud, but pulled the covers back on the other side of the queen-size bed. Kelly smiled and crawled in next to Megs. She fluffed her pillow behind her head then brought the quilt up to her chin. Stared at the ceiling. Wondered if her sister had fallen asleep, or if she couldn't quiet her mind from the memories like herself.

She got her answer when Megs flopped on her back and exhaled through her nose. "You're thinking too loud."

"And you're not?"

She rolled onto her side, facing Kelly. "I can't believe she's really gone. I keep waiting to hear her calling me to help her figure out her meds. Or that we're late getting to the bakery."

"I keep expecting to see her in her favorite apron. The blue one—"

"With the butterflies. I know." Megs sighed and fingered the edge of the quilt. "First Pop, then Daddy. Now Grammy. They're all leaving me. And you will, too."

Kelly glared at the ceiling. "I'm not leaving. Not right away."

"But you will, and I'll be all alone."

Kelly moved onto her side to face her sister. If anyone was alone, it was her. Megs had a whole community behind her. What did she have? "The town's in love with you and your pastries. You're not alone."

"Doesn't feel that way."

Kelly knew what she meant. She squeezed her eyes shut to try to hold back the tears. "Don't get me started crying."

"Maybe that's what you need."

The first wet drop followed the slope of her nose then down her cheek onto the pillow. Soon another followed just as silent.

Megs shifted onto her back. "Every night, after I gave Grammy her meds, I kissed her and came upstairs. I'd stand at the top of the stairs and yell down, 'Good night. I love you.' And she'd answer back, 'Love you, too, Meggie.' Tonight, I paused at the top of the stairs, but then realized I'm never going to hear that again."

The only sound filling the house was the ticking of the grandfather clock downstairs. Suddenly, Megs called out, "Good night, Grammy! We love you!"

Silence answered back. In the dark, Kelly reached over and squeezed her sister's hand. She raised her voice. "Love you always."

They held each other's hands and cried until they fell asleep.

CHAPTER FOUR

GRAMMY'S FUNERAL WAS held on a rainy Thursday morning. The number of people that showed up to pay their respects amazed Kelly. Addy Sweet had been a part of the community of Lake Mildred for over eighty years. She'd seen the town grow from a few hundred souls to over ten thousand. She'd survived the lean years and enjoyed the plenty. She'd been a fixture at the Sweetheart, and no one could imagine what the bakery would be like without her. Megs had inherited her baking gene, thank goodness. Because if they were depending on Kelly to create pastries then they would go hungry waiting.

Kelly tugged at the dark green cardigan that she'd thrown on over the simple black dress. The harsh colors probably washed her out, but then she looked pale no matter what she wore or how much makeup she put on. She hummed the beginning bars of her solo until a sob choked her, and she took a moment to calm herself. She could do this. She could sit through her grandmother's funeral and sing her favorite song. She could say good-bye to the woman who had raised her since being a teen.

Oh, Grammy.

She entered the church and found Megs sitting in a pew at the front, kneading her bare foot. "I don't know how people can wear heels all day."

"I don't know how you can stand all day making dough, so we're even." She took a seat next to her sister and tried to count the number of people in the other pews. "I figured there would be a good turnout, but this is too many."

"She's baked the cake for every wedding in Lake Mildred for sixty-plus years," Megs said with a shrug. "As well as first birthday cakes, Valentine cookies and warm bread for the sick. People shared their joys and their sorrows with her. They loved her."

"We loved her more."

Megs gave a soft smile, then nodded to-ward the back. "I asked Sam to be one of the pallbearers. As well as Rick and some others who admired Grammy. But if you wanted to be one, I can add your name to the list."

Kelly shook her head. "No. I'm having enough trouble getting up the courage to sing. I've had stage fright before, but I'm not sure I can do this."

"You have to. Grammy would have wanted you to."

"I know." She inhaled and held a breath, letting it go in a hum. She started to cough, then waved her hand at Megs. "I need some air."

The organ began playing, and both sisters paled. Megs gave her a shrug. "No time. Can you do this?"

Kelly nodded and squeezed her sister's hand before walking up the three steps to the dais where the microphone waited for her. She grasped it, removing it from the stand. Bowing her head, she let the bars of the intro play. Told herself that this was like any other singing gig. She'd been born to do this. Then it was her cue. She lifted her head and opened her mouth.

Nothing came out.

She glanced at the organist who played the intro again. She closed her eyes. She knew the words. She'd sung them thousands of times. She opened her mouth, but while the words were on the tip of her tongue, there was no sound. Her eyes wide now, she looked at Megs who watched her with a frown. She glanced at Sam who waited in the back of the sanctuary with the coffin. She shook her head, and hot tears filled her eyes. She looked at the floor, letting her hand with the microphone drop.

Then Megs was standing next to her, putting her arm around her. Megs led the congregation, singing the first words of "Amazing Grace" as the pallbearers carried the casket with Grammy to the front.

EVERYONE GATHERED AT the Sweetheart after the cemetery, so it was a good thing that Megs had gone crazy with baking the last couple of days. Kelly rushed around pouring coffee and tea. Refilling napkin stands and plates. Making sure trays of pastries stayed full. Playing the ultimate hostess to her grandmother's wake. She and Megs had debated about providing a luncheon, but anyone who knew Grammy would want pastry.

Someone gently touched her arm. "Kelly, I'm so sorry for your loss." Rick Allyn tried to give her a smile. "Your grandmother was really special."

"Thanks, Rick." She eyed him from head to toe. "You've certainly grown up since high school. And Megs told me you got married."

He gestured to a short woman with long dark hair choosing a pastry. "That's my Lizzie right there." He waved her over and introduced her to Kelly. "Kelly and I dated briefly in middle school."

Kelly laughed. "Very, very briefly. It lasted all of a week." She turned to Lizzie and smiled. "Jennifer Harrison suddenly grew boobs."

Lizzie laughed and almost choked on her bite of kruszczki. "These things are amazing. What are they called?" she asked.

"They're Polish angel wings." Kelly glanced at the buffet of strudel, baklava, napoleons and mille feuille. "We always said Grammy was the United Nations of baking. And I guess my sister has kept up the tradition."

"Your grandmother made our wedding cake. It was fabulous." Lizzie snuggled closer to Rick's side. "But then the whole day was magical."

Kelly swallowed at the lump in her throat as the happy couple walked through the crowd, hand in hand. She'd never had a chance to do that. She was almost thirty and had never even had something close to love. What would her life be like if she had pursued romance as hard as she'd pursued her singing career? Maybe she'd have someone to hold her hand and help her through this day.

She pivoted on her heel and banged into a wall of chest muscle. Before she could stop herself, she started to fall, but strong arms caught her and pulled her close. She looked up into startled hazel eyes. "You?"

"Me."

She backed away from Sam. "You don't need to keep an eye on me."

He shrugged. "Seems like every time I'm near you, something pushes us together, Kelly."

"Well, it needs to stop." She ran her hands down her dress, smoothing it. She eyed him warily. "Maybe it's you that's doing that. How do I know that you aren't pushing us together?"

"I'm not that desperate for female attention."

No, he certainly didn't look like he was desperate. She'd noticed the appreciative glances of women as he walked by them. The way they tried to get his attention. But he seemed oblivious to their drooling. She didn't want to join the crowd and become one of their bunch. "The only attention you seem to want is mine."

"That's not what's going on." He looked at her as if she talked gibberish. "It's not like I'm seeking you out or anything."

But his actions made his words seem hollow. She didn't reply; didn't have any more time for this kind of debate. "Have you seen Megs? We're running low on Black Forest cake, and I need more tea bags."

"Don't worry about that right now. How are you holding up?"

"Fine. I'm fine." But she wasn't. That's why she wanted to keep moving and concentrate on anything else. "But I need Megan."

He took her hand and led her over to a quiet corner. She tried not to let the warmth of his hand in hers mean anything more than comfort. "You're not fine, Kel. And staying busy won't change anything."

"It's what I have to do for now." She let go

of his hand reluctantly. "I don't want to think too much."

He searched her eyes. She glanced down, uncomfortable at how intimate his gaze felt.

"I understand what you're thinking. When I lost my grandfather, it felt as if the bottom had dropped out of my world. Sound familiar?"

Yes. But she couldn't peek up at him. Otherwise, she'd lose what little control she had of her emotions and be weeping in his arms. She needed to stay confident. And not give in to the despair that tinged the edges of her life. "I need to find my sister." She rose and started to leave, but stopped and faced him. "Thanks, Sam."

"I didn't do anything."

"Exactly. That was exactly what I needed right now." She pushed through the swinging doors to the kitchen where she found Megs sitting on a stool and staring at the floor. "Hiding?"

"No." Her sister glanced away, wiping at her eyes. "I needed a moment alone."

Kelly noted the empty kitchen and sighed. "There was always something going on back here. It doesn't seem right to see it like this.

Cold ovens. Empty trays. There's no warmth without her."

"You know Gina, right? My cashier? She asked me this morning if we're closing the bakery. And I'm sure the other baker Tom is wondering the same thing, too."

Kelly frowned. "What? No. Not possible."

Megs rested her chin on her fist, leaning on the marble work counter. "I don't know how to run a bakery. I've been working next to Grammy for twelve years, but I don't know the first thing about what she really did. I know her recipes. I know the rotation of the menu. But the business side of things?" She gave a shrug. "Nothing."

"You know more than you realize." Kelly approached her and took her hands in hers, then flipped them over to expose her sister's wrist. "Your veins are filled with butter and cream because this bakery is your life. Grammy always said to find your passion and this is where it is."

Her sister looked up at her, eyes shining with fear and something else. Doubt?

Megs let her hands drop to her sides. "Is it?"

Kelly hated to see her sister like this, full

of worries and second-guessing herself. How could someone so talented with flour and sugar be so insecure in her future? This wasn't the Megan she knew. "The reading of the will isn't until tomorrow, but we both know she's going to leave you this place."

"It's not that simple." Megs rose to her feet and straightened her dress. "Come on, let's get back to work."

SAM GLANCED BEHIND MEGS, looking to see if her sister would be joining her. She gave him a soft smile. "Searching for someone?"

He frowned. "Who?" She eyed him until he sighed. "It's not what you think. I'm worried about her. That's all."

"If you say so."

"You know, Addy always said Kelly was beautiful, but I assumed she was being a proud grandmother. Puffing her up so I'd like her, you know?" He ran a hand over his jaw. "But she's more than what I expected. I'm uncertain as to what to do about her."

"Well…she's my sister."

"Right." He leaned in closer to Megs and dropped the volume of his voice. "She's gorgeous. And it's got me rattled."

Megs wrinkled her nose. "Gross."

"Come on, you're my best friend. If I can't talk to you about this kind of thing, who can I talk to?"

She peered at him, then broke into a smile. "You're trying to distract me."

He put a hand on her shoulder. That had been part of it. "Did it work?"

"Maybe a little. It may sound weird, but I still wish Grammy could be here to see this. She'd be so grateful, and probably taken aback by everyone showing up for her." She collected a couple of empty coffee mugs on the table closest to them. "I've got to get back to playing hostess."

She started to walk away, then glanced back at him. "I think the lawyer told you about the reading of the will tomorrow?"

Zac Hall, the family lawyer, had approached Sam at the funeral home and mentioned that he would need to be there, since Grammy had named him in her will. Not that she owed him anything or that he deserved it. "Which doesn't make any sense. Why do I have to be there?"

"Just remember that Grammy wanted what was best for all of us. And that includes you, too." She paused to watch Kelly behind the glass pastry cases, handling a new box of tea bags. "Tomorrow is going to change a lot of things around here. I hope we can still all be friends at the end of the day."

She rushed over to a table at the far side of the bakery, and he was left confused. What in the world was that all about?

KELLY COLLECTED THE last of the china tea cups and brought the full tray into the kitchen where Megs was washing and placing them on the rack next to the sink. Her sister had told her that Grammy had meant to replace the old dishwasher, but had never gotten around to it. Now she never would.

Kelly grabbed a dish towel and started drying the cups and other dishes, and stacking them neatly on the standing carts. They worked in silence until every bowl, fork and last cookie tray was put away.

Megs gave her a soft smile, collapsing onto a stool. "Glad that's over."

"It's been a long day." Kelly yawned and rolled her shoulders, trying to ease away some of the tension that seemed to have lodged there.

"More like a long three days." Megs pulled her hair off her neck and twisted it into a knot on top of her head. "We could have a late dinner at the diner before going home."

"I'm not hungry."

Megs stood and grabbed up a cleaning rag. "Nah. Me, either."

Kelly stretched her arms above her head and gestured to the front of the bakery. "Sam's almost finished sweeping out there. He said he'd mop, too. I don't know where he's got all this energy after a day like this."

Megs wiped down the last counter then turned to her. "I told Gina and Tom that we'll reopen Saturday at four a.m. I need one more day before we attempt normal life."

"Everybody understands that."

Megs flicked the rag back and forth. "The longer we stay closed, the less money the bakery brings in, which means the less available to pay my employees. And our suppliers."

"And you said you don't know anything about running the business."

"I'm serious." Megs slowly ran a hand down the clean counter top. "I won't lose the bakery because Grammy isn't here anymore. I'll do everything required to keep it going."

Now that sounded like the Megs she knew and loved. "So take a small-business class or something. Get educated so you can manage it all better."

Megs bit her lip, looking hesitant. "You think I could do that?"

"Doesn't the library offer things like that? Or the community college?" Kelly took out her phone and started the search app. "I know they've got stuff like that online at least." She found one course and held the phone out to her sister. "You can do it on your own time at your own pace."

Megs took the phone and read the screen, then gave a shrug. "What own time? With Grammy gone, it's all on me. I won't have time to breathe much less take a class. I can't do this."

"Yes, you can." Kelly walked over to her sister and took her phone back, slipping it into one of the front pockets of her apron. "You can do anything. Especially if you have help."

Her sister stared at her with undisguised skepticism. "Who's going to help me?"

Kelly took a deep breath and pointed at her chest. "Me."

Megs laughed as she scooted away to retrieve the stack of dry trays that needed to be stored away. She continued to chortle while she placed them on the shelves. Kelly frowned. "It's not that funny."

"You don't know the first thing about the science of baking. Or what it requires to create a superior product."

There was a science to it? She'd barely passed that particular class more than once. "Okay, so I don't." Kelly narrowed her eyes. "But you do. And so do Gina and Tom. Surely there's something I can do to lend a hand around here."

Her sister grimaced and put her hands on her waist. "And what about Nashville?"

"I've been thinking about that for the past few days, and Nashville will still be there once you get the bakery going again." She hoped the panic that rose in her chest wouldn't show on her face. She would go back to her singing, eventually, but it wouldn't hurt to take some time to assist Megs. Or make it something more permanent. She frowned. "Besides, it could be time for me to come back home. Give up that pipe dream."

Megs shook her head. "Oh, no. No way. If I have to keep Grammy's bakery dream alive, then you have to keep pursuing your music."

"Maybe I'm done with music. Or maybe it's done with me. You heard what happened at the funeral when I tried to sing." She'd barely been able to choke out the words after being rescued by her sister and the congregation. "Are you actually turning down my help? After everything you've said to me about not doing my fair share?"

For a long moment, the swish of Sam's mop was the only sound that could be heard, until Megs sighed. "Fine." She held up one finger. "But it's only temporary. Grammy would never forgive me if I let you give up on your talent."

"Don't you think she'd appreciate that I'm helping you, so that you don't?"

Sam pushed through the swinging doors. "It's all set up front. Do you need my help back here?"

Megs and Kelly kept their eyes on each other rather than turning to face him. Sam asked, "Uh. Am I interrupting something?"

Megs gave him a quick smile. "Thanks for staying and cleaning up."

Sam grinned. "Have to be honest. It wasn't without an ulterior motive."

Of course, Kelly thought. No one ever helped out for free. She crossed her arms over her chest, waiting for him to continue. All of a sudden, he looked sheepish. "I was hoping to take home some of those leftover cheese croissants for my breakfast tomorrow."

Megs's smile widened and she hurried to retrieve a white paper bag. She took several pieces of wax paper and carefully wrapped three rolls. Once they were inside the bag, she folded the top over a couple of times and then handed it to him. "Payment in kind. Thanks again for your assistance."

He clutched the bag to his heart. "I'm getting the better end of this deal." He peered around the kitchen. "Are you done in here? I'll follow you two back home."

Kelly couldn't stifle a yawn. "I'm done in. Megs?"

She shook her head and swept a look around the kitchen. "You two go ahead. I have something I need to do. Alone."

Kelly put her hand on her sister's arm. "It can wait until tomorrow, can't it?"

She felt someone pulling at her other hand. Sam.

"Let's give her some time. I'll get you back to the house."

She took her hand away from his, then

watched her sister who was fussing with canisters and some cutlery on the marble counter. Megs waved her off. "Go. I'll be five, maybe ten minutes behind you."

Kelly retrieved her sweater from the hook by the back door as well as her purse then followed Sam out to his pickup. She waited while he hit the button on his key fob to unlock the doors. She turned to look at the bakery. When Sam got in on the driver's side, she got into the passenger seat, but kept her gaze out the window. "Do you think she'll be okay there alone?"

"She'll be fine." He started the truck and it growled to life. "I think she needs to say goodbye to your grandmother in her own way. She's afraid that she's going to lose the bakery without Addy."

"She mentioned that. Yes."

He drove down Main Street in the direction of the farmhouse. "What about you? Isn't there something besides singing that you've wanted to do?"

"Never. If you don't keep your focus on this business, then you miss opportunities. There's no room for doubts."

"There are other careers out there."

"Not for me." She reached over and snapped on the radio. A mournful male voice sang about letting go of regrets. She switched it off. "You think you know Megs so well, and me. I'm telling you that you have no idea."

He glanced at her, then back to the road. "I'm starting to realize that."

He pulled into the driveway and parked the truck near the garage. The faint lights from the dashboard sent splashes of blue and red over the hard planes of his face. She ignored it before she did something crazy like reach out and touch those sharp cheekbones and strong jaw.

She swallowed hard. What was wrong with her? This was Saint Sam, the man who was supposedly the second love of her grandmother's life. He wasn't a potential love interest for herself though. He probably thought of her like a sister, anyway, like he did with Megs. If that's even what he really thought about her.

He put his arm across the back of the bench seat. "Kelly."

She twisted to face him and wished for a moment that he could be more than a family friend. He was more than handsome. And he'd been so sweet during all this funeral business. Some of Grammy's effusive compliments for him seemed to be true. The potential of more hung in the air between them for a moment, but she broke the tension and held out her hand. "Good night, Sam. Thank you for the ride home."

He slid his warm hand into hers and held on to it. "If you ever need someone to talk to, I'm available. Call or text me anytime."

"I don't have your number."

He took her phone sticking out from the top of her purse and typed in his phone number. "Now you do. And I mean it. Anytime."

He handed the phone to her, his fingers touching hers again briefly. She almost dropped the phone from the touch. "Thanks."

They got out of the truck, and Kelly walked to the house and the side door that led into the kitchen. Sam began to head up the stairs to his apartment. He called out, "See you tomorrow at the lawyer's."

Confusion followed Kelly as she went inside.

SAM PACED OUTSIDE of the lawyer's office until he spotted Megs and Kelly strolling down Main Street from the Sweetheart. Must be one of the perks of working in downtown Lake Mildred. But then, his job took him all over the county rather than keeping him cooped up in an office. And that's the way he liked it.

Megs walked up and gave him a hug while Kelly watched him intently as if trying to figure out something. Good. He didn't know what or why he'd be inheriting anything, either.

He opened the glass door and let them both pass in front of him into the office. Sam removed his leather jacket and folded it over one arm. He also adjusted his tie, which he'd worn out of respect for Addy.

A secretary ushered them into a private office and shut the door behind them. Sam held out a chair for Megs. She thanked him before he held out another for Kelly. Sam pulled a third chair closer to Megs and draped his jacket over the back of it.

Megs watched him. "You don't look like you slept much."

Sleep? What was sleep after all? He shrugged. "No big deal. I had a lot of things on my mind." He yawned for emphasis and stretched his arms out.

"I know the feeling." Megs gave him a soft smile as the door opened, and Zac Hall stepped inside. Sam stood and held out his hand. "Good to see you, Zac."

"Wish it was under better circumstances." Zac held Meg's hand first. "I'm sorry for your loss, Megs. Your grandmother was a treasure."

"Thanks, Zac."

He turned and held out his hand to Kelly. "Ms. Sweet, I'm your grandmother's lawyer, Zac Hall."

Kelly gaped at him. "Where's Lloyd? He's been Grammy's lawyer since before I was born." She shook Zac's hand but acted as if she was expecting old Mr. Hall to enter the room.

"My grandfather retired last year, and I took over his practice."

A similar history would repeat itself with Megs; unless Sam had been right about her changing her mind, her future. Maybe it was only a projection of his desire to forge his own path rather than following the one his father had handed to him. Maybe Megs did have big plans for herself and the bakery.

As Zac started flipping through papers,

Sam focused on Kelly who was staring out the window. The grief and fatigue etched on her face made her appear more vulnerable. She gave him the impression of being a little lost. But then death had a way of upturning people's plans and goals.

Zac placed the papers on the desk beside him. "I've reviewed the details of the will, and I believe there will be few surprises." He placed his hand on the file. "Before we go over Addy's will, I want to set some ground rules. First, hold on to all comments until the end of the reading." Zac glanced at Kelly, then Megs and then at Sam. "Second, let me assure you that Adelaide Sweet was not coerced into anything that has been written here. Believe me, these were all her ideas."

Zac leaned forward. "And lastly, I admired Mrs. Sweet. She always remembered my birthday and the fact that I loved strawberry cupcakes with vanilla frosting. I won't tolerate anyone twisting her words or her intentions. Understood?"

Both sisters nodded, and Sam settled into his seat. Zac took a deep breath and opened the file. Over the next few minutes, they reviewed the basic terms of the last will and testament of Adelaide Sweet. The sisters would receive her possessions and money in equal parts except for a thousand dollars each as a bonus to her current employees Tom and Gina. The bakery would belong to Megs to do with it as she wished.

Ownership of the farmhouse and the land it sat on was to be divided equally between Sam and Kelly.

They both stood up and Zac protested. "I haven't finished reading yet."

"But how can she split…" Kelly clamped her jaw shut and took a seat when Zac stared at her.

The lawyer continued to read. "Kelly cannot sell the house or land without the permission of Sam. Nor shall Sam sell without the permission of Kelly."

Oh, Addy. What were you thinking? Matchmaking beyond the grave? Sam winced and noticed Megs who seemed strangely calm. As if she…knew. He narrowed his eyes at her as he speculated.

Zac placed the will back inside the file and drew out three sealed envelopes. He handed one to each of them. "She asked that I give these to you after the reading, but she also suggested that you look at them only after you've left the office."

Sam glanced down at the spidery handwriting on the front of his envelope. He traced his name with one finger. What would she say? Could she say? She had linked his name with Kelly's without asking him first.

"Does anyone have any questions?" Zac asked as he cleared his throat.

Kelly stood and glared at him. "Absolutely, I do. How is it legal to pass a house to two people when only one of them deserves it?" She was going to get a headache with all that squinting, he thought. "How is that even possible? He's not even family. And you said she knew what she was doing?"

"I believe Mrs. Sweet saw it as a way to repay Sam," Zac answered.

Her eyebrows shot up. "Repayment for what?"

Now Sam stood and approached her. "I did a lot of work on the house to help her out and never charged her a cent."

"No, but you lived there rent free."

"Giving me the house wasn't in my original agreement with her."

Kelly stood on her tiptoes to get closer to his height. "*Half* the house."

Zac called a time out, using his hands to form a T. "Folks, I know this is a very emotional time, so feelings are bound to run high. But let's concentrate on Mrs. Sweet's wishes. I understand that the clause about the farmhouse and property complicates the issue, but she expected the two of you to work it out somehow."

Kelly continued to glare at Zac. "I don't see how that's possible."

Megs rose slowly to her feet and kept her gaze on the lawyer. "I think Grammy was right. She only had your best interests in mind...both of you. Think about it and maybe you'll see in a few days, when things aren't so..." She sighed. "Heated." She held out her hand to grip Zac's, and they shook briefly. "Thank you, Zac. Your grandfather would be proud. I'll see myself out."

Megs left the room and Sam peered over at Kelly who was staring down at her envelope. She shook her head and wiped at the corners of her eyes. Despite the uneasiness the reading of the will had caused, Sam wanted to comfort her. She'd lost her grandmother already, and now she probably thought she'd also lost half her inheritance as well. He hated to cause her more pain. He shook Zac's hand. "Could I have a moment alone with Kelly?" When Zac gave a nod, Sam patted him on the shoulder. "That didn't go quite like I expected."

"These things usually don't. I'll make sure that you're not disturbed," Zac told him, and he came around to the other side of the desk and picked up his leather messenger bag. "I'll see you at basketball practice tomorrow night?"

Sam agreed.

The lawyer walked to the open door and closed it quietly behind him.

Sam approached Kelly who still kept her gaze on the envelope. He took the seat that Megs had vacated. "I'm sorry."

"For what?" She glanced over her shoulder at him. "You didn't make her take half of my inheritance away from me. Right?"

"I had no idea she was going to do this. I need you to believe that. Believe me." He hadn't realized how important it was that she know that he hadn't betrayed her until he'd said the words. "I would have told you if I had known."

For several long moments, she stayed silent, then she whispered, "I believe you."

He sagged slightly in his chair, relieved that she'd given him that, even though he could see that it could cost her. "If there's anything I can do, just say the word."

She tried to smile. "You mean besides let me have the house?" She leaned over and grabbed her purse from where she'd set it earlier under her chair. She opened it and rummaged through it until she found a small compact mirror. She shuddered at her image. "I can't let anyone see me like this. I don't want them to think I have a red nose and mascara-smudged eyes all the time." She removed a small package of tissues and wiped under her eyes, making herself presentable.

But to him, she was always beautiful. Strong. And resilient. "We'll talk later?"

"Okay."

They both left the office then and he walked down to the Sweetheart, while she headed off in the opposite direction.

Once he reached the bakery, he let himself in via the unlocked back door. He found Megs sitting on a stool, paging through Addy's recipe book. She raised her head as soon as she spotted him. "Before you ask, Grammy told me not to tell you."

"I still don't quite get it. I wasn't expecting anything from her, you know."

"I told her that. I also told her that Kelly would be distraught. You saw her." She flipped the recipe book closed. "Grammy admired you and wanted to do something to make up for all that you'd done for her. It was more than fixing the door that wouldn't close and rehabbing the apartment above the garage. You gave her a man to dote on again. She loved that. Made her feel feminine."

What? He shook his head. "I didn't mean to do that."

"That's why it was so sweet." Megs gave him a warm smile. "You must have known."

He looked down at his feet, his cheeks heating under her scrutiny. "Maybe I did know that."

"You couldn't help it."

He crossed the quiet kitchen and took a seat on an adjoining stool. He pointed at her envelope. "You going to open that?"

"Later. You?"

He held his sealed envelope up for her to see. "I'm a little afraid of what I might find in here."

Would Addy tell him why she split the house and property between him and Kelly? What had she been thinking would happen by throwing them together? Addy had talked about her granddaughter so much that he thought he knew her, at least, a little bit. But what if he didn't know anything? He tapped his knee with the letter. "Your sister didn't look happy."

"She'll get over it."

"You know her best." He let out a deep moan then bounded to his feet. "I've got to head out to a job site. Will you be home later? Maybe you and Kelly and I can have dinner. I'll even spring for the pizza."

"Not tonight. I have plans."

His eyebrows rose at this news. "Hot date? It's about time you got back into the scene." He'd known her for almost two years, but he'd never seen her go out with anyone. She deserved to find someone. He wondered if Zac was available.

She laughed. "Not quite. More like an appointment with my accountant Jack to go over the bakery's finances. Now that this place is mine, I need to know where I stand."

She certainly wasn't wasting any time. He gave a quick nod. "Good for you. Smart. But it can wait, can't it?"

"I need answers so that I can make my mind up about some things. But before I can do that, I need to do a little restorative baking."

He frowned at her. "Is that some kind of new recipe?"

She started to push him out the door. "It means I want to sink my hands in a bowl of dough to make me feel better. Now get out. I also need solitude."

"Too much isn't good for you, you know." The way she brought out all the brotherly feelings in him only cemented their friendship.

She hustled him to the back door. "I'm asking nicely. Don't make me get mean."

"As if you could." He put his arm around her shoulder and squeezed. "If you need to talk."

"I know where to find you."

He opened the back door and stared out into the gray weather. "Don't close yourself off from everyone."

"Okay, Mr. Bossy Pants. Go to your job and let me get to mine."

KELLY'S WORLD FELT as if it had been turned upside down by a few words in her grandmother's will. Made sense. She ambled along Main, not sure where to turn to. She wanted to go back to the farmhouse. To pack up her stuff and get out of Lake Mildred as quickly as she could. But a promise to help her sister would keep her in town.

That, and the fact that Megs had driven them both in her car that morning.

She gave a nod to several people as she walked down Main and continued to the park. She and Megs had loved this park as kids, and she'd gotten her first kiss under the giant oak near the benches.

The nostalgia threatened to bring back the tears, so she turned sharply on to Lincoln where the Sweetheart was tucked. She took the alley to get to the back entrance where she finally found Megs baking something with cinnamon and sugar if her nose could be relied on. "New recipe?"

"It's an oldie, but a goodie. Cinnamon rolls." She took the metal bowl from the stand mixer to the sink. "They'll be ready in about an hour, once they finish rising and get out of the oven. Want one?"

"Sure. Thought I'd read what Grammy wrote in my letter. Did you read yours?"

Megs held up her unopened envelope. "Not yet. Figured I'll do it tonight before I go to bed. But go ahead. I've got some things to do here, so I'll give you your privacy."

Once Megs left the kitchen, Kelly took a seat on one of the stools at the marble worktable and pulled out the envelope from her jacket pocket. *Grammy, what do you want from me?*

Only one way to find out. She slipped a finger under one side of the envelope flap and moved it to the right to loosen it. She took out the single sheet of purple stationary and unfolded it.

After fearing reading the letter to see what it said, it only took seconds to do it. Two lines. That's all her grandmother had written to her.

Never give up on your dreams. Take care of your sister.

She checked the envelope to find out if there had been something else left behind. But it was empty. She brought the letter to her nose and inhaled deeply. It smelled of honey.

Grammy.

She closed her eyes and placed the letter in her lap. The swinging doors that led to the front space of the bakery opened, and Kelly glanced up to find Megs approaching with a cookie that must have been left over from the funeral the day before. Megs held it out to her. "I thought you might want something."

Kelly took the chocolate chip cookie from her. She nibbled at it, then handed her letter to Megs. "Have a look."

Her sister didn't open the piece of paper, instead she placed the letter back in Kelly's hand. "It's yours, not mine."

"I don't get it, Megs. None of this makes sense." Kelly read the contents out loud. "Why would she tell me to keep pursuing my dreams of music, but go and leave me her house? After hearing the terms of her will, I figured she wanted me to come home at last. But how do I chase my dreams in Lake Mildred?" She grimaced. "Do you know how many times I called and said I was giving up and coming home? And just as many times she told me that I had to stay and keep at it." She waved the letter under Megs's nose. "Does this sound like something Grammy would say?"

"Maybe she thought her death would change things. Change us."

"How?" She didn't want to think of what else lay before them. "It's not like we're going to fight over money."

"Some families do. They get torn apart when it comes to splitting an estate." Megs nudged her shoulder. "But that's not us."

"And now she wants me to keep my dreams, yet she's trapped me in this town by giving me that place." She paused. "Or, half of it, anyway."

"She trapped both of us, you know?"

"But you wanted the bakery."

"I did. Do." Megs ran her hands through her hair, then took a seat on the stool next to Kelly. "I always knew that she would give me the bakery, so I grew to expect it. Like you always expected her to push you to sing even though you asked to come back home."

"I guess." Kelly laid the letter out flat on the worktable and smoothed the creases from it. "And she would have wanted to make things fair between us." She peered at Megs. "Did you want the house?"

"It's yours and Sam's. I have no claim."

"You don't have to go moving out anytime soon. I have no idea what we'll do with it." She rested her hand on her chin. "Sell? Rent? Keep?"

They sat side by side for a moment, neither of them saying a word. Then Megs stood. "I need to check on the cinnamon rolls. They're supposed to double in size before I bake them. Want to check with me?"

Kelly shrugged. Might as well. What else did she have to do? And maybe this was part of her grandmother's admonition to take care of Megs.

SAM CLEANED UP after finishing his repairs to the dock. He put a foot on the wooden planks and pushed with all his strength. Solid. Firm. No more rot.

Satisfied, he carried his box of tools to the bed of the truck and secured them before slamming the tailgate up and hearing it click into place. Another job well done. He got in the truck and frowned when he heard the crumple of paper.

He looked around and on the seat underneath him, he found the envelope from Addy. He pulled it free and tapped it on the steering wheel. What on earth had Addy needed to say in the end that she hadn't already told him?

He opened the envelope and took out the single purple page. He closed his eyes at the sight of her handwriting. Even the paper smelled of her and brought back the image of her beckoning him into the house to fix one more thing. He dismissed the memory, cleared his mind, then opened the letter.

Not that it was much of a letter. Only three words. *Keep them close.*

He didn't need to ask. He knew who she meant. Wasn't making him split the house with Kelly enough?

He started the truck, put it in gear and pulled around the drive to head back to town. It was long past lunchtime, but he had business to conclude with the part-time mayor, part-time diner owner.

He found Rick in a booth at the back of the restaurant, eating a late lunch. Sam took the seat across from him and laid the final bill on top of the table and slid it over to him. "It's all done."

Rick stopped chewing his BLT mid-bite and pulled the bill towards him. He wiped his hands on a napkin and continued to chew as he read over the final numbers. "Already? I wasn't expecting you to be finished for at least a week."

Sam shrugged. "Didn't require as much work as I thought, and it went fast. Besides, it was therapeutic." He pointed to the bottom of the page. "As you can see, I discounted the amount to reflect the difference in time of labor."

"Some men would have kept it the same."

"That's not how I work." He glanced around as a waitress approached the table. "Shirley, can I get what Rick's having?"

"You betcha." She shifted her weight to the other hip. "When you going to check out my back door? That thing sticks something horrible."

He glanced at the clock on the wall. "What time are you done here?"

"In an hour."

They made arrangements to meet at her house. If it was what Sam thought it was, the fix would take fifteen minutes tops. He could shave the bottom of the door, then make it home in time for the baseball game on the tube. Maybe pick up a pizza in town before driving back to the farmhouse.

Rick waited until Shirley left them to put in Sam's order. Rick looked him over. "You know, Will is interested in able bodies to help with his senior citizen project. He needs people with skills to help fix things up for them."

Will, the town inspector, had approached him a few weeks ago regarding the work weekend to give seniors a hand, who may not be able to afford a contractor. "Already signed up."

"Good man."

"Hardly. But I'm good with my hands." Shirley brought him a glass of ice water. He took several long sips.

Rick watched him, then leaned in closer. "You're tight with the Sweet girls. How are they doing?"

Megs was a like a sister, sure. But Kelly? He still hadn't figured it out quite yet. "As well as can be expected, I guess. Addy was a force of nature, and they're feeling her absence."

"We all are."

"I think they get the right to miss her more."

"I didn't mean they didn't. It's just that Addy was a part of our community for so long. She was there behind the scenes for so many people. And now that she's gone, I don't know who will fill the gap that she's left."

"We all live our lives, hoping we have an impact on those around us. But few of us ever leave the hole that Addy did." Sam stared down at the napkin in his lap. "She will be missed."

The men kept their moment of silence broken only as Shirley brought Sam's sandwich and fries. He glanced up at Rick. "Megs seems to be planning on keeping things much like they were before, when Addy was still with us."

"She's definitely a woman after Addy's own image."

Sam wondered how much of that was what Megs really wanted.

SAM KNOCKED ON the back door of the bakery, then let himself in. Cinnamon assaulted his senses as he stepped inside. He found the Sweet sisters huddled around Addy's recipe book. Kelly glanced up first. "Hey, Sam. Whatcha got?"

He put the plastic bag of takeout from the diner on the counter next to the book. "Thought you might need some lunch. Rick makes the best burgers."

"That's sweet of you. Isn't that sweet, Kelly?"

Kelly took out the two Styrofoam boxes from the bag and handed one to Megs. "Thanks, Sam."

"It's nothing." He took a seat on one of the stools. "You both still have to eat."

Kelly opened her box and sniffed it. "It smells heavenly." She brought out the burger and took a big bite. She moaned as she closed her eyes, and Sam tried not to grin. She appreciated good food as much as he did. Another item in the plus column.

He turned to find Megs watching him as he stared at her sister. He took a deep breath. "Megs, can I borrow your sister for a little while? I thought I'd take her for a drive so we can talk."

"Can't we talk here? You just brought me lunch." Kelly put her burger back in the box.

He smiled softly at her. "I was hoping for some privacy."

Megs wiped her mouth with the edge of her

apron. "Go ahead and take her. Just be sure to bring her home before dinner."

"Thanks."

Kelly stood and glanced between them. "Don't I get a say in all this?"

Sam took her jacket off the peg by the back door and tossed it at her. "No. Bring your lunch. You can eat in my truck. I've got a quick job to take care of on the way."

Kelly grumbled under her breath, but she put on her jacket and tucked the takeout box under her arm as she followed him outside to his truck. He opened the door for her, then gave her a hand to help her up into the cab. She placed the Styrofoam box next to her on the seat before reaching over to pull the seat belt across her chest.

Sam shut the passenger door, then walked around the truck to get in on the driver's side. He turned the key in the ignition as Kelly put her lunch in her lap and continued to eat. He watched her for a moment. "I appreciate you coming with me."

"Like I had a choice?"

He gave her a grin then pulled out on to Lincoln, then Main. She dug into her fries as he drove down a tree-lined road to Shirley's house. Kelly made a face as he pulled into the driveway next to a worn-down bungalow. He parked the truck, then hopped out and retrieved his tool box from the back. Through the open door, he said, "I should only be five minutes. You can stay here and eat, if you'd like."

Kelly closed the lid over her lunch and put aside the takeout box. "That's okay. I'm curious to see what it is that you actually do."

Sam whistled as he walked to the back door. He pulled open the screen door and knocked on the wooden one. Shirley answered, still dressed in what she'd worn at the diner. "I appreciate you fixing this for me."

Sam gestured at Kelly. "I brought a helper with me. Hope you don't mind."

Shirley held out her hand to her. "I knew your grandmother, Kelly. She sure did brag on you and your career."

Kelly shook the woman's hand. "Most of it was exaggerated, I'm sure." She stepped back to give Sam enough room to work.

He ran a hand along the bottom of the wooden door and noted the difference between its edge and the frame. "Does it stick more during damp weather?"

"Sometimes so much so that I have to lean

on the door to get it locked." Shirley came down the steps and stood next to Kelly, asking him, "You think you can take care of it?"

He brought out a mallet so that he could remove the door from the hinges. It took a few minutes, but once the door had been propped against the house, he used the planer to shave a fraction of a centimeter from the bottom. Then he replaced the door on its hinges and shut it. It clicked into place without any effort.

Shirley clapped her hands. "Perfect. How much do I owe you?"

He made a circle with his fingers. "Not a thing. It was a simple fix."

"Hardly simple. I couldn't have done what you did." Shirley trotted up the stairs and opened, then closed the door again. "Seriously, what do you want for doing this?"

Sam bit his lip, pretending to consider an amount. "How about a coffee to go from the diner on my next morning run?"

"You got it, Sam." Shirley turned to Kelly. "Your man is something else, isn't he? You're a lucky woman."

Shirley stole back into the house before either Sam or Kelly could protest.

Her man? Sam wondered where that had

come from. He packed his tools rather than commenting and then led Kelly to the truck.

Once his tool box was stored safely in the truck bed, he and Kelly got into the cab. He put the key in the ignition, but didn't move. "She thought you were my girlfriend."

"You bought me lunch. You brought me out on one of your jobs. It's a small town, so she assumed that we were more than whatever it is we are." She looked at him. "What are we, Sam? Friends?"

He let out his breath in a rush and started the truck. "I don't know."

"Me, either." Kelly opened her lunch up and offered him the takeout box. "Want some of my fries?"

He took a handful and ate them as he pulled onto the street and headed toward the freeway.

Kelly was peering out the window as she asked, "Where are we going?"

Instead of answering, he opted to ask a few questions of his own. He needed to find out a few things before he made up his mind about her. "What's your life like in Nashville?"

Kelly swallowed the fry she'd been eating. "What does that have to do with anything?"

He snuck glances at her, but mostly kept

his eyes on the road. "You don't talk about it much. Do you have an agent? A band? Is someone waiting for you back there?"

"Like a boyfriend?"

Not what he meant, but he was curious to find out the answer to that, too. "When did you plan on going back?"

"Not for a while. I promised Megs that I'd help her out at the bakery."

"And your singing career is on hold? Isn't that making a big mistake when you could be losing any momentum that you've established there?"

"What do you know about Nashville?" She crossed her arms over her chest, as if shutting him out. "I haven't had a singing gig in the last four months. I got fired from my last band because they wanted someone younger and hotter up front."

The pain in her voice made him want to stop the truck and put his arms around her. Tell her that the music industry had a way of hurting people. He knew from experience.

Not that he'd tell her that specifically about himself. That part of his life was dead and gone.

"Did you tell Addy that?"

"I did, but she believed that every setback was temporary. That I was only a breath away from stardom and hadn't found my niche yet."

"And what would that be?"

"I don't know. I never figured it out." She rubbed her forehead. "Why are we talking about this?"

"I'd like to understand what you plan on doing with your half of the house. Are you interested in selling it so that you can go back to Nashville? Or are you giving all that up and moving home?" Sam checked his rear-view mirror, signaled and moved into the next lane. "Your decision about the house affects me after all, and I'm curious as to whether you've thought about it."

"It's only been what? A few hours since we found out about Grammy's will?" Kelly groaned. "There have been so many changes this week, I haven't the first clue about what's going to happen or what I'm going to do." She glanced at him. "Is that enough of an answer?"

He reached over and patted her hand. "For now, yes."

They drove in silence for a few minutes

before Kelly asked, "Have you thought about what you want to do?"

He'd done nothing but think. However, she wasn't ready to hear his ideas just yet.

He had plans he wanted to make and goals he hoped to accomplish.

Addy's house was a step in the direction he wanted to go in. He dreamed of making the old farmhouse sparkle and shine, be a testament to the work he was capable of and thus bring in more business.

Though instead of saying all that, he gave a one shoulder shrug. "Some. But we have plenty of time to think things through."

Kelly visibly relaxed beside him, and she rested her head on the back of the seat. "Good. Thinking I can do. Deciding? Not yet."

CHAPTER FIVE

KELLY GROANED AS her alarm clock blared at three-thirty in the morning. A sharp knock on her bedroom door followed. She put her pillow over her head, but she could still hear her sister's voice. "I'm leaving in ten minutes."

Kelly rolled over and slammed her hand down on the digital clock. Why in the world had she volunteered at the bakery? Especially at this horrible hour. Another knock. Kelly got out of bed and answered the door. Megs looked at her sternly. "I mean it. Ten minutes."

Kelly shut the door and immediately pawed through her suitcase to find a pair of jeans and a top that could stand up to the rigors of working in the food industry. Finding the necessary outfit, she dressed quickly and pulled her hair back into a ponytail as she all but crawled down the stairs to the kitchen. She'd set the coffee machine's timer last night before bed, thank goodness. This cup would only be the first of many she'd need to get through the day.

Megs appeared in the doorway looking as if she'd had a full night's rest. She frowned at Kelly. "I'll find you a Sweetheart shirt to wear when we get there."

Kelly cupped the travel mug in her hands and held it up to her nose, letting the steamed warmth and aroma float over her face. "Why do we have to leave this early? You don't open up until seven."

"Because I have a full morning of baking ahead of me. And I don't serve leftovers."

Megs turned abruptly and left. Kelly poured sugar into her travel mug and ran after her sister. Megs had the car started already, and Kelly jumped into the passenger seat. Megs reached behind her to retrieve the ice scraper for the fine layer of frost that covered the windows. Not even the middle of October, and already there'd been the prediction of snow for the end of the week.

They didn't talk as they drove into town. Kelly sipped her coffee, tapping her fingers against the side of the travel mug to the beat of the song on the radio. Megs glanced at her once, but otherwise kept her gaze on the road.

Once they were parked in the lot behind the bakery, Megs waited for Kelly to get out of the car then hit the fob twice to lock the doors, the horn honking once.

Inside the dark kitchen, Megs walked over and switched on the overhead lights. Kelly winced at the brightness.

Megs brought out several large books as well as a notebook that she consulted. Kelly glanced over her shoulder.

A menu for Saturday. Kelly whistled. There had to be at least two dozen pastries listed and another dozen kinds of bread. She looked at Megs. "You make these every day?"

Her sister nodded. "And I have the rolls and cakes to make for the diner." She went to a shelf and pulled down two aprons and handed one to Kelly. "I'm going to have you mix up the batches of bread dough in the big mixers. Do you remember the drill?"

Kelly had spent her teenage years in this kitchen, but it had been a while since she'd done anything like this. "I can figure it out. I'm sure it will come back to me."

"I need you to follow the recipes exactly.

No changes." Megs glanced back at the lists, pulling out three laminated sheets of paper. "People are expecting that things won't change with Grammy gone, so that's what we have to give them."

She heard the words her sister spoke, but the tone didn't match; it seemed to imply something else altogether. "Is that what you want?"

Megs shrugged. "Doesn't matter. It's what we have to do."

For the next three hours, the sisters sifted flour, creamed sugar and butter, and greased pans. They put pastries in the ovens, then removed them to leave them on trays in a tall rolling cart to be put out once Tom and Gina arrived. Kelly was ready for a break after all the hard work, but opening the bakery meant brewing coffee and refilling supplies for the day.

Once those tasks were done, Megs flipped the sign over to Open. Everything was ready.

Megs called Kelly into the kitchen as Gina helped their first customer. Megs handed her a pink T-shirt emblazoned with a red heart and the bakery's name in the center. "You can put it on upstairs if you need to. I should have given you one of these yesterday."

Kelly nodded, then left to change. It felt familiar yet strange to again don the bakery's uniform. She remembered Grammy giving her the first T-shirt when she'd turned fifteen. Only weeks after her mom left, and she'd been feeling lost. Grammy had put her to work sweeping up after school. She eventually graduated to running the cash register and helping roll out cookie dough. She'd never felt comfortable making the recipes though. Not like Megs, who had relished the opportunity.

Kelly returned to the kitchen as Megs removed a tray of three cinnamon babka from the oven and placed it on the counter to cool. They'd tried her test ones yesterday and agreed that babka might be a good addition to the menu.

Loud voices from the front caught their attention. Kelly went to investigate. Standing at the cash register, Mrs. Sweeney was glaring at Gina who was trying to give her a pastry box tied with white string. Mrs. Sweeney turned to Kelly. "Is this how you plan on ruining your grandmother's bakery? Messing with a good thing?"

Kelly looked at Gina who shook her head and told her, "It's the same menu we've had for weeks."

"Where's my lemon squares? I always buy them Saturday morning to serve my husband. They're his favorite after a long week of work." Mrs. Sweeney's gaze swept over the display cases. "I don't see them."

"Because we didn't make them." Megs stepped out of the kitchen and the swinging doors swung shut behind her. "They need to be made two days in advance, but I wasn't able to. We'll be sure to have them next week."

The older woman pursed her lips. "But I always have them on Saturday night after dinner. Mr. Sweeney expects them."

Kelly bristled and opened her mouth to tell the old lady that they'd been too busy burying their grandmother two days ago to worry about her lemon squares, when Megs put a hand on her shoulder. "I've got this. Can you check with Tom to see what he needs next?"

Kelly went into the kitchen where Tom hurried away from the swinging doors and returned to the mixers that whirred as they kneaded more dough. She sighed and walked to the counter and tried a maple and bacon cookie that was cooling on one of the trays. It was her reward for biting her tongue. She was leaning against the counter stuffing her mouth when her sister returned. "I can't believe that old bat," Kelly said.

Megs shrugged and pulled out a cookbook from the shelf above the desk. "She's a customer."

"With that attitude, we can do without her business." Kelly and took another bite of the delicious cookie. "It's just lemon squares."

"No, it's her way of telling Mr. Sweeney that she appreciates the job he does at the factory every day." Megs flipped through several pages of the cookbook, then finding what she evidently wanted, laid it flat on the island. "It's how she keeps her marriage together."

"If all it takes is pastries made from lemon, then you're even more of a miracle worker than I thought."

Megs looked up at her, studying her. "It's also another reason to keep everything the same." She glanced at the tray of babkas and sighed. "Maybe we shouldn't put these out. They all want things to stay as they were."

Kelly moved to her sister's side to gently bump her hip. "Do you want things to remain unchanged from the way things were with Grammy?"

"I want the business to succeed. So I guess that's the same thing." Her sister left her and disappeared into the walk-in cooler and brought out a bowl of lemons. She started to grate the rind into zest.

Kelly stared at the yellow snow falling from the grater. "You're making the lemon squares."

It wasn't a question since few recipes at the Sweetheart required lemon zest. Megs replied, "A promise is a promise whether it was made by me or Grammy. These won't be quite the same, but I think I can do the recipe justice."

Kelly shook her head. She finished her cookie before starting the next recipe.

Hours later, Kelly stretched out on the pink velvet sofa in the loft above the bakery and rested her head. Pop Pop had built the loft as a break room when things got too hot in the kitchen, both literally and figuratively. Kelly remembered finding Grammy sitting on this very same sofa and putting her feet up on the ancient scarred coffee table.

Kelly could close her eyes and sleep for years if given the chance. Instead, she sat up and ate the sandwich she'd thrown together before retreating upstairs to the loft. Still smarting over Mrs. Sweeney, she'd wanted to yell at the woman. *You can't let go of the past, if you're hanging on to the memories holding you there.*

She paused. That sounded like a song lyric. If only she had some paper to write it down. She had a habit of writing phrases down when they came to mind, albeit nothing ever resulted from those scraps.

She quickly popped the rest of her sandwich in her mouth and searched the large one room space to see if Grammy had left a notebook or bit of paper as well as something to write with. She opened the chest of drawers, but didn't find anything that she could use. She searched the galley kitchen cupboards and came up with a forgotten half-opened package of cocktail napkins. In her apron, she found the pen she'd been using to take orders with and wrote the few words she'd thought of.

She stuffed the napkin in her front jeans pocket when she heard footsteps on the stairs. Her sister looked as tired as Kelly felt. "I'm running low on supplies, so I'm going to Robert Falls to pick up what we need to get through Monday morning before the usual delivery arrives," said Megs.

"Do you want company?"

"I've been doing this by myself for a while, so I should be okay. Besides, I'll need you here to cover the cash register when Gina gets off at two." Megs glanced around the loft. "You know, I've always wondered what it would be like to get this place fixed up like an apartment. I could live up here and work downstairs. The perfect commute, especially in the winter."

"You should talk to Sam."

Megs nodded. "I think I will. Be back in a few."

Her sister's footsteps echoed on the stairs. Kelly smiled, took her cell phone from her back pocket and dialed Sam's number. He didn't answer, so she left a brief message asking him to call her back.

THERE WAS NO way in the world this guy was going to get by him. Sam crouched lower and swayed side to side as his opponent dribbled the basketball and feinted to the left. The guy might have been good, but Sam was better and intercepted the ball and passed it to his teammate Zac, who was positioned near their own basket.

Score! Sam raised his hands and whooped.

Zac wiped his face with the hem of his T-shirt. "Whatever. We're still down by eight."

"For now."

The referee blew the whistle to signal the end of the game. Zac smirked. "For good." They shook hands and pounded each other on the back. "Good game."

Sam jogged to the sidelines of the high school gym and retrieved his duffel bag. He'd joined the men's community basketball league about a month ago, after Addy had suggested he might find more friends besides an elderly woman and her granddaughter. Zac sat beside him on the bench as they pulled on joggers over their shorts. "A bunch of us are going to the Penalty Box tonight. Want to join us?"

That sounded good. Too good. When was

the last time he'd had beers with the guys? Tempting as it was, he couldn't set foot in a bar. One drink would ruin all the hard work he'd done to get sober. "Can't. I got a call from Kelly about some things she wants done at the bakery. I promised to stop by before it got too late."

Zac raised one eyebrow at this. "What about working on the house? How's that going?"

"We haven't even talked about that yet." He took off his jersey and stuffed it into his bag before pulling on a sweatshirt that would keep him warmer. "Can I ask you why she did it, Zac? Split the house between Kelly and I? Did Addy tell you anything?"

Zac paused as if weighing what to say. "Didn't she say something in the letter she left?"

Keep them close.

He thought he understood what she'd meant, but it didn't explain why she would leave half her house to a stranger. Well, maybe not a stranger but hardly a grandson or a relative. Not blood, anyway. "No. Nothing that explains why."

"Maybe she felt like she owed you for all your hard work."

Or maybe she hoped that she'd get a grand-son-in-law by insinuating him into Kelly's life to keep them both linked to the town. "I didn't do that much for her really."

"Maybe she expects you to do more." Zac pulled on his coat, yelling a greeting to a few of the guys who were ready to leave. "In the end, it doesn't matter why. You get half the house regardless." He slugged Sam on the shoulder. "I'll catch you later."

Sam gathered his stuff. He stepped outside, into the cold, and a few stray snowflakes drifted down from the clouds to land on his bare hands. He'd agreed to stay in the arctic North for what reason? He got into his truck and cranked up the heater before pulling out of the parking lot.

As he headed out of town he had to pass by The Penalty Box, where he spotted a few guys from his team. No regrets about turning down Zac's invite, he pressed down on the accelerator.

When he eventually stopped in the drive-way next to the farmhouse, he noticed that Megs's car was absent again. That girl was going to wear herself out by the time she was thirty if she didn't watch out. He parked beside Kelly's truck and admired it before walking to the side door and knocking on it. Kelly answered and smiled at him. "Thanks for coming over, but can we take this to your place?"

Sam frowned. What kind of conversation did she think they were going to have? "Um, sure."

She closed the door behind them, then followed him up the stairs to his apartment. He swung the door open without having to unlock it. She stared at him. "You don't lock your door?"

"It's Lake Mildred. And I don't have much to take." He ushered her inside and gave her the five second tour. "I'm glad you called. I've been meaning to talk to you, too."

"About the loft?"

He opened his mouth, but then shut it. What loft? "About the farmhouse. Our house."

Kelly's eyes narrowed. "It's not your house."

"It's not just yours, either." He took off his coat and threw it across the back of the couch. "And why do we have to talk up here?"

"I want to surprise Megs. I'd like you to fix up the loft that's above the bakery." She did a circuit of his apartment. After running a finger along the kitchen counter, she returned to the armchair and took a seat. "Maybe not quite as cozy, but open like this."

"The loft?" He ran a hand through his hair. He should have taken a shower after the game and before he met with Kelly. Not that he wanted to impress her, but still, it was only common courtesy. "Megs might have mentioned it one time."

"She's always lived here, so I thought it might be nice to give her her own place."

Sam whistled and shook his head. "You're kicking her out already? Wow."

Kelly jumped up. "Who said anything about kicking her out? She's the one who said it would be nice to live above the bakery instead of having to drive into town every day. I didn't say she had to leave." Kelly paced back and forth, eventually stopping in front of his guitar, plucking it from its stand. "Do you play?"

When had the conversation changed? Had he missed it? "I play a little." He put his hands on his hips and watched her strum a few chords. "Kelly, what's going on?"

She looked up at him, then returned his guitar to its stand. "I want to do something for her. She gave up a lot so she deserves to have something that's all hers."

"Uh-huh. And how do you plan on paying me?"

She bit her lip and shrugged. "My inheritance?"

"Do you know how much that is? And how long it could take before you get anything?" Sam grimaced. "I appreciate what you're saying about doing something for your sister, but you really have no idea what you're talking about."

"Maybe I know better than most." She glanced around the place, then claimed her seat again. "I wanted, want to give her something like this. A retreat. Something that is just hers." She stood and crossed the room to the windows that overlooked the driveway. "You're right. I don't know anything. But I was hoping that you could help me with it, since you keep saying that I need to try harder with her." Her blue eyes shone with tears. "I've lost my sister somehow and I don't know how to get her back. That's why I thought the loft would be a kind of olive branch."

It was a noble gesture, even he could see that. Sam gestured to the couch. "Why don't you take a seat? There is something I wanted to talk to you about." Kelly crossed the room and sat down, perched forward as if she might need to get up and run out at a moment's notice. He hesitated, weighing how to approach the topic. "It's about the farmhouse we own. We have some decisions to make about the future."

She frowned. "Decisions?"

"Do we keep it? Sell it? Does one of us buy the other out?"

She held out her hands wide. "I have no money. Less than nothing if you include what I still owe. I couldn't afford to buy your half."

But he could afford to buy her half, though he didn't want to play that card just yet. Instead, he plopped down in his favorite chair and hooked one leg over the armrest. "I have some ideas if you want to hear them."

"As much as I would like to, there are other decisions I need to make first. I don't know if I'll be staying here in Michigan or returning to Nashville after everything is done. It wouldn't be fair to you to agree on something, then change it when my plans do." She got up from the sofa and approached him. "I need some time, Sam. Then we can discuss your ideas."

He escorted her to the door and opened it for to pass through. She went down a few steps before she stopped to look at him over her shoulder. "We'll talk soon. Promise."

He watched her open the side door to the farmhouse and kept his gaze on the kitchen window for a second as the light glowed within it.

He did have ideas about the farmhouse as well as the beautiful woman he shared ownership with. But could he hold on to one without losing the other?

KELLY SAT IN the living room in front of the empty fireplace. She'd thought about laying a fire, but it was easier to wrap herself in a blanket and stare at the cold hearth. The side door opened and closed, then Megs appeared in the doorway. "You waiting up for me?"

Kelly clutched the blanket tighter around her shoulders. "Do you know what time it is? Where have you been?"

"You don't have to worry about me. I'm a big girl." Megs removed her boots and placed them on the rubber mat in the foyer before stalking off upstairs where she slammed the door to her bedroom.

Kelly sat for another minute, then rose and turned off the lights in the living room. She entered the kitchen and set the timer for the morning coffee before retiring to her bedroom as well. She paused outside Megs's door and lifted her hand to knock on it. If Megs wanted her to know what she was doing, then she'd have told her.

Still, something niggled at Kelly. She knocked on the door anyway and tried the knob. "Where were you tonight?"

Kelly froze in the open doorway as Megs paused in turning down her bed to look at her. "Why do you want to know?"

"Because I'm your big sister, and I have a right to know."

"What right?" Megs yanked the coverlet down and rearranged the pillows. "Good night, Kelly. If you plan on joining me for church tomorrow, I leave at eight-thirty on the dot."

"Don't you ever sleep in?"

"Seven is sleeping in for me." Megs got into bed and settled under the covers. She paused and asked, "What did you do tonight?"

"I talked to Sam."

Her eyebrows shot up at this. "Interesting. I didn't think you two were close or whatever."

Kelly wasn't sure what to call whatever it was between her and Sam, either. They had a bond because of the house and Megs. But Kelly had a yearning for something more. "I had an idea about something, and I wanted to talk to him." She shrugged. "Doesn't matter because I don't think I can do it. Now it's your turn. Where were you?"

Megs played with the edge of the quilt, folding it over into pleats. "I went to the cemetery. I know I probably shouldn't but I wanted to talk to Grammy. I know she can't answer, I don't care though, I wanted her input."

"Oh."

Megs glanced up at her. "And I called Mom."

Kelly needed to sit down, so she claimed a corner of the bed. Okay, that wasn't what she'd expected to hear. Megs usually avoided their mother rather than seeking her out. "What did she say?"

"She's sorry that she couldn't make it back

for the funeral. And that she might come up for a visit during the holidays."

Kelly had heard that before, but something always came up to prevent her mother visiting. Usually it was a new man in her life. "Fine."

"She asked about you."

Probably to find out if she'd made it big in Nashville yet. Kelly sighed. It wasn't nice to think such things about her own mother, but history had shown that Lisa Sweet was selfish with a long streak towards self-preservation. "Sometimes I wonder if Daddy hadn't died whether she would have left us anyway."

"Daddy was her whole world. After he died, it's like she did, too."

"She was our mother, she should have stuck it out with us. She had two kids who were depending on her." Kelly frowned, the familiar anger starting to burn in her chest. "She probably thought Grammy would step in if she couldn't raise us. Which she did."

"And we're both better for it."

Thank goodness for Grammy. Kelly got to her feet. "I'll be ready for church when you are tomorrow."

Megs rolled over and switched off the light.

Taking that as her cue, Kelly left the bedroom and shut the door behind her.

SAM PICKED UP the guitar where Kelly had left it on its stand. He strummed a few chords then put it back. Better to leave it there. Not think about it.

His cell phone rang, and he glanced at the caller ID before answering it. Great. Not what he needed tonight. He swiped his finger over the front of the phone and held it to his ear. "Hi, Dad."

"Junior."

"The answer is still no."

"I haven't asked you anything."

"Not yet." His dad was well-known for being focused, determined and relentless. "Every phone call from you is the same."

"Your mother misses you."

Sam missed her, too. She had brought kindness and compassion to his harsh reality. While his father had only pushed him harder and further. "She understands what I'm doing here. Unlike you."

"You have an obligation to the record label."

"I fulfilled my contract, and I am allowed to choose my own life and live it the way I see fit." And that meant living here in this small northern Michigan town and building a business from the ground up. He'd cling to his passion despite the naysayers, including his father. And he'd avoid the demons that waited for him in Nashville.

"What about your fans? Don't they deserve something more than this silence?"

Sam laughed, but it sounded bitter to his own ears. "They deserved to have a man they could look up to. Not one who was broken and useless."

"You're stronger now."

He thought back to his conversation with Zac, the pull to go to the bar with the guys even once. It was that pull that had gotten him into trouble before. That thirst, that need to belong and be admired. Worshipped even. Deep down, Sam knew he hadn't changed. Not really. But he could overcome the demons by remaining here and working hard. "I'm not coming back. I love my life in Lake Mildred."

"Listen, son. That may be true now. But one day, you're going to wake up with regret."

No, he'd done that enough in Nashville after a night of binge drinking. "I don't think so. All those could have beens don't appeal to me."

The silent tension between the two men lasted a long while. Sam eventually got off the armchair and went over to the windows to check on the farmhouse. No light shone from the dark windows, which meant that the sisters had gone to bed, a notion that appealed to him, too. It had been a long day, a long week. And sleep beckoned like a neglected child. "Tell Mom I love her."

"You should tell her yourself. In person."

Yep, focused, determined and relentless. "Soon."

"Don't forget the launch party for Tyler's album. Your friend wants you there. And son, so do your mother and I."

"I'll think about it."

His dad huffed, "Good night, Junior. And think about what I said."

Sam ended the call and stared at the phone for a second, then he glanced at his guitar. The only obligation he had was to himself and to becoming the man he'd once lost. He walked past the guitar and collapsed on the bed. He didn't change before he drifted into sweet oblivion.

THOUGH THE SWEETHEART was closed on Sunday, it was filled with women and presents wrapped in shades of pastel pink and blue. Kelly set out a selection of teas before returning to the kitchen to check on Megs, who'd scurried by with plates of scones, cupcakes and tarts. Kelly caught up to her sister and grabbed two of the plates.

The guest of honor, Suzy Bylin—now Suzy Stone, Kelly reminded herself—sat plump and smiling on a chair surrounded by friends and family. She glowed under all the attention.

Lizzie Allyn approached Kelly and sighed. "She looks too happy."

"I think that's because she is." Kelly turned to Lizzie. "And don't tell me you're jealous. I've seen you with Rick."

Lizzie blushed. "I'm ecstatic with him. Usually. And we've talked about babies, but I must be hearing the clock tick louder lately or something."

A tall woman with red hair handed Suzy another gift. The blue ribbon broke, and the women clapped. "That makes six blue and two pink," Eva Stone, the expectant mom's mother-in-law announced. "I just know it's going to be a boy."

Suzy chuckled. "Maybe."

The redhead's mouth dropped open. "You peeked at the results of the ultrasound, didn't you? And after you promised Will that you'd keep it a secret."

"I didn't peek." She slid her finger under the gift wrapping decorated with teddy bears and sail boats. "Will did first, and then he couldn't keep it a secret."

Everyone leaned forward as Eva clutched her chest. "And?"

Suzy paled. "Oh, no. He'd kill me if I said anything." She let the wrapping paper fall and cooed over the gender-neutral onesies and booties inside. "Thank you, Penny. It's all perfect."

Another woman sitting next to a lady who could only be the woman's sister nodded, but she didn't look happy. Kelly had the feeling that this party was in fact causing her discomfort, maybe even pain. Kelly took a plate of scones and offered it to her. "Here, try one of these."

The woman looked up and gave a wry

smile. "I wondered when you'd be back in town."

Kelly dropped to the empty seat next to hers. Penelope Novakowski. She should have recognized her instantly. Together, they had dominated the choir room and been rivals as well as friends. "Megs told me you got married a while ago."

Penny nodded. "To Matt. I'm Penny Sorenson now."

"Matt the Stud Sorenson? How did you make that happen?"

The light in Penny's eyes dimmed. "By getting pregnant." She turned her attention back to Suzy who broke another blue ribbon. The women cheered, but Penny glanced at Kelly, then got up from her chair and fled to the restroom. Kelly leaned toward Shelby, Penny's younger sister. "Did I say something wrong?"

Shelby waved off Kelly's concern. "She gets sensitive at these things. She and Matt, they've had a hard time. She just needs a moment."

Kelly nodded as if she understood, but really she had no clue. In high school, she and Penny had been inseparable. Unless they were fighting over a guy or a solo, then they had avoided each other. But it only lasted for so long before they reconciled, stronger than ever. After Kelly left town for college and then Nashville, however, they'd lost touch. She hadn't felt the loss of the friendship until now.

Kelly's thoughts were interrupted by a high, keening noise. She turned to find Suzy clutching the last gift to her belly. "Not now. It's too soon."

Eva bounded to her feet and rushed to her daughter-in-law. "Contractions?"

Suzy nodded. "I've had a backache since last night, but I think either my water broke or my bladder is too full."

This motivated the party into action. Eva called her son on her cell phone while the tall redhead helped Suzy to her feet. "Tell him we'll meet him at the hospital. I'll drive her there myself."

Lizzie directed guests to push their chairs out of the way. She pointed at the huge pile of gifts. "I'll call Rick, and we'll deliver these to your house later this afternoon. You concentrate on having a healthy baby."

Suzy nodded again and paused in her walking to clutch her belly. "Please wait, little one. Wait for Daddy."

A young woman with long curly blond hair followed her. "That's right, Suzy. Talk to the baby and calm *him*? Her?"

Suzy scoffed at her friend. "Nice try, Page. But I'm not even telling you."

Suzy waddled under the supervision of the redhead, Eva and another woman who Kelly assumed must be a sister-in-law. Megs pointed to the swinging doors. "Go out through the kitchen. It'll be closer to your car that way."

Kelly sprinted to hold one of the doors open for them to walk through. Suzy and her entourage made it out to the car amid the concerned looks of the guests. Once the guest of honor was off to deliver her baby, the shower held little appeal. The women gathered their coats and purses while Megs sent them home with bags, filled with pastries.

With the bakery finally empty, except for she and Meg, Lizzie began to organize the gifts into manageable piles. A knock on the front door, and Megs let Rick inside. He lit up as his gaze fell on his wife. "Never a dull event with you around."

Lizzie smiled and gestured to the presents.

"We can fit those in your truck, and I'm sure my car can fit these. Did Will give you their house key?"

"I am mayor. So I do have the keys to the city." He waggled his eyebrows which made her roll her eyes. "Yes, I picked it up from him as you ordered. Though given he was speeding to the hospital, I hope he doesn't get pulled over."

The Allyns carried gifts to their cars as Megs and Kelly tidied the bakery for the following day. They took the dishes and cups into the kitchen for washing. But when Kelly started to fill the sinks with hot water, Megs shook her head. "They can wait until tomorrow morning."

"You need to invest in a dishwasher."

"That's why I hired you." Megs returned to the front of the bakery. Lizzie and Rick had the final presents in their arms when Kelly joined them.

Lizzie said, "Thank you both for hosting us today. Maybe it will be my turn soon."

Rick planted a kiss on the top of her head, and Kelly hurried to the front door to let them out. She turned to find Megs sitting in a chair, scrutinizing the place. "You all right?"

Her sister looked up at her and shrugged. "Despite how it ended, today's shower was nice. I enjoyed myself even though I was technically working."

Kelly's back and feet ached from standing so long, but she agreed. "Have you hosted a lot of these types of events?"

Megs got to her feet and rearranged a couple of chairs. "Usually I deliver the pastries to a person's home or the hall. But I like the idea of being able to rent out this space for something like this."

"More changes?"

"Maybe." Megs continued to put tables and chairs back into position. "I'll need to think about that."

Kelly walked into the kitchen to fetch the broom and dustpan.

THE LONG LINES at the bakery didn't stop at all Monday morning, leaving Kelly drained and wishing for a moment to herself. One where she didn't have to fill an order of doughnuts or wrap a loaf of bread in pink tissue paper, or ring up a purchase on the cash register that Megs should really consider replacing with a newer model. Kelly thought of coffee with an extra spoonful of sugar, a smile creeping over her face before she could control it.

"Okay, take a break."

Kelly turned to look at her sister. "Excuse me?"

"You look like you could use one." Megs pointed at the display cases. "Get a doughnut and take fifteen. You deserve it."

Kelly spied the line of customers still waiting. "What about you?"

"I'll go after you." Megs used plastic tongs to put a honey cruller, Kelly's favorite, onto a piece of pink tissue paper, then she handed her the sweet treat. "Now. Go while you have a chance."

She didn't have to be told a third time. Kelly took the doughnut and bit into it as she pressed on the swinging doors to enter the kitchen and claim one of the stools. She thought better of it and walked upstairs to the loft to relax on the pink velvet sofa. She propped her feet on the old coffee table and settled back into the cushions.

Contentment found in a circle of dough. Simple pleasures came in small packages.

There it was again. Like a line from a song, but she knew that she'd just created it. She searched and found more napkins and wrote the words down. They perfectly summed up her life in that moment.

Footsteps on the stairs. Had it really been fifteen minutes already? She stuffed the napkin into her pocket and took another bite of the doughnut, trying to appear nonchalant, rather than guilty. Why should she feel guilty for writing some song lyrics? But she did.

Sam appeared on the landing instead of Megs. He scanned the loft and whistled. "Nice digs."

Kelly shrugged. "I told you it has potential."

He agreed and moved towards the large picture window that overlooked Lincoln Street. "I can see that." He turned back and held up his hands as if blocking a camera shot. "We could make it an open concept living room and kitchen. Granite counters with maple cabinets. A door to a bedroom off on the left." He glanced up to the ceiling, then to the walls. "Keep the exposed brick and beams look." He grinned. "It could be a beauty."

"A vision you reminded me that I can't afford." Kelly got to her feet. "Is Megs looking for me downstairs?"

"Nah, I asked where you were, and she directed me up here."

Kelly frowned. "Why?"

He took a seat on the sofa and coughed as dust rose off it. He took out a bandana from his back pocket and used it to wipe his nose. "I have a proposal for you."

She eyed him. This sounded sort of promising. "What kind of proposal?"

"A business one."

He leaned forward and rested his arms on his thighs. She glanced at the muscles that seemed to strain under the denim. Did he work out? Or was it his construction job that kept him so toned? She tried to think of the last time she'd gone to a gym or exercised. She'd had to give up her gym membership a long time ago when money got tight. She looked up to find him watching her assess him. Heat flooded her cheeks. "What kind of business?"

"House renovation. Well, more like restoration."

"Whose house?"

But she knew which one he meant before he could get the words out. "Addy's. Ours really."

Kelly rose to her feet, shaking her head. "No, I don't think so. I told you I needed time to figure out my life."

"You haven't even heard me out."

Was he crazy? She didn't need to hear a word to know this was a bad idea. "I don't need to. We're not tearing down Grammy's house. Her grandfather built that house."

"I'm not suggesting we tear it down. But it is showing its age. What I'm proposing is to restore it to the condition it used to be in." He stood up and approached her. "Whatever you end up deciding to do with the place, you're looking at having to fix things up."

"The house is fine."

He pulled out a piece of folded paper from his back pocket. "I made a list months ago of the things Addy would need to have repaired." He held the sheet of paper out to her. "I prioritized it by putting the more pressing issues on top."

She took the list and perused it. It filled both sides of the page. She waved it in front of him. "The house doesn't need this much work. It's fine."

Sam took it from her and started to read aloud. "The foundation in the front is sagging. That means the wood slats of the porch are becoming warped, and the steps are pulling away, causing a safety issue. Shoring it up from the basement below would take care of most of that, then, of course, there's replacing and painting the porch." He glanced up at her. "And that's only the first item on here."

"So? You said the house is showing its age."

"Actually, it's doing more than that." Sam folded the paper and put it back in his pocket. "These aren't cosmetic things we're talking about. Though there are plenty of those on this list, too. But issues of safety—yours and your sister's—concern me."

She sat back down on the sofa. "And we'd take care of these issues with what money? As you pointed out to me, I don't have a dime right now."

"But I do." He shifted an inch closer to her. "My business is doing well, and I have some money from before. We could write a contract between us that any proceeds from the purchase or sale will be divided between us after the cost of the renovation." He held out his hand to her. "What do you say? Partners?"

She glanced at his hand, unsure about this.

The idea of updating the house seemed good on paper, but what if Sam changed it too much? Would the memories she had disappear along with the old cabinets and appliances? Desperate, Kelly grasped at any straw available. "Don't you have work that you already have to do? You're going to take time off from that to do this?"

He reached out to her, but stopped himself. "The winter is approaching, so the jobs I'm signed on for are dwindling."

"I don't know." She rubbed her arms at the sudden chill that seemed to permeate the loft. "What brought this on?"

SAM SIGHED. HE knew it would be a hard sell, but he hadn't expected such reluctance on Kelly's part. Why balk at the idea of doing this and making them a bigger profit in the long run?

Unless she really was determined to keep the house?

He'd woken up that morning with the image of the sparkling, polished farmhouse lingering after his dream. A home that would once again build memories and a legacy. The one now seemed to be dying with Addy, unless they did something.

Kelly looked at him as if waiting for him to say something. Right. Why he wanted to do this. He gave her a smile that he hoped she'd find reassuring. "I think it's what Addy would have wanted in the long run."

"If that's true, she would have had you crossing off things on that list, rather than applying bandages."

An argument he'd had with Addy often. To do all the upgrades that he'd wanted and she'd needed would have taken money and time. Addy had been short on both, as it turned out. "I worked within what she gave me. And it wasn't nearly enough."

Kelly clasped her hands in front of her and glanced down at them. "I don't know."

It was better than an outright refusal. "Like I said, the foundation is a serious issue that would need to be addressed whatever you, we, decide to do with the farmhouse."

"I can't think about this right now."

He took a few steps toward her and held her by her upper arms. "Why not? Don't you have plans? A life to get back to?"

She removed herself from his grip and

walked away from him. Glancing at her empty coffee cup, she said, "I've got to get back downstairs. Megs will be waiting for me."

"She knows you're up here with me."

Kelly looked up at him. "I can't talk about this right now." She walked down the stairs, leaving him alone.

He scanned the loft again and took a few measurements. Kelly was right about making this a retreat for Megs. Just like he was right about what the farmhouse needed.

As he started down the staircase he saw a napkin on one of the steps. He picked the napkin up and unfolded it to read the words written there. He read them again and smiled at their simplicity.

Addy had never mentioned that her granddaughter could write songs as well as sing. So, Miss Kelly had some things she was keeping to herself, too.

He hummed a new tune as he finished his descent to the bakery.

MONDAY NIGHT, AND Kelly struggled to stay awake in front of the television. She glanced at the time. Only eight o'clock? When had she turned seventy? She sat up on the edge of the couch and stretched, smirking at Megs who snored in the armchair next to her. What a charmed life they led.

She walked into the kitchen and opened the refrigerator to stare inside. Closed it when nothing appealed. It's not like she was hungry. Just bored. And worn out.

She leaned back against the kitchen counter and surveyed the room. Tried to see it through Sam's eyes. His proposal to fix up the place had thrown her. He couldn't just come in and change everything because Grammy was gone. But she did acknowledge the dated appliances. Admitted the shelves in the pantry sagged with age and use. Could hear the creaks in the floorboards as she pushed off the counter and approached the wall of double ovens, Grammy's pride and joy.

Kelly ran a hand along the chrome and assumed they couldn't remodel the kitchen without losing them. And that was something she couldn't agree to.

A truck approaching in the driveway pulled her up short. She peered out the window and saw Sam get out and head to his apartment with a pizza box.

She couldn't invite herself over to his place,

even if the thought of pizza made her mouth water.

Unless…she wanted to discuss his proposal.

She peeked into the living room and saw that Megs was still asleep in the chair. She was out the side door and up the stairs before she could talk herself out of this.

Sam answered on the third knock. He glanced behind her, then opened the door wider to let her in. "I wasn't expecting you."

"I hate to invite myself over." Yeah, right. She'd planned on it. She crossed the threshold into his apartment. "But I wanted to talk to you about what you said earlier today."

He motioned to the pizza box on the coffee table. "I was about to have some dinner. Hungry?"

She didn't answer, but kept her gaze on the box as he opened it and chose a slice. She took the piece of pizza from him. "Okay, maybe just one."

Sam smiled and left the living room to retrieve a roll of paper towels from the kitchen. "Plates and napkins all in one." He ripped off one square and handed it to her.

Such a guy. "That list you showed me today. How much of it on there is necessary?"

"Depends on what we plan to do with the house." He stuffed a bite of pizza into his mouth and searched his leather jacket until he found the list. He handed it to her. She unfolded it and put it on one knee while she ate her piece of pizza. "There are things we could do that wouldn't cost as much but would only be that bandage you were talking about. There are others that would cost a little more, but would add to the value of the home when it came time to sell."

Another thought that didn't settle well. "If we sell."

He nodded. "Right. If."

He took a seat across from her and watched her as she read over the list. Feeling his eyes on her, she looked up at him after she had finished reading it. "I'm not an expert on this stuff, but you are. I'd have to trust you with whatever you decided."

"You can trust me."

"I don't know you." She wiped the sides of her mouth. "But Grammy did. And Megs thinks you can do no wrong."

He helped himself to another slice of pizza as she weighed over her options. She couldn't afford to buy his half and keep the house herself. He might be able to buy her out, but didn't seem inclined to do so. "Maybe the best choice is for us to sell, and make the most profit, which means renovating the house." She crumpled the paper towel in her hand. "But the house was a piece of Grammy that she had left behind for me. I don't know if I can let it go." She groaned. "I don't know."

"It's a big decision. I get it. And we don't have to rush into anything right now." He sat forward a little, almost leaning closer to her. She backed away slightly. "And there's a lot of emotions wrapped up in this. I understand that, too. Take your time."

"I don't know."

He reached out and put a hand on her shoulder. "It's okay. We don't have to decide tonight. But I don't want to wait too long on this, either."

She searched his eyes as if they held the answer to her problem. She glanced down at her hands. "The foundation issue."

"I wouldn't wait on that, no matter what. I can start on it by Thursday at the latest."

That she could live with, so she stood. "Thanks for the pizza. I'm sorry for interrupting your evening."

He shrugged. "My pleasure."

She walked to the front door then turned back to face him. "Don't tell anything to Megs yet. She's dealing with enough as it is."

"If she asks, I won't lie."

"Fine, but don't volunteer our plans. She won't understand."

He got up from the armchair and went to open the door for her. "She'll have to be told eventually, Kel. But I agree, not until we know for sure what we want to do."

Kelly nodded and left. Oddly, she reflected, she longed to stay in the tiny apartment and spend the evening doing nothing with Sam.

CHAPTER SIX

THE RADIO BLARED with a country top ten hit, and Megs sashayed around the kitchen as she put pans of bread dough in the oven to bake. Kelly smiled as she dropped balls of dough into the deep fryer. "You're in a good mood," she told her sister.

Megs shut the oven door and turned to her. She rubbed her hands together to remove some of the flour that coated them. "I guess. Suzy and Will welcomed their baby boy Benjamin early yesterday, and I'm feeling hopeful."

"This is the first time you've danced since I've come back to town." Kelly checked the doughnuts to see if they were floating and bubbling in the oil.

Her sister's smile faded, and she brought her hands to her cheeks. "It's not like that."

"It's okay, Megs. Life has to go on even if Grammy isn't here." She used the slotted spoon to remove the balls of fried dough. She looked up at her sister. "And that includes dancing because you feel like it."

Megs returned to the counter to check the list of items they had left to make for the day. "And what about you? I haven't heard you sing."

Kelly brought the doughnuts over to the rolling cart to sit and cool before being filled with jelly or cream. "I haven't felt like it." She faced her sister, putting a hand on her arm. "Besides, you heard me at the funeral. I could barely croak out the words to the song."

"You were emotional."

"It was more than that." She raised her hand and massaged her throat. "I can't sing."

Megs raised an eyebrow then started to measure out the ingredients for the next recipe. "Grammy always said you were born to sing."

"Not anymore." Kelly untied the strings on her apron and headed toward the back door. "I'm taking a break."

"Your talent for singing didn't die with Grammy."

She turned and stared at her sister. "You're going to throw that at me? What about you?"

Megs looked around the kitchen. "What about me? I'm still baking. Still keeping the Sweetheart alive and running."

Didn't she see it? Yes, Megs was here physically, but otherwise? "Your heart's not in it any more than mine is."

"You don't know what you're talking about." Megs took eggs from the cooler and cracked several into a metal bowl. She started to whisk them as if it was their fault she was stuck in the kitchen. "Aren't I doing things like she always did?"

Kelly rounded the kitchen island and slapped the counter. "Exactly. You're running the bakery perfectly according to Grammy's ways. But what about your ways?"

Her sister poured the eggs in the indented center of a mound of flour. She mixed and kneaded the dough until Kelly could swear it begged for mercy. "I'm doing it the way I should."

"But not the way you want."

She'd seen how Megs had eliminated items from the menu that she herself had introduced. How she returned to the pastries that their grandmother had been famous for. How she kept everything, including the items in the cupboard, in their same spaces. The spices in the same order. The bowls and pans on the same shelves. Grammy used to brag about how Megs had inspired recipes that they would try and won rave reviews. But no one would sample them now.

She approached her sister who started to roll the dough into a long snake. She put her hand on Megs's and stilled it for a moment. "The Sweetheart belongs to you. You can try things however you want to."

Megs snapped back, "You don't get to come to town and tell me what you think you know about me. Because you know nothing at all."

"I know that you're retreating into a shell of who you once were."

Megs's eyes flared with a gleam of brown light. "That's really ironic coming from you. You say you can't sing anymore? Maybe you can't, but you're letting your dream die along with Grammy."

Kelly bristled and clenched her hands into fists. "Then we're both messed up." She retrieved her coat from the hook by the back door. "I'm out of here."

"It was only a matter of time."

Kelly slammed the door on her way out.

She retrieved her car keys from the pocket of her coat and used the fob to unlock the doors. She slammed the door shut twice before it stuck, then started the truck and peeled out of the parking lot. She didn't stop driving until she was in front of the Grammy's house. The pickup in the drive meant that Sam hadn't left for work yet. She took the stairs two at a time and paused outside the door to his apartment when she heard the music from inside.

She tried the doorknob and found it unlocked. She opened the door and stared at Sam, who strummed his guitar, eyes closed, singing about second chances. How could she have missed this? It must be the grief, she thought.

She pressed forward and sagged onto a kitchen stool. The scrape of the legs alerted Sam to her presence. His eyes opened, and he stopped playing.

She was sure she was gaping at him, her mouth open, probably letting in flies. She tried to chuckle. "You don't have to stop on my account, Junior."

He set the guitar aside, then stood. "It's not what you think."

"I'm so stupid. Frank Etchason Junior has

been living above my grandmother's garage for months, and I didn't know." She looked up at the ceiling as if it held the answers. "How big of an idiot am I?"

"I'm not that man anymore. I'm Sam now."

Who was he trying to kid? "Really? Because I have a CD of yours back in Nashville that would disagree." No wonder he'd looked familiar to her. Not only had he released an album that she loved, but he was the son of a Nashville record executive. "What in the world are you doing in Lake Mildred, Junior?"

He retrieved his leather jacket and stuffed his arms into the sleeves. "I'm not Junior. I'm Sam."

"Right." She stood and looked him over. "You disappeared from the Nashville scene, and I always wondered why."

He retrieved his bag of tools and slung them over his shoulder. "I'm late for work. And you need to leave."

"Why? Because I finally figured out your secret?" She laughed, but she felt no joy in it. "I knew you were too good to be true."

"You want to talk about secrets?" He left the room and returned from the bedroom with a crumpled napkin. "What about your song-writing?"

"I'm no songwriter."

He thrust the napkin into her hand. "The evidence would suggest otherwise."

She unfolded it and read the few words. "It's nothing. Just a few thoughts I had one day. Big deal."

"With some work, it could be." He stared down at her.

She took a step away from him, not liking how he towered over her. "My secret is smaller than yours."

"Are we really going to compare size?"

She blushed and stuffed the napkin into her pocket. "Seriously, Sam. Why are you here doing manual labor instead of composing songs? Does anyone else in town know who you are?"

"No. And it stays between us."

"Did Grammy know?"

He nodded. "I told her, eventually. She had that way of getting things out of people that they didn't want to share."

Kelly had been on the receiving end of that a time or ten herself. "Does my sister know?"

"No. I wanted to put as much distance between Junior and myself as I could. I couldn't tell her."

The fact that he was Frank Junior blew Kelly's mind, but that he didn't want anyone to know? "Why? You're an amazing singer."

"Kelly, why are you here?"

Nice change of topic. She shrugged. "Megs and I had a fight, and I used to run to Grammy, but she's not around, and you—"

"I am."

She nodded, and he took a step toward her. "As much as I'd like to talk about all this right now, I really do have to get to my next job." He went to the front door and held it open for her. "We can talk later."

She crossed her arms, but left the apartment, anyway. "Fine. But I want answers."

"So do I."

Kelly returned to the Sweetheart after leaving Sam's place. It was hard to think of him as Junior, the singer who had filled some of her solitude with his stunning voice.

She let herself in the bakery's back door, wary of seeing her sister after their fight, but found Tom alone, scooping chocolate chip dough onto greased cookie sheets. She looked around. "Megs?"

He didn't glance up or pause in his work. "At the bank. She should be here by the time these come out of the oven."

Kelly hung up her coat and approached the work island. "Where are we on today's recipes?" she asked.

SAM TOOK THE long way home once he'd finished his visit to the lumber store in Robert Falls. After Kelly's discovery of his identity that morning, he'd needed to reclaim the life he'd worked so hard to build. To put Junior back in the box where he belonged.

He shouldn't have been foolish enough to play the guitar. Worse to have tried to sing after so long. His vocals sounded rusty after two years of disuse. Not that it mattered. That wasn't who he was anymore.

He pulled into the driveway and glanced at the farmhouse before getting out of the truck and approaching the side door. He knocked once, but there was no answer. He glanced behind him and saw that both the sisters' vehicles were parked next to his. Oh-kay. He knocked again, but this time turned the knob and entered the kitchen.

"If you don't like it, pack up and get out

of here!" Megs pointed toward the door that Sam had just walked through seconds before.

Kelly scowled at her sister. "If anyone is going to pack up and leave, it won't be me. This is my house!"

Sam raised one finger. "Actually, it's ours."

She turned and glared at him. "Stay out of it."

He moved his fingers in front of his mouth as if locking them shut. The two sisters continued to stare at each other from opposite sides of the kitchen. Megs growled, "I knew you would throw that in my face eventually. You want me out? Fine." She stormed from the room and stomped upstairs to her bedroom, where they heard the door slam.

Sam looked over at Kelly. "What was that all about?"

"Sister bonding."

He snorted. He'd grown up with a sister himself, but he doubted the Sweet sisters' argument he'd walked in on could be called anything close to bonding. "You can't let her leave."

Kelly's eyes showed lightning flashes of anger. "What would you know about it?"

"So then tell me."

She shook her head and searched for her coat behind him, where it looked as if she'd casually tossed it over a stool. "I need to get out of here."

He handed her the coat, and she threw it on. "Megs said you always run when things get difficult."

She whirled on him before zipping up the coat. "Is that what you think I'm doing?"

"I haven't got a clue what you're doing. But it looks like you're leaving." He held his hands up in surrender. "If you need a sounding board though, I'm good at listening."

She bristled and cocked her ear as if trying to hear what was happening above them. "Do you think she'll really move out?"

"This has been her home for fifteen years. What do you think?" He glanced to the ceiling. "But give me five minutes before you take off."

"All right." Sam left Kelly in the kitchen and walked into the foyer. He took the stairs briskly, then strolled to the only closed door off the hallway. Knocking softly, he inched the door open. "I come in peace."

Megs's tear-stained face appeared. "What do you want?"

He opened the door the rest of the way and saw the open suitcase on her bed. It was still empty. He cocked his head to the side. "You can't move out."

"I'm not a prisoner here."

Interesting choice of words. "Is that how you feel?"

"Don't shrink me, Sam. I'm not in the mood." She went to her closet and tore open the door. "Kelly was allowed to leave town. Now it's my turn."

"Is that what you really want?" He was sure he had the answer, but he wanted to hear her say the words out loud. If not to convince him, then to assure herself.

She turned and shook her head. "Of course not."

He let out a breath that he hadn't known he'd been holding. "So why are you doing it?"

She took out several clothes on hangers and threw it all in her suitcase. "Aren't I supposed to leave the nest eventually? Kids go off to college or a job or get married. Isn't that what normal people do?"

"Since when have you been normal?"

She squelched a grin. "Okay, you got me

with that one." She collapsed on the edge of the bed. "Is Kelly still downstairs?"

He nodded and sat down beside Megs. He took her hand in his. "What's going on with you?"

"It's like I don't know my place in this world without Grammy. I don't understand how to live in a place she's missing from." She put her head in her hands. "And then, my sister is here, but for how long? And when she goes back to her own life, where does that leave me?"

Sam put his arms around Megs and pulled her close to his side. He rested his chin on top of her head. "Where do you want to be?"

"I don't know. I honestly don't."

She clung to him and sobbed. Finally, her cries subsided but she still sniffled. Sam let go of her and took a tissue from the box on her nightstand and handed it to her. She wiped her eyes, then blew her nose. She ran a hand through her hair. "I look a fright."

"You're fine." He took another tissue and handed it to her.

"I'm a lot of things, but fine is not one of them." She looked up at him. "I didn't mean to blubber on your shoulder."

He picked at the wet spot on his shirt. "That's what friends are for."

She blew her nose again, and then folded the tissue in squares several times. "Could you tell Kelly that we'll talk tomorrow?"

He pointed behind him toward the open doorway. "Don't you want to talk to her yourself?"

"No!" Megs lowered her voice. "I can't. Not yet. Tomorrow."

Sam nodded, leaned on the edge of the dresser. He looked around the bedroom. "This is the first time I've been in here."

"Don't get used to it."

He smiled, and she tried to give one back to him. "Never crossed my mind," he said. But at the way her face fell, he grimaced slightly. "I didn't mean it like that. It's like you're my sister, so I don't think of you like a woman." He shook his head and held up his hands as if surrendering. "That sounded worse than what I meant." He ran a hand along his jaw. "Can you help me out here?"

"Why? You're doing such a wonderful job on your own."

"You know what I mean."

She grinned. "I regard you like a brother,

so yes I do. But something tells me that you don't think of my sister in the same way."

"No, I don't look at Kelly like I would a sister. She could maybe be something more." He paused. "Are you okay with that?"

"Why wouldn't I be?"

They looked at each other for a moment, then he pushed himself off the dresser. "I'm going to check on Kelly. Are you okay?"

She shrugged. "I'm going to change into pajamas and crawl into bed. I can't think about any more of this tonight."

"Sleep tight."

He shut the door behind him, only to be stopped by Kelly who was waiting at the top of the stairs. "How is she? You were gone longer than five minutes."

"She needs to be left alone right now."

Kelly offered a weak smile, but kept her gaze on Megs's door. "I don't want her to leave, you know." She gazed up at him, unshed tears shining in her eyes. "She's all I have."

"I know."

Suddenly, she leaned forward and her shoulders shook with her cries. What was it with the Sweet women and their tears? He put his arm around her and led her down the stairs to the kitchen. He handed her a wad of tissues. She wiped her nose on one and crumpled it in her fist. "I don't know what I'm doing," she said.

"Megs feels the same way."

She nodded and wiped the corners of her eyes. "Grammy kept us together. And now that she's gone, it's like we don't have that connection anymore."

"So find a new one."

She frowned. "The Sweetheart?"

"How about the fact that you're sisters through thick and thin? That the blood bond you share is more important than any other you'll find in this life?" He shook his head. "You know what? You two do what you want. I feel like I'm wasting my breath on the both of you."

He started to walk away, but Kelly grabbed the sleeve of his shirt. "Don't leave me."

"Why not?"

"I don't want to be alone right now." She moved into his embrace, but he didn't put his arms around her. "Please stay."

"Kelly, you're treading on dangerous ground."

She looked up at him, and he instantly, magically lost a piece of himself in those blue eyes. He swore softly then wrapped his arms around her tiny body. She snuggled into him, resting her cheek on his chest. He closed his eyes and rocked her gently. "Better?"

She and gave a soft sigh. He assumed that was a yes.

While he'd felt brotherly with Megs upstairs, with Kelly, their nearness generated different feelings, using opposite hormones. With Kelly, he wanted to not only help her and protect her but he also wanted to hold her and kiss her. To make her important in his life. He opened his eyes and tried to think of something else besides lifting her chin, so he could kiss that tempting mouth of hers. Concentrating on the ceiling instead of how the light made her blond hair golden and call out to his fingers. He tensed his hand into a fist.

Suddenly, she stepped back and he tried to think of something to say to her, but it all sounded trite. Cliché. So he stuffed his hands into his jean pockets and rocked back on to his heels. "I guess I'll go home, unless you need me still?"

"Take me somewhere."

He raised one eyebrow at this. "Excuse me?"

She bit her lip, and then said, "I'm not running away if I plan on returning. But I need to get out of this house at least for a little bit."

"Where should we go?"

"Anywhere other than here." She turned and grabbed her coat from where she'd tossed it after the fight with Megs. She struggled with the left sleeve, so he helped her with it. "Don't you want to go do something?" she asked.

Did he all right, but he doubted they were thinking the same thing. "Sure." He slipped on his leather jacket. "What were you thinking?"

"The Penalty Box?"

He shook his head. "I don't go to bars."

She frowned, but then quickly brightened. "Okay. The diner?"

"It's past nine so it's closed."

"And *this* is why I had to leave this town. There's nothing to do." She put her hands on her hips. "I give. Where do you want to go?"

"This is your party. You tell me."

She squirmed under his gaze. He could see when inspiration struck. "There is one place with lots of peace and quiet. Secluded. I'll drive."

He held up his key ring and dangled it at her. "Nice try, but I'll drive."

KELLY DIDN'T KNOW why leaving the house and spending time with Sam had become important, but it had. She didn't want to be alone. Yet she didn't want to be with just anyone. Only Sam. She tried to figure out why the man who had stolen half her inheritance had become essential in her life. When she was upset, she turned to him. When she needed advice, it was his that she sought. Shouldn't she want to be far away from him, rather than sitting next to him as he drove them to Lover's Leap?

She couldn't seem to stop looking at him. Man, he was beautiful. When he turned to look at her, she glanced out the window. "There's a mailbox coming up on the left. Take the dirt path, and we'll be there in about a minute or two."

"You can tell you've lived here a long time, you sure know your way around this place better than I do."

She glanced at him and saw him turn away

quickly. So she wasn't the only one looking at the other. They passed the mailbox, and he steered left onto the dirt road. She kept her gaze forward. "Did Megs seem okay when you left her?"

"She's hurting just like you."

"Not just like me."

Sam slowed the truck, peering out into the darkness. "You've both lost the same grandmother. You feel like you've lost your way, just like Megs. You're more alike than you realize." He stopped the truck. "Where are we?"

"Megs doesn't have my doubts about what to do with her future." Kelly motioned to a break in the pine trees on their right that the headlights of his truck lit up. "You can park over there, but keep your lights on so we can see the path. Then we can get out and walk."

"You sure about Megs not having doubts, Kel? Just because she never left town and has been at the bakery doesn't mean she knows what to do any more than you do."

"She's stronger than you give her credit for."

"Or maybe you want to give her more credit, rather than facing the truth." He got out of the truck. He looked around the woods then started walking.

Kelly watched him go, mouth open, then she got out and ran up to him. "You've known my sister how long? And you think you know her better than I do?"

"You've all but admitted she's a stranger to you now."

"Oh sure. Throw that in my face."

He scanned the area before looking back at her. "Where to now?"

"Follow me." She pushed away some of the branches of a pine tree and let the glow of the truck's headlights and the moon guide her way. Soon they had reached the edge of a drop that lead to a clearing. She took a seat and dangled her legs over the side. "Isn't this beautiful?"

Sam took a seat next to her but kept his gaze on her. "Gorgeous."

She looked out into the night and sighed. "I used to come here and think." She glanced at him. "Until it became a make-out place. And even then, I came up here a time or two with Seth Danz."

Sam gave a chuckle.

"It's a quiet place. Gave me somewhere to think."

"So why bring me up here?"

She pulled up one leg and rested her chin on her knee. "Maybe to capture that feeling I had when I was a teenager. I had the whole world at my feet. All I had to do was grab it. And now? I have nothing. Not even my voice."

Sam sat down, reached over and took her hand. "You're going to be okay. You're a strong, independent woman who knows what you want and goes after it."

She wished he was right, but he didn't know the half of it. How the doubts and fears kept her awake at night, tossing and turning her in bed before she fell into exhaustion and her mind shut off. Was being strong doing what she had to do despite the doubts? "I did know once. But it's over."

Sam laughed, the sound of it echoing around them. "Are you kidding me? You've barely started."

She stared at him hard. "I tried to make a music career for eight years. After college, I pushed at it and nothing happened."

"Nothing?"

"I got a lot of callbacks and some short-term gigs, but no, nothing lasting." She removed her hand from his. "And what about you? Who are you really? Just because I haven't brought the topic up doesn't mean I've forgotten your secret, Junior."

He hushed her. She should have admonished him, but he was so cute, so sweet that she laughed. "You think the forest creatures are going to figure it out and call the tabloids? Sure, you had a hit with one song. Everybody remembers the words, but they don't remember who sang it."

He ducked his head. "And wrote it."

"What I don't understand is that you could have stayed on top of the charts. You had the talent and Daddy's connections." She leaned toward him. "So, what happened?"

"I don't want to talk about it."

"Why not? We've talked about me." She watched him. While the light from the dashboard had made him handsome, the moonlight brought out something else. He looked breathtaking. Focusing on his mouth, she licked her lips. "Couldn't handle the fame?"

"I said I'm not talking about it." He rose to his feet and dusted off the dirt and grass from his jeans. "You stay as long as you need to. I'm going back to the truck."

She stood and called out to him, "Was I

right? You couldn't handle being in the spot-light?"

Sam stalked over to her, and she stepped up to meet him. He pointed his finger in her face. "You don't know anything."

No, she didn't, which was her point. "So explain it to me."

He looked down at her, opened and closed his mouth as if trying to find the words. Then he grabbed her and kissed her soundly on the mouth.

The pressure of his lips on hers made her forget everything else. She let her eyes close and she savored the kiss. After all, he had only done it to shut her up.

Right?

She brought her hand up to the back of his head, his hair tickling her palm. She gave a sigh. He only pushed her away and trudged back to his car.

She touched her lips that still tingled.

What had just happened?

SAM CALLED HIMSELF a bunch of names as he swung open the truck door and climbed inside the cab, slamming the door after him. What had he been thinking?

That was the problem. He hadn't been thinking. He'd wanted to get her to stop talking. To fluster her as much as she was doing to him. And instead, he'd ended up kissing her.

Sure, he'd been thinking about it. A lot, especially lately. More than necessary. But the reality had been different than what he'd expected. Softer. Sweeter. And so addicting. He was already thinking about going back there and trying it again.

Keep your eyes on the prize, Etchason. Falling for Addy's granddaughter didn't fit into his plans. He needed to establish his business and make it thrive so he could prove to his father that he wasn't wasting his life.

But it wouldn't hurt to steal one more kiss, right?

He groaned and rested his head on the steering wheel. He blamed Kelly for making him lose his mind in that moment. She'd brought up this place being an old make-out haunt. And he'd had it on the brain. That's it. It was her fault.

The passenger door opened, and Kelly got inside the truck. She didn't look at him, but kept her gaze out her window. "Just take me back home."

He put the key in the ignition, but didn't turn it. The smart thing would be to do as she'd said and take her home. To return to his apartment and try to forget how that kiss had rocked his world. But he'd never claimed to be that smart.

He put his arm across the back of the seat and turned to her. "After we talk."

"What is there to talk about?"

He hesitated. "I didn't answer your question before. Instead, I—"

"You kissed me."

"To avoid answering you, yes." He put his hand on her shoulder, but she still wouldn't look at him. "The reasons I left my life in Nashville are complicated. And I don't talk about them with anyone."

She faced him then, hurt clear in her eyes. "Do you think I'm going to sell your story to the tabloids or something? I'm not like that."

"I know, but there are things that I don't talk about. Can't talk about." He reached up and pushed a golden strand of her hair behind her ear. "I'm not ready to. But when I am, you'll be the person I'll tell."

She seemed to be holding her breath and let it out in a rush. "Okay. I can be patient, I suppose."

He nodded, then turned back and started the ignition. "And I'm not sorry about that kiss."

There was a moment of silence, then she said softly, "Me, either."

CHAPTER SEVEN

THE KITCHEN DOORS swung open, and Megs brought out another tray of cinnamon rolls fresh from the oven. Kelly double-checked the coffee carafes to make sure they were full as well as the cups, stirrers and lids. Another Monday morning yet Kelly was ready for the weekend. Not that she'd had much of one since returning to Lake Mildred. Working six days at the bakery meant she had only one day off, and had to wait awhile until she could enjoy another one.

Megs carried a tray of sliced coffee cake to one of the display cases, then glanced at her watch. "It's almost seven, so you might as well unlock the doors."

Kelly nodded and did so. She turned the sign over to "Open" then returned to her position behind the counter as the bell above the front door tinkled, alerting them to their first customer.

Kelly looked up to find Rick already perusing the doughnut selections behind the glass. She raised one eyebrow. "Don't you serve breakfast at your diner?"

Rick grinned. "A guy needs fat and sugar sometimes." He pointed to a bear claw. "I'll take one of those."

Kelly used a piece of wax paper from the box and picked up the pastry, then put it in a pink paper bag. "Any others you'd want to add?"

He glanced over the offerings, but shook his head. "Nah. Lizzie will kill me if she finds out about this one."

"She's got you on a diet?"

"No, but I've got to keep in shape for her." He winked at Kelly, then accepted the pink paper bag and walked with it to the cash register. "Is Megs around? I was hoping to talk to you both about something coming up for the town."

Kelly rang him up and handed Rick his change. "I'll go get her."

She walked into the kitchen to find Megs elbow deep in dough. "Rick's asking for you."

Megs nodded. "Probably wants to go over his order for the diner."

"He wants to talk to both of us."

Megs frowned and walked to the sink to wash her hands. She took the towel with her, as she went out to the front of the bakery. Kelly followed her.

Rick smiled at them both as they entered. "I don't know if you've heard, but the library is holding a fund-raiser next month for the upgrades needed on the computer system. We're having a formal dinner with an evening of entertainment."

Megs smiled. "Great. Let us know when, so I can make sure to come and donate."

Rick grinned even wider. "I was hoping that your donation could be towards the dinner. I'm talking rolls to be served with dinner, and then cakes and pastries for dessert." He held up his hand. "I'm not expecting anything fancy, but it would help us keep our costs for the dinner down if you could do that."

"How many are you expecting?"

"We have about twenty-five signed up so far, but we're hoping to get at least fifty or more."

Megs bit her lip while Kelly wondered how much product that would cost them. Finally, her sister nodded and held out her hand. "Deal. I'll need final numbers the week before."

They shook on it. Then Rick turned to Kelly. "As for the entertainment portion after dinner, I hoped that I could convince you to sing a couple songs?"

A hot punch in her belly almost made Kelly bend at the waist. Her? Sing? Hadn't he seen how she couldn't perform at Grammy's funeral? She could feel beads of sweat pop up at the corners of her forehead. Was the room getting warm? Rick watched her, waiting. She gave a short nod. "Um, sure?"

He laughed. "That sounded more like a question than an answer."

Megs put her hand on Kelly's arm, but she flicked it off. "It's fine. I can sing."

"Great. I knew you two would step up for the community. You're definitely Addy's girls." He held out his hand and shook both of their hands in turn. Then he held up his pastry bag. "Thanks for breakfast, too."

"We'll see you later, Rick." Megs waited until the door shut before she asked Kelly, "Why did you agree to sing?"

"It's not like I could back out." Kelly

shrugged. "Besides, maybe my voice will be back by then."

Megs stared at her, but then returned to the kitchen. Kelly huffed and wiped the counters down. Her voice *could* return in a month. It had to. Because she didn't know what else she could do with her life beyond music.

THE MORNING PASSED by slowly. Eventually though, Kelly's lunch break arrived and she took her sandwich upstairs to the loft. She ate as she watched over Lincoln Street from the window upstairs. She could see the display at Roxy's department store across the way, decorated for the Fall season. Mannequins dressed in wool sweaters and jeans, surrounding a bushel of fresh-picked apples. Another display had a witch in costume with two small goblins. In a few weeks, the displays would be changed for Roxy's infamous Christmas windows. She wondered what the theme this year would be.

The hardware store was also down the street, and she noticed Sam's pickup parked near the front door. The aquarium shop was a recent addition since she'd left town, along with the cards and candles store. All small businesses, all with their own quaint charm.

Once she finished her sandwich, she wadded up her paper towel and threw it away in the wastebasket. She dug in her apron and pulled out a small soft-bound journal she'd found in her old bedroom and a pen, and sat down on the velvet sofa to write. Clicking the pen, she bit on the tip until the words started to come. She wrote about her Grammy. About the hole in her life that her grandmother's passing had left. And the hollow of her heart that yearned to be filled after the absence. How she still reached for her phone to see if Grammy had left a text or voicemail. How she would slip into the bakery's kitchen and expect to see her standing in her apron with dough covering her hands as she kneaded and molded it into submission.

Kelly put her head down and let the tears come. Let them dampen the page, giving life to her words.

A creak on the stairs brought her head up. "Who's there?" she called as she shut the journal and tucked it under the sofa cushion.

Megs came slowly up the steps. "Mind if I intrude on your break?"

Kelly shook her head and patted the cushion next to her. Megs brought her sandwich over and groaned, biting into it. She leaned back, closing her eyes. "I can't believe how busy it's been and how good this tastes."

"When are you going to hire someone to take Grammy's place?"

Megs opened one eye and peered at Kelly. "I did. You."

She shook her head. "We both know I'm temporary at best. You need a professional baker who can do what Grammy did if you want to keep on doing things like before."

Megs stopped chewing and laid her sandwich down on her plate. "We need to talk."

A warm feeling spread through Kelly's belly. Uh-oh. Nothing good ever came after those words. That's what people said before they broke up or someone got fired. She shook her head again and rose to her feet. "I think I need to get back to work."

Megs reached out and grabbed Kelly's hand, trapping her there. "I can't keep going like we have been. I'm exhausted."

"That's why I said to hire someone."

Megs pulled Kelly back down onto the

sofa. "I need you to step up and do more, Little."

Kelly stopped at hearing the long forgotten nickname. They had called each other Little, Kelly because she was shorter, Megs because she was younger. She must be serious if she was pulling that out now. She frowned. "Haven't I been working with you this whole time? I come in when you do. Stay until you do. I can't do all the recipes like you and Grammy did, but I follow them and remember how she kept things here."

Megs sighed and let go of Kelly's hand. "What if I want to change how things are done?"

Kelly's jaw dropped, then she shut her mouth, considering her words. Even though she had been trying to convince her sister to do the same thing, to finally hear the words come out of Megs's mouth made her pause. "You want to change the Sweetheart?"

Megs stared at her, then nodded slowly. "I've been thinking about it for a while. Grammy was a powerhouse even in her later years, but I can't step into her shoes. You can't, either. So something has to give."

"Like what? The wedding cakes? The morning doughnuts?" Kelly spread her arms out. "Where would you make cuts? You promised people that nothing was going to change."

Megs dropped her head into her hands and moaned. "I know. But I can't keep this up."

"That's why you need another baker."

"We can barely afford Gina and Tom now."

Silence reigned for several minutes, and Megs eventually stood. "You know what? Never mind. I've said too much. I'll deal with this on my own. It's what I'm used to."

She started down the stairs. Kelly called her name, but Megs didn't stop and turn around.

Kelly sighed and brought out her journal. It didn't take long before she admitted she couldn't concentrate anymore. Grammy had left a bigger hole than she'd realized in her life. She looked to the top of the stairs where Megs had disappeared and rose to join her.

Downstairs, the kitchen was empty. No Megs. Not even Tom, who might have been outside on a smoke break. The daily binder was open on the counter. Kelly walked to it and glanced at the list of items that had been prepared for sale that day. There had to be at least three dozen different items. No wonder Megs was at her wit's end.

Kelly left the kitchen to check the front of the bakery for her sister. Only Gina stood there, first checking the coffee supplies and then wiping the counters. "Hey, you seen Megs?"

Gina replied, "Yeah. She said she was going to take her lunch break upstairs."

Great. Kelly returned to the kitchen. Still, no Megs. She felt for her phone in her jeans pocket then pulled it out and dialed her sister's phone number. Straight to voicemail. Kelly quit the call and texted her sister, not expecting, but hoping for a response.

Then she texted Sam. Help. Megs missing.

The response came a second later. When U last see her?

We just had a fight.

Kelly watched her phone, waiting for his answer. But there wasn't one. She tried to be patient and checked the binder for tomorrow's baking list. Where were they? What needed to be prepped ahead of time? Her phone dinged, and she glanced at it. She wants space. Txt you later.

So Megs would answer Sam, but not her. Kelly frowned but didn't have time to get upset. Almost four hours remained of her day at the bakery, not including time spent on clean-up. Kelly double-checked the list and saw that the rolls for the diner's order still needed to be made, plus the afternoon cookie rush would start after school got out later. She also had to factor in starting the dough for the next day's baking.

Megs was right. This was too much. Trying to keep up with Grammy was exhausting, if not impossible. She groaned and looked up the recipe for the yeast rolls.

SAM SAT IN his truck across the street and watched as Kelly locked up the bakery, flipping the sign to Closed. He'd called Megs to make sure she was okay after her runaway stunt earlier, but it had been Kelly that he was worried about.

He knew Megs would figure things out and be fine. But her older sister was floundering in her life and he didn't want her to drown under the pressure.

He pulled out into traffic then parked behind the bakery. He walked to the back door and knocked. Kelly appeared after several minutes. She frowned at his appearance, but stepped aside to let him in. She went over to the double sink area where a mountain of dirty bowls, whisks, spoons, dishes and baking trays waited. "What do you want?" she asked.

"Maybe it's more what you need." He took off his leather jacket and hung it up on a hook next to her wool pea coat. "I'm a mean dishwasher."

She paused in her spraying down of a tray and gave him a wary glance. He tried to smile to show his willingness, which must have worked, since she nodded toward the sink where a pile of dishes were soaking. "You wash, I'll rinse."

"Good. I'll turn up the music." He flipped the radio on and turned the dial to a country station. A popular song played, and he nodded and snapped his fingers. "Love this tune."

He hummed a few bars as he went over and stood next to her, using a wire bristle brush to get the harder bits off the first dish. He even swung his hips side to side to the beat.

"You're certainly in a good mood."

Her tone sounded like she wasn't. He shrugged and handed her the bowl he'd scrubbed. "Guess my day wasn't as bad as yours."

"I can't believe she abandoned me like that."

He noticed the faint tracks of tears on her face. "She was upset. Can you really expect her to behave otherwise?"

She glared at him. "She left me."

He really didn't want to get in the middle of this. Not between these two sisters who should be talking about what was going on, rather than pretending everything was okay. Or that they would deal with it later. "I'm sure she thought the same things when you moved to Nashville."

Kelly almost dropped the dish she was rinsing, but saved it at the last second. "That is not the same thing. I didn't leave her in the middle of work, making her do everything."

"Oh, really?"

"Shut up." Kelly grasped the spoons he handed to her and she sprayed them clean before putting them in the dish rack. "That's totally different."

"Okay."

Another good song started to play; one of Sam's favorites. He kept up the hip action. It was almost the end of tune when she finally turned to him. "I didn't abandon her. I left for school. For a career. She understood that."

"Listen, I'm only saying that's what she might have thought."

"Whatever."

They continued with the dishes until only a stack of the trays from the display cases remained. Sam started with the first, handed it to her. But she didn't take it from him. He turned to see what the problem was. Kelly was grasping the edge of the sink, her head down. He nudged her. "Maybe I'm all wet."

"No." She brought up the spray hose and hit him in the chest with a shot of hot water. "*Now* you're wet."

"Do you really want to go there?" He scooped up a handful of suds.

She held up the spray hose. "Do you?" she warned.

They stared at each other for a moment. Then Kelly broke into a grin. "Truce?"

He nodded and plunged his hands back into the soapy water. Plucking the washed tray from the suds, he handed it to her. She started to spray it with the hose, but then turned the water on him. "Whoops!"

"Oh, that's it. You've got it coming now."

He used another tray to scoop water from the sink and drenched her. She squealed, but hit him with another spray from the hose. Two could play that game. She backed up, aiming the hose right at him, but he lunged for it anyway, and pulled her to him.

He looked down at her, her gold hair wet and stringy, the pink cotton of her apron clinging to her slight form. She laughed up in his face, and then let the hose go in order to pull him down into a kiss.

He let it all go and tightened his arms around her, kissing the side of her mouth, the tip of her nose. She moaned against his mouth and put her hands on his chest. Sanity quickly returned, and he took a step back.

"What are you doing?" she asked. "I didn't think I was that out of practice." She used her thumb to wipe the corner of her mouth. "I thought we were kissing."

He took even more steps back, then reached under the sink to find a dry dish towel and wiped his face. "You don't need kissing right now."

"No? Then what do I need?"

He tossed her the dry towel. "To talk to your sister. To work out what you want. Because until you do, whatever might happen between you and me is...uncertain."

"You don't know that."

He retrieved the mop from the storage closet and began tackling the puddles on the floor. "What do you want, Kelly? What are your future plans?"

She bit her lip as she dried off her hair, squeezing out the excess water. "Do I have to know that right now?"

"I suppose not, but it means you're merely content with someone to fill in the gaps. And I'm not that guy." He'd all but finished the floor and paused to focus on her. Why did she have to look so cute when she was wet? Couldn't she have gotten the drowned rat effect instead, he lamented. "And if we're going to be partners with the house..."

Her head snapped up, her eyes full of fire. "Partners?"

"We do own equal shares." He leaned on the mop. "So yes, I'd say we were partners in this."

"We haven't even decided what we're going to do."

"And don't you think it's time we did decide?" He squeezed the mop into the empty sink and returned the mop to the closet. "Listen, I'm not the kind of guy who can wait around until you make a decision when it's convenient for you. I need answers. And I'm going to need them sooner rather than later."

She shook her head and took a step toward the last of the trays. "Well, I'm not sure."

He took a step forward and intercepted her. "Then you'll just have to make up your mind. I'm tired of your hemming and hawing when I've made a list, which we can go over anytime."

"But what about Megs?"

"It's not her choice. It's ours." He let her go, and she stumbled. "Unless you've decided to buy my half out."

"You know I can't afford that."

"So that's that, then." He took a deep breath. "Today's Monday. You have until Wednesday night to make your decision." He stalked off toward the back door and got his jacket from the hook it hung upon. He glanced over his shoulder to see Kelly watching him. "Figure out what you want, Kel. You've got two days."

He threw his jacket on and stomped out the back door.

KELLY KEPT HER EYES on Sam. Part of her wanted to run after him. But mostly she was glad to see him go. How dare he give her a deadline? This was her future they were talking about.

She paused. Their future. He'd been right about that part. Her choice affected him as much as it did her.

She finished drying the dishes and putting them away, then double-checked the kitchen to make sure everything had been prepared for the following morning. Satisfied, she put on her coat then stepped out into the cool air. She could feel the tips of her wet hair starting to freeze. The temperature must have been dropping all day, since she'd left the house early that morning.

She checked the back door to make sure it was locked, then she turned and ran to her car. Once inside, she checked her phone. A text message from Megs: I'm home.

On my way.

Kelly started her car, but didn't leave just yet. She stared up at the bakery and tried to picture it as if she were her sister. All along, she'd thought that Megs had viewed it as her home and haven. But what if she did see it as her prison instead?

Kelly pulled out of the parking lot and onto Main. She switched the radio on as she drove, finding the station that Sam had been singing to. She touched her throat and wondered. Following along with the song, she hummed at first. Didn't sound so bad. She started to add words, but could feel her throat closing up on her.

Better not to press the issue. She remained silent the rest of the way home.

She noticed Sam's truck and glanced up at his apartment, but shook her head. He'd made it clear that he wanted some answers first. And she needed to find some.

She let herself in by the side door and found Megs standing over the stove. She gestured to the pot she was stirring. "I made dinner."

Kelly took her jacket off and got settled, but still Megs kept quiet. "So, you abandon me at the bakery, and all you have to say is you made dinner?" Kelly had told herself not to get upset as she drove home, to let her sister have a chance to explain her side of things, but seeing her acting as if nothing had happened changed all of that.

Megs didn't respond. Only stirred whatever smelled so good in the pot. "Eat or don't eat, I don't care."

"Right." Kelly crossed the kitchen to stand next to her sister. "What is going on?"

Megs stopped stirring, and her shoulders sagged. "I don't know how to do this without Grammy."

"Yes, you do." Grammy might have been in charge, but Kelly knew it had been her sister who had run the bakery. Grammy's health had been declining, and she'd been giving more of the responsibility to Megs. Why couldn't her sister see that for herself?

Megs turned, her face stained with tears long shed. "You've said that before, but that doesn't change the fact that I'm drowning." She sagged on to the closest stool. "I can't keep doing this."

The despair in her voice broke Kelly's heart. "Doing what?"

Megs buried her face in her hands and started rocking back and forth. "I can't do this on my own. I can't be what everyone wants me to be."

Finally something that made sense. Kelly walked over to her sister and put her arms around the quaking shoulders. "Then don't be. Be who *you* need to be." Her sister looked up, and Kelly squeezed her tighter. "Don't try to be Grammy because the town can't let her go yet. Be who you are. Make the bakery. No, make your life how you want it."

"Easy for you to say."

Kelly took the stool next to hers. "To say, yes. But I'm still trying to figure out how to live that one out."

"But what if I change things and we lose customers?"

"We'll survive." Kelly took her sister's hand in hers. "But the important part is that you will be happier. And that's more important than how many pastries we sell." She peered into Megs's face. "Am I right?"

The nod came reluctantly. Megs wiped her face. "So what about you? What are you going to do?"

"You're the second person to ask me that

tonight, and my answer is the same. I'm not sure." She looked around the kitchen. "You know that Sam is talking about updating the house. Maybe selling it afterwards."

Megs nodded. "That's the only way for you both to get anything out of Grammy's will. Unless you two get married and live here?"

Kelly laughed and scoffed, "And now you're going to be a matchmaker? Try that on someone else."

"Why not you and Sam? You like him, and I can see he likes you, too." Megs wiggled her eyebrows, but rather than being suggestive it came across as comic.

Kelly thought of the kiss in the bakery earlier. "He is hot. But he's not what I need."

"And what is that?"

"Don't know. But I don't think it's Sam." She studied her sister. "Would you be okay with us fixing up Grammy's house?"

"Depends. You okay with me changing the bakery?"

Kelly held out her hand. "Deal."

Megs pulled her into a hug and didn't let go for a long while. Kelly told her, "I need to go do something before I lose my nerve, but I promise I'll be right back."

She left Megs in the kitchen and ran out the door and up the stairs to Sam's place. She knocked and waited. Knocked one more time. He answered the door, but kept his gaze on the television that blared a football game. "Couldn't this wait until halftime?"

"I don't need two days to decide what's right, partner." She thrust out her hand.

He turned to look at her and gave her a smile. "I'll start tomorrow on making our punch list."

"A what?"

"It's a list of everything that needs to be done to complete a job on a construction site." He winked at her. "Stick with me, partner. I'll teach you all about the renovation business." Then he shook her hand.

Later that night, Kelly slipped between the sheets and tugged the covers over her head. She let the darkness settle on her. The air heating from her own breath. It was time for the Sweet sisters to make some choices. Take a stand and show this town who they were.

CHAPTER EIGHT

"Why does change have to come so early?" Kelly propped her head up on one fist as she leaned on the bakery's kitchen island. "Couldn't you delay opening hours at least so we can sleep in a little more?"

No response beyond the whir of a mixer. Megs checked her dough, then shook her head. "I have a plan. But I don't mind the hours."

Kelly did. Big time. She groaned and went to pour a third cup of coffee from the station out front. She'd tossed and turned last night rather than sleeping, and her body felt it. She doctored her java with cream and sugar and carried it back to the kitchen with her, stirring as she walked. "What's your plan?"

"We're going to close the bakery early."

The coffee cup almost dropped from Kelly's hands. "Maybe I got less sleep than I thought because I think you just said we're going home early."

Megs held her hand up in warning. "We'll try it out first. Leave earlier so that we're not putting in as many hours and wearing ourselves out."

"Oh." The sense of relief she felt shouldn't have been so strong. After all, the bakery was Megs's life. Not hers. "What else do you plan to do?"

"Simplify. I can't keep up with all the varieties of baking that Grammy did." She walked to the ovens and checked the temperatures. "But what I do, I do well. And that's what customers respond to."

Kelly approved. Megs consulted the recipes and looked up once more. "And the Sweetheart is no longer doing wedding cakes."

Now she was just talking crazy. "But you have to. Every wedding in Lake Mildred has had its cake from the Sweetheart for over fifty years."

"Then it's time to give someone else a chance." Megs took the coffee mug from Kelly before she spilled it. "Grammy had the skills and the passion for cake decorating. I don't." Megs shrugged. "You said that I need to be who I am." Megs held out her hands and motioned to her body. "This is it."

Sure, she had to throw her words back at her. Kelly was still stunned. "But you have to."

"No, I don't." She took a seat next to Kelly. "Isn't that what you were telling me last night?"

"Yes, but what about tradition?"

"I'll still make those we have under contract, but I'm not taking on any more." She giggled. "You have no idea how freeing this is making me feel."

Kelly closed her eyes. When she'd told her sister to be who she was, she hadn't meant to throw decades of tradition out the window.

Had she?

Still, the drawn look on Megs's face had disappeared. She seemed content. As if she really knew who she was and what she wanted. Kelly longed to run to the bathroom to see if that same expression was on her face, but she doubted it. She had decided to fix up the house and sell it. But what would happen after that?

Kelly's cell phone buzzed, and she took it out of her jeans pocket. A text from Sam: Going through the house now and making my list. Any suggestions?

More changes. She grimaced. Suddenly, her vow to make a stand in this town felt hollow. What had she gotten herself into?

SAM MEASURED THE wall and put the figures in his notebook, then he replaced the pencil behind his ear. If they moved this wall back six inches, it would open up the living room. He glanced up. Or what if they took it down and made this an open-concept first floor? Living room flows into dining room and into the kitchen. He got the pencil and made some notes.

His cell phone buzzed with a reply text from Kelly. Don't do anything drastic.

He paused. Was she changing her mind already? Granted, they would need to come to an agreement about what needed to be done, but he was the builder. She needed to trust him that he knew what would work.

He sighed as he texted back: Just getting ideas right now. Talk later.

His phone buzzed again, but he put it in his pocket. She wasn't going to bring down his enthusiasm. When it kept vibrating, he checked it and groaned at his dad's phone number. "Hi, Dad. Can I call you later? I'm in the middle of a job."

"You need to come home."

Sam took a step back and braced himself against the wall. "Is it Mom? Is she okay?"

"What? Your mother's fine. It's you that must be sick." His dad cleared his throat and continued. "You've played around enough. It's time for you to come back to Nashville. To your music career."

Sam laughed and shook his head. "What career? I left all that behind."

"It's waiting for you if you want it."

"Which I don't." Sam scribbled in his notebook as he perched the cell phone between his ear and shoulder. "I have my life here now. So no thank you."

"That's not why I called exactly. I just hate to see you throwing away your talent, Junior." Another cough. "What I wanted was to make sure you are coming to Tyler's album launch. You never sent your RSVP."

Sam let the phone slip back into his hand as he propped one fist against the wall and tapped his head against it. Tyler had been a kid in the industry when Sam had left. After Sam got sober, it was Tyler who reached out to him for advice on music. Sam had been fine with offering assistance from afar. "Tyler doesn't need my help anymore."

"That may be, but he wants you here."

It was always something. His father would never let him go. Maybe if he went back this once. "I don't know."

"The party is on a Friday night. You could come down and stay with us for the weekend. Your mother would love to have the opportunity to spoil you for a few days."

Sure. Start using the guilt. "I'll check my schedule."

"From what you said, you're your own boss. Surely you can come down for one weekend."

It would be one weekend. Then a week, then a month. And eventually it would take over his life again until he found himself lying on the floor of a bathroom confused about how he'd let himself get there. "Like I said, I'll check my schedule."

"Tyler's your friend, a good one. He would appreciate it."

Tyler had been a friend who believed in him when Sam couldn't do it himself. "Yeah, all right. I'll be there. Gotta go." He hung up before he could do something even more stupid, like agree to move back home.

Sam focused on work. Once he finished checking out the first floor, he went down to the basement. And frowned as he saw the floor joists. Not good.

The age of the house was clearly showing, and they would need to shore up the foundation if they wanted to be able to save the house, let alone sell it. And that meant time and money. Lots of it.

He wrote a few points in his notebook then plucked his cell phone from his back pocket. Bad news. I need you to see something. Can Megs spare you to come out to the house?

He waited for a reply but kept checking the front supports. Winced and made more points. His phone buzzed. After the lunch rush. Want me to pick something up?

He smiled and typed his reply: Craving a BLT. I'll pay you back when you get here.

My treat. And how bad are we talking?

Bad enough. Sam used his phone to snap several pictures of the worst damage. He would need to draw up some estimates. He only hoped that Kelly would agree with him.

KELLY CHOKED AS she looked over the figures. "Are you kidding me? All of this for something that we won't even see? It makes no sense."

Sam paused in eating his sandwich and laid it down in the Styrofoam container. "It will when you can't walk in the front door without falling through the floor."

"But you're talking tens of thousands of dollars that we don't have." She turned the page over to see if there was something on the back of it that would cheer her up. "You haven't even started to figure out the renovations, and we're already in the hole."

"Projects start out this way sometimes." He wiped his mouth with a napkin. "But if we don't do this, then whatever else we do won't matter."

Kelly rubbed between her eyes and moaned. "Why couldn't it be an easy fix for once? Why does it always have to be hard?"

He put his hand on her shoulder, but she stepped away and left the kitchen. Downstairs in the basement, she peered up at the ceiling to the wood beams that Sam had an issue with. She squinted to see if it would help, but it didn't. It only made her eyes water. The thud of feet descending the steps alerted her to Sam's presence. "Okay, Sam. If you really think it's necessary."

"Kel, this is just the beginning of what the old house needs. And none of it is cheap."

"How much?"

Sam frowned at her and pointed at the sheet he'd handed to her when she arrived. "That's only the estimate for the foundation. Then we have dry rot in one of the walls upstairs, have to completely gut the kitchen. Expand the master bedroom upstairs and add a master bath. And we'll have to increase the insulation, as well as update if not replace the furnace and central air system. And the hot-water heater has maybe another two or three years left. And then carpet and paint and new fixtures." He shook his head. "We're talking over a hundred thousand dollars here."

Her jaw dropped as she realized the magnitude of what he was talking about. "Hundred...?" She stomped up the stairs to the first floor and glanced around the rooms. Was he insane? How would they be able to do this?

As well as hope that it would sell for what they wanted and leave them with something to split? She sank onto the sofa. He might as well have told her it would cost a million dollars. Impossible.

Sam took a seat next to her. "It's not impossible."

"You're reading minds now, too?" She tilted her head back and stared at the ceiling, at least it was intact. Or so she thought. "You ask for too much."

"I could ask for more, but I know I wouldn't get it." Sam took the sheet from her hand before she could crumple it. "It all comes down to what you want. Do you want to make this house dazzle so a buyer will snap it up? Or do it on the cheap and hope for a quick sale?" He spread the sheet out and smoothed it with his hands. "Either way, the foundation is where we have to start. No home inspector would let the house pass with these issues."

"But it can't be all that bad here, right? I mean, Grammy and Megs have lived here for years without anything bad happening."

"And I want you both to be able to enjoy it for many more if that's what you want." He stood and looked down at her. "It all comes down to what do you want, remember?"

Right in that moment, she'd give up her own life if it meant she could see her grandmother one more time. To lay her head on her chest and ask for her wisdom. Instead, she had to be a grown-up. To make her own choices. That sucked. "Fine. Fix the foundation. And then we'll decide the rest of it once that's finished."

He gave a short nod. "I'll start after I eat my sandwich."

"And you owe me four-fifty for it. If I'm going to be giving up thousands to you for this house, the least you can do is pay for your own lunch."

"Deal."

CLOSING THE BAKERY EARLY, Megs and Kelly arrived back at the farmhouse and let themselves into the kitchen. They could hear banging coming from the basement. Megs poked her head down the stairs. "You okay?"

Footsteps sounded, and Sam appeared without his shirt. A tool belt was slung low on his hips. Kelly stood behind her sister and swallowed at the sight before turning away to hang up her coat. Anything to distract her from the sight of that gorgeous man.

"Found something you girls might like." He disappeared and brought up a photo album covered in dust. He handed it to Megs, but glanced at Kelly. *Was the room getting warm?* Kelly fanned herself.

Megs opened the book and squealed. "Grammy's scrapbook. I wondered where this had gone to."

Kelly peered over her sister's shoulder. "Which one is it?"

Megs paged through the book and said, "From when Daddy was still alive. Look."

Sure enough, there was a picture of their father and mother standing before a large pine Christmas tree. The two sisters stood in front of them, Kelly crying, while Megs watched her with a couple of fingers in her mouth. "I was maybe three?" Megs smiled and ran a finger down the photo. "Why were you crying?"

"Because I wanted to open presents instead of getting my picture taken," Kelly answered, and she glanced at the picture then up at Sam. "At least that's my guess."

"I found more of those books down there

in a trunk. I could bring it up here later if you're interested."

Megs nodded vigorously as Kelly took the scrapbook from her and went to the couch to peruse it some more. Pictures of their family as it used to be. Memories that were hazy at best, but grew stronger with the images in the book. She pointed to a picture of her singing with a toy microphone. "Destined for greatness, even at six."

She turned the book so that Sam and Megs could see it. She grinned and shook her head, then turned the book back to face her. Had she really been that young and naive? To believe that holding a microphone in her hand meant something? She checked out more pages then set the book beside her. "What else was in the trunk?"

Sam shrugged. "More photo albums. Some old baby clothes. A couple of cassette tapes."

Kelly's mouth became an O, then she got off the couch and ran down the stairs to where the trunk was propped open, inviting a search though its contents. She pushed the books aside and grabbed the four cassette tapes on the bottom. There was handwriting on the cassette covers. Kelly, age 7. Kelly, age 8.

Kelly, age 9. Kelly, age 12. She clutched them to her chest and ran back up the stairs. "Megs, where did Grammy keep her boom box?"

Megs frowned. "She got rid of that thing years ago."

Kelly looked at her sister. Grammy never got rid of anything. She ran down the hall to the master bedroom. She paused for a moment outside her Grammy's bedroom before pushing the door open. The bed was still unmade from that morning when Megs had found her. Her laundry hamper had clothes peeking out. A glass of water sat on the nightstand by her bed. Kelly closed her eyes. She'd think of that later.

She walked to the closet and opened the door, elbowing clothes aside until she found what she'd been hoping would be there. Grammy never got rid of anything, indeed. Kelly sat on the bed and put the first cassette tape inside the antiquated device. Pressed play.

A younger version of herself belted out a country tune along with the radio. Kelly closed her eyes and let the song play over her. Remembering the joy she once felt singing for her family, her friends, anyone who would listen. The tone of her voice was pure. She could hear the passion behind the notes.

To feel like that again.

The song she'd been singing with ended, but the recording continued. "Someday, you're going to be a star, baby. And I'm going to hear you sing on the radio."

Then her seven-year-old voice said, "Just watch me shine, Grammy."

Kelly choked back the tears. This was what she was meant to be, to do. And she'd been ready to give it up.

But not anymore. She would be a singer no matter what.

And no one or nothing would stand in her way.

CHAPTER NINE

WITH FEWER HOURS at the bakery thanks to Megs's re-visioning period, Kelly found herself with time on her hands and no idea what to do with it. Sam was hard at work shoring up the first floor so that they could start on the other rooms. She used his cue and began researching ideas for the rest of the renovation. If they could expand the closet in her room, that would appeal to today's buyer.

What if they took down a few of the walls on the first floor to create a more open concept that seemed so popular? She remembered that point on Sam's list somewhere.

She used her sister's laptop to scour social media for ideas as well as decorating and home renovation websites. She collected the ideas that appealed the most and planned to show it all to Sam. She hadn't calculated the price tag for these ideas, but he would know. He also had a finger on the pulse of what was selling now. She was grateful to have him on her team.

She heard steps coming up from the basement and turned to find Sam leaning on the doorway of the living room. "I could really use a glass of water. It's getting warm down there."

Kelly nodded and rose from the couch. "I'll get us each a glass. Taking a break?"

He nodded and wiped his forehead. "Need one. But it's looking better down there."

"Good." She brought down two glasses from the cupboard then walked to the sink and got them each a drink. She handed one glass to Sam, and kept her eyes on him above the rim of her own. "I've been doing some research."

"I saw." He shrugged when she frowned at him. "I peeked over your shoulder when you were on the computer earlier. The closet organizer pictures."

"I have lots of ideas. Buyers these days want more closet space than what this old lady offers. I thought maybe if we expanded what we had..."

"Without sacrificing square footage in the

bedroom?" He winced but took another drink of his water. "I'd have to check. Maybe."

"I bet I'm right. And we need a master bedroom with its own bath." She pointed at him. "You already talked about that one."

"I did." He finished his drink and put the empty glass on the counter. "We have time to sort this stuff out. The house won't be out of probate court for at least five more months, so we can't sell it until after that."

"I don't have five months."

He cocked an eyebrow at her. "You're not sick. And anything else you might have in mind can wait."

"I promised Grammy that I would be a professional singer by the time I was thirty. And I only have little more than two months." Kelly finished her own drink and put the glass on the counter. "It may not mean anything to you, but this is my life."

He stepped closer to her. "You don't know what you're asking for. That life can destroy you."

She glared at him. "Chasing my dreams isn't a bad thing."

"It's not. But giving up everything else

to pursue them? Even your sister? Or your soul?"

"What does my soul have to do with it? I want to sing on a stage in front of an audience. How is that selling my soul?"

"I know what the music business can do to a person more than you do. And I'm telling you, it has the potential to ruin you." He took his glass to the kitchen sink and rinsed it off before turning back to face her. "The strongest people are sometimes the ones who fall the hardest. And I can't let that happen to you."

What? Since when had he become the guardian of her soul? Not that it was in danger. "I'll be fine."

"And how often did you come home to see your family before?" When she didn't answer, he gave her a look. "You almost lost your sister once. Do you really want to risk that again?"

Okay, now he was treading a fine line between friendly concern and butting in where he wasn't wanted. "I never lost Megs."

"Sure. My mistake."

He walked to the top of the basement stairs and turned to face her one more time.

"There's nothing wrong with going after what you want, but there's always a price. Make sure you're willing to pay it."

He walked down the stairs as Kelly stared at the open door. Just because he hadn't been able to handle the business didn't mean she couldn't.

Right?

SAM PICKED UP the sledgehammer and brought it down on the partial wall he'd been tearing down since the night before. He paused for a moment, then picked the tool up and did it again. Paused. Nope. He still wanted to go upstairs and shake Kelly. Instead, he took out his frustrations on the partial wall that once down would make the basement much bigger.

By the time the wall had been knocked down completely, his anger had cooled slightly. Kelly thought she knew what she was doing. She had no clue. She didn't know the temptations that the business could bring. The loneliness that led to pursuing things best left alone. What she saw was the glitz of fame. The glamour of a microphone.

The reality was long hours in a studio or a tour bus. Sleeping marginally when he could because he had another appearance or interview. Love for something could become hate after a while.

He dragged the broken pieces of wood and drywall to a corner to be taken up to the Dumpster to be delivered later that afternoon. He stopped and sat on one of the stairs. With the partial wall down, he could work on adding support beams to the floor above. Strengthen the joists and eventually put in a drop ceiling. If he could convince Kelly to finish the basement the way he'd planned, he could reconfigure the space for a laundry room as well as a family room.

From above him, Megs whistled as she spied his progress. "You were right. Without that wall, it really opens up the space down here."

"That and it gives me room to fix the floor joists." He shifted over so she could join him on the step. "Figure out the new menu?" he asked.

"Some of it." She looked him over. "Are you the reason why Kelly is slamming doors upstairs?"

He glanced at the ceiling. Good. Maybe

he'd gotten to her, at least, a little bit. "She's ticked off at me."

"Tell me something I don't know."

He sighed. "Sometimes, she makes me so angry that I can't stand the sight of her. Then other times, I want to grab her and kiss her blind."

Megs wrinkled her nose. "Ew, gross. That's my sister you're talking about."

"I'm aware of that, yes. And that's another reason for me to stay far, far away from her." He shook his head. "I don't understand how she's getting under my skin in such a short time."

"Because she's Kelly, and she's good at it."

As if the answer was that simple. "Nope. That's not it."

Megs studied him, and he wanted to squirm under her perusal. She put her arm around his shoulder. "I know my sister, and she's not that easy to get along with. I'm surprised you've made it this far, to be honest. But eventually, she will get to you. She will drive you nuts. And I guess it depends on what you want from her to see if you'll last."

"*I'll* last? I think she's the one you need to worry about because this partnership isn't going to fall apart based on me." Sam stood up and picked up the sledgehammer. "If I need to, I'll invest in more of these."

She smirked at him. "I'll ask you if you feel the same way in a few weeks."

He groaned and hefted the sledgehammer over his shoulder. "She's just a woman. How bad can it be?"

SAM STARED AT Kelly as if she'd sprung a fourth head. The woman shrugged as if she hadn't just spouted insanity from that cute mouth of hers. "What? All I said was that I think it's a good idea if we don't do as much that people aren't going to see."

"A furnace might not be sexy, Kel, but it's a basic need to have a good one." Sam glanced around the basement. "Without making these repairs, we won't be able to sell the house. And if we can't sell it, then we won't get back the money we're putting into it."

"I don't understand what's wrong with the current one. So it breaks down every once in a while." She shrugged as if she didn't see the big deal. "They're not going to care if it's old."

"They will if it's an issue the inspector

brings up that will keep somebody from buying the house." He shifted his weight from one foot to the other. "I think I know what I'm talking about."

"You know more than me, you mean?"

"You're the one who said it."

The standoff continued until he could feel the air heating around them. But he wasn't going to be the first one to look away.

Eventually, she narrowed her eyes until he finally blinked. He grimaced as a smile spread on her face, as if she'd won. "You know that at least part of what I'm saying is right. I've seen the list you've been making, Sam, and a lot of it is the same thing. Like water heater, plumbing." She groaned. "It's boring."

"It's necessary to update the house."

"That would be fine if we planned on living here, but we're selling it. We need more bang for our buck."

The thought of them living here, though tempting, wouldn't help either one of them get what each wanted. "We need to sell a house that isn't stuck in the fifties. We'll get more money my way."

"Not the way you're spending it before it's even sold."

He rubbed the back of his neck where an ache formed and threatened to spread if he wasn't careful with his next words. "Well, we need to finalize a budget." When she pouted, he held up a finger. "So we know how much to spend and can prioritize where."

She opened her mouth, paused, then agreed. "That makes sense."

He searched his back pocket for his tiny notepad and pencil. When she frowned, he shrugged. "I figured I'd record this moment since you thought I was right."

"I said you made sense. I didn't say you were right." She took a seat on a basement step and stretched her legs. "I didn't realize this was going to take so much work."

"The good news is that we have the time to do it right." He joined her on the step.

The neighborhood around the property would help, as well; it was made up of lots of open space and adjoining farms, rather than houses on top of one another. "Tell you what. I'm ready for a break. Why don't I use the rest of today to come up with what we talked about? I'll look up the prices of local homes that've sold and determine what we would need to do to compare with them," he offered.

She smiled. "Then we'll meet tomorrow and hammer out the details."

He held out his hand. "Deal."

They shook on it, and he hated to let her hand go. But keeping her with him would only make things even more confusing between them. He was starting to like her. Way too much. And he needed some space to figure it out.

He stood and helped her to her feet. When she came up, she loomed close to him and he had to take a step back before he did something crazy like kiss her again.

She looked up at him. "Dinner tonight?"

"Uh, no." He hated to see the disappointment in her eyes, but he really needed that space. Inspiration struck. "I already have plans."

Thank goodness for intramural basketball.

BORED. AND RESTLESS. Kelly flung the magazine onto the sofa next to her. Megs glanced up from the recliner by the bay window and raised an eyebrow at her. "Who do you think he's out with?" Kelly asked her sister.

Megs returned to the thick cookbook she had open on her lap. She flagged a page. "Why didn't you ask him?"

"Because it's none of my business."

Not looking at her, Megs chortled and turned another page. "You trying to convince yourself of that?" She pressed the book close to her face, as if checking something. "I could make this."

Kelly got off the sofa and came to stand beside her. Megs pointed to the picture of a loaf of bread braided. It was only bread, but the gleam in Megs's eye meant it was something more to her. "Can you imagine the different varieties we could make?" She turned the page quickly and pointed to bread that had been baked into an elaborate star shape. "Oh. Or this!"

Kelly returned to the sofa. Try as she might, she couldn't get excited. "So, you're thinking of specializing in bread?"

Megs glanced up and shrugged. "Don't know, but it's an idea." She scrutinized page after page, and Kelly knew she had lost her.

Kelly found the television remote and pressed On, flipping channels until she found an old movie. She pulled the afghan off the back of the sofa and tugged it around her. Settling in, she let the images sweep her away. She'd always loved watching old movies with Grammy. Cary Grant had been Kelly's favorite actor, although Grammy was partial to Jimmy Stewart.

The phone rang beside Megs, and she paused in her reading to answer it. "Hi…Mom."

Kelly rolled her eyes. What did she want now? It's not like they had received any of Grammy's money yet and wouldn't likely for a while.

Megs nodded and said coolly into the phone, "Why, yes, she's right here."

Kelly shook her head and mouthed, "No," but Megs handed her the phone anyway. She covered it briefly and took a deep breath before she could say anything. "Mom."

"Well this is a surprise to find you still there in Lake Mildred. I figured you'd be long gone back to Louisville."

Kelly squelched a groan. "It's Nashville. And plans change. I'm helping Megs at the Sweetheart for a while." Her mother sniffed on the other end, but Kelly pretended interest. "How's Florida?"

"Glorious." Her mother's throaty laugh

came over the line. "I've met the greatest man in the world."

Another one? "What happened to Roy?"

"Heart attack. It was quick." Her mother's tone was somber. "But lucky for me, he left me a fortune."

Of course he had. "Good for you, Mom. What do you want?"

"Nothing. I just wanted to see how my oldest daughter was doing."

"What about Megs? Want to talk to her again?" She was more than agreeable to handing back the phone to her sister. "Don't you need to catch up on what she's got going on?"

Megs waved a fist at her from the other side of the room.

"You call me at least once a month, Mom, to catch up. What about your other daughter?"

"It sounds like you're trying to get rid of me."

That's because she was. Phone conversations with her mother tended to leave her feeling hollow and empty. "What do you want, Mom?" Kelly repeated.

Her mom was silent for a long while before she said, "I realize you're going through a huge loss right now, so I wanted to make sure you're okay."

The words were spoken so softly that Kelly wasn't sure she'd heard them correctly. It sounded as if her mother cared after all. Not that she'd showed much of that when Kelly had been fifteen and grieving for her father. She was thankful every day that Grammy had stepped in where her mother couldn't and raised her and Megs. But Kelly still tried to make an effort, since she was her mother. She let out a breath really slow. "I'm okay."

"Do you think you'll get a chance to come down and visit me? You and your sister? The holidays are coming up. Or I could visit up there."

Kelly couldn't remember the last time her mother had asked them to see her or vice versa. Usually, years went by without an invitation like that. The last time she'd seen her mother was for her wedding to Roy two years ago. And Kelly had only been in town overnight. "I'll talk to Megs and see what she says. With her owning the bakery now, things are complicated."

"Right, right." More silence. "Addy and I didn't agree on a lot of things, but she raised the both of you so well."

Afraid she'd start crying, Kelly swallowed

and breathed through her mouth. "Yes, she did." She'd never heard her mother admit those words before. "Megs is here if you want to tell her, too."

"That'd be great, sweetie."

Megs shook her head, but finally accepted the phone. She covered it with one hand and glared at Kelly. "I'll get you for this later."

"Oooh, I'm scared." She turned off the television and left the room to give Megs privacy.

Kelly walked upstairs to her room and lay on the bed, staring at the ceiling. The phone call from her mom unnerved her. Their calls usually ended in an argument and one of them hanging up on the other. While Kelly might try to cut her mother some slack, she still had a short temper with her. Losing Addy had either mellowed her or her mom, if not both of them.

Thoughts of Addy brought reminders of her promise to pursue her music. Kelly rolled onto her side and peered into the darkness. If she was in Nashville right now, she'd be getting ready to go out. To an open-mike night at a local bar or to hear another up-and-comer sing. She tried to imagine what her life would be like once she went back. Would she stay in her apartment or get a better place? Her current one was cheap, which meant more money to put into her career. Would she get new headshots? Try to find an agent again?

Possibilities swam in her head until she sat up and closed her eyes. What could she do differently that she hadn't already tried? Thousands of dollars poured into a music career that had never started.

KELLY BROUGHT A tray of cookies and cups of coffee to the kitchen table where Sam had several charts and pages of figures. He separated them into three different piles and put his laptop in the center. "Cream and sugar?" she asked him.

He glanced up from what he was doing. "Black is good for me."

Kelly set his mug in front of him then got the flavored creamer she'd bought that morning. Poured a healthy dose in her mug then used a spoon from the cutlery drawer to stir the coffee, turning the dark brown liquid into a light tan. The spoon clanked on the sides of the mug, then she let it still. Took a sip and sighed. Pumpkin spice. Her favorite flavor this time of year.

She took a seat at the table as she took another sip of the hot coffee and looked over at Sam. He waited for her to put her mug down then pulled up a rendering of the kitchen. He turned to her. "I drew up a couple of ideas based on three different budgets with three different styles. Like you said, it depends on where we want to spend our money."

When she opened her mouth to make a comment, he held her off. "Except for the foundation. That's not negotiable."

She huffed and folded her arms across her chest. "Fine."

He moved the laptop towards her so she could see a current photo of Grammy's kitchen. He pressed a button and it shifted to a digitally designed alteration. She gave a soft sigh of delight. The kitchen appeared bigger, more open. The cupboard space was almost double and had a stove with a hood above it. Very modern.

Sam pressed another button to show a blueprint of the same room. "Kitchens and bathrooms sell a house more than any other feature of a home. Ask any real estate agent, and they'll tell you the same."

"Would a modern aesthetic work in this

space though?" She glanced around. This was still a farmhouse.

Sam nodded and clicked on another button. This time the modern lines softened. The picture still kept the open concept, but the style looked more country. "We could change some of the design ideas and make it fit the home as well."

He showed her a third idea, this one with a true rustic appeal. "Or go in another direction."

"That's nice. What are the costs for all this?"

"We'll get to that." The next image he showed her was a current picture of the living room, then it morphed into a modern design, followed by country and finally rustic. "Again, we can use the space differently. Open it up more to appeal to today's buyer, but design in whatever style we wish." He produced a current photo of the foyer and did the same thing. "Depending on what direction we go in, we can use the same theme throughout to make it cohesive."

"I liked the wood-burning stove in the rustic one, but why lose the fireplace that we already have?"

He nodded and continued with his presentation. He pulled up a picture of Grammy's bedroom. Kelly tried to ignore the ache it brought and took a sip of coffee to mask it. He clicked on a blueprint showing the room now with its own bathroom and walk-in closet. She frowned. "What happened to not wanting to sacrifice space to add those in?"

"You had a point. We could sell it for more this way." He pushed another button and went past several slides until he showed a blueprint that kept the rooms as they were. "Or keep the space but lose out on possible dollars."

"I like the master suite with its own bath better."

"I do, too." He flipped back to a modern design of the space. "We could choose fixtures and colors to go in whatever direction you want."

She raised one eyebrow at this. "You're letting me decide?"

He gave a one shoulder shrug. "In some ways, you have ideas closer to what today's buyer wants. I like your ideas."

"The closet organizer?"

He tried to hide a grin. "We'll see."

He put the laptop aside and gave her a spreadsheet showing a total that made her choke and cough. "This much?" She shook her head. "For which design?"

"That's what we would need to get the bare bones, not including how much we would spend on fixtures, depending on the design idea you choose." He gave her another sheet. "This is what we would need to spend to make it top of line." Then another sheet on top of that. "And this is one in the middle."

When had fixing a house gotten so expensive? She read a few of the line items and the costs associated with them. She wrinkled her nose. "You're hiring a painter?"

"To get what we need done, I would have to have some outside help."

"Why not me?" She read through the list of costs and flipped to the cheapest design. "We could eliminate several thousand dollars if I painted and did some of this work."

Sam took a seat across from her. "Do you understand what you're saying? This is a lot and you're already at the bakery at least eight hours a day. And what happens when you return to Nashville?"

"I can't go back until we sell this place, so I'm invested." She bit her lip and kept reading through the spreadsheets. She looked up at him. "You said we were partners in this, or weren't you serious? If I'm going to contribute, I'll find a way. And I'm pretty good with a paintbrush. Neat and straight."

"We are partners in this. And that means we need to work together. Not giving your opinion just because it's different from mine."

"A partnership doesn't mean I have to go along with everything you say. It means that I might have different ideas that complement yours. Kind of like a harmony. It adds to the melody to blend into something even better."

"Okay. You can paint."

She glanced at the other piles of paper. "So what are those?"

He pulled one of the documents closer to her then scooted his seat around the table to be next to her. "These are some breakdowns of ideas depending on our design theme. Items I found online that we could use depending on what budget we agree on."

His head bent so close to hers that she could smell the scent of the shampoo he'd used that morning. She closed her eyes for a moment and breathed in something that reminded her of the ocean. When she opened her eyes, she found him watching her. She focused her gaze to what he'd been showing her, making a few sounds of interest.

Once they had finished going through his presentation, she sat back in the chair and grabbed her coffee mug. "It's a bit much, isn't it? Are we crazy for tackling this big of a project?"

"We won't know if we don't try."

"Fine. If I'm going to help with some of the labor, why don't we go with the middle of the road budget."

"And the design?"

She bit her lip. "I'll need to sleep on that."

IN THE WEE hours of the morning, Sam flopped onto his back, wide awake. He needed to stop thinking so he could get some sleep. His phone buzzed, so he reached over to the night stand and checked the message.

It was from Ty and it said, U coming or what?

Sam made a face. The kid wasn't giving up. Sam thought about going back to Nashville, waited for the panic that usually set in, but found that it didn't bother him. He took a deep breath and texted back. Do U know what time it is?

Can't sleep. U coming?

U know I will. Give U deets l8r.

Knowing that sleep was futile now, he rose and changed into his work clothes, then left his apartment to walk over to Addy's for his usual morning. When he opened the side door, Megs walked into the kitchen in her bathrobe and gave a huge yawn. She stumbled to the refrigerator and peered inside. She looked as good as he felt. In other words, like they could both use another night's sleep. "Didn't sleep well?" he asked.

She shook her head and brought out a small container of yogurt, her eyes half open. "Maybe I should have changed my opening times rather than when I close. Maybe then I could get some sleep." She walked to a drawer and pulled out a spoon. "I still haven't finalized the changes I want to make."

"Staff?"

"I'd never get rid of them." She stifled another yawn. "I meant the menu."

He nodded as if he knew, but he had no clue really. He didn't know what it took to run a bakery. But he did know what it took to run your own business, and he understood the fear of making changes that customers may or may not like. He put his hand on her shoulder. "They may not all like what you're going to do, but they'll come back eventually."

She wrinkled her nose. "Thanks?"

His thoughts returned to the early call from Ty and the launch party coming up. "What would you say if I took your sister out of town with me this weekend? Unless you can't spare her."

Her eyebrows shot up into her hairline. "You want to take Kelly somewhere? By choice?"

He smiled. "It was just a thought. I have to go to Nashville for a few days, and I figured maybe she'd like to come with me."

"Why?"

"Because she's from there, and she can pick up a few things from her place if she wants. Maybe I could introduce her to some people in the music business." At Kelly's insistence, he'd finally opened up about some of his past to Megs. It was actually a relief that he didn't have to hide who he was from one of his best friends. "I thought maybe I could smooth some roads for her. You know she's still determined to go back there eventually."

"I know." Megs didn't sound too happy about it, either. "Why are you going?"

"Promised a friend I'd be at his party Friday night. We can fly out Thursday and be back by Sunday afternoon."

Megs looked him, over then broke into a grin. "Why are you asking me for permission to take her?"

"I'm not asking your permission." He wasn't. Kelly was a grown woman, and she could make her own decisions. Just like he could.

"Aren't you?"

Frustrated, he sighed and headed for the door. "Forget it."

She reached out a hand and caught his arm. "No, I think it might be a good idea. I was only teasing you."

"What do you think she'll say when I ask her?"

KELLY'S EYES BULGED OUT. "You want me to go where with you?"

Sam shrugged as if it was no big deal. But he didn't understand what he was asking. Taking her to a Nashville album launch party where she could rub elbows with movers and shakers in the business? It was a dream that she was almost afraid to reach out and grab. Then she narrowed her eyes. "And what do you get out of it?"

He leaned on Addy's kitchen counter. "I don't want to go alone. That's all. I'm not asking for anything else."

She bit her lip and considered her current financial situation. She could stay in her apartment, which would cut down on expenses for a hotel room and meals. But the cost of the flight made her belly ache. "I don't know."

"This is a chance of a lifetime for you. Why aren't you jumping all over this?"

She considered what to tell him. It wasn't his business how tight money was, but she didn't want him to think she wasn't grateful for asking her. "It's complicated."

"We can stay at my parents, so you don't have to worry about a hotel." Sam searched her eyes as if he could figure out her hesitancy there. "Separate bedrooms, I promise."

She tried to keep the warmth from her cheeks unless it should betray her. She appreciated the separate bedrooms, but she wouldn't mind kissing him a little more than she had. They'd shared two kisses, and she looked forward to more. But still she shook her head. "I don't know. How much are the plane tickets?"

He looked at her and relaxed, his shoulders losing some of their tension. "Is that what this is? You're worried about how much it will cost? Don't worry about it."

"I do worry about it. The flight can't be cheap."

He waved off her concerns. "I've got points to use up so I'm sure I can get a great discount."

She wasn't certain if she believed him, but she let it go for now. "Why do you want to take me?"

"I thought you loved Nashville. You've been chomping to get back there since you arrived."

"That's not true." When he looked at her skeptically, she rolled her eyes. "Well, it's not completely true. But you've been dead set against me going back. Why the change?"

"I guess I figured I could show you some of what that life is like." He watched her as she let this sink in. It would be a great insider's view of the life of a country music singer.

He gripped her upper arm. "But it's not all parties and fun. There's a darker side to it."

"So you keep telling me." She stepped away from him and he released her. "If I agree to go, and it's still a big if, what would we do?"

"The launch party is Friday night for my friend Ty's album. Then I'd take you around to meet some people on Saturday. Maybe get your foot in a few doors in case you do go back."

"You mean when I go back."

He gave a single nod. "And we could get some things from your apartment, if you like."

Or she could pack it all up and ship it here. Get rid of that monthly expense since the apartment stood empty and would for a while. She'd be silly to pass this up. Finally, she nodded. "All right, but you'll let me know how much my ticket is. I'll find the money somehow."

He held out his hand. "Deal."

"Deal."

CHAPTER TEN

SAM PUT HIS hand at the small of Kelly's back as they walked out from the airplane hangar at the Nashville airport. She turned to look at him but didn't say anything about the proprietary gesture. As if they were together. Putting his stamp on her. She ignored the fluttering in her chest that the thought brought and concentrated on finding where the baggage claim was located.

They took the escalator down and found a young man in a cowboy hat holding a sign with "Etchason" scrawled on it. Sam didn't see him, so Kelly tugged on his arm and pointed to the sign. Sam broke into a smile and rushed forward, arms outstretched towards the man. "Funny."

They embraced, pounding each other on the back at a force that made her wince. They broke apart, and the young man held out his hand to her. "Tyler."

She shook his hand, finding his hold firm. "Congratulations on the album."

Tyler winced as he let go of her hand. "Don't say anything just yet. You might jinx it."

Sam put his arm around Tyler's neck. "If you've put the work into the album already, then you don't have to worry."

The young man gave a wary smile. "Try telling that to my record producer."

"My father is always harder than he needs to be on his artists. Says it keeps them humble and willing to work hard."

A whistle sounded, and the slats of the luggage carousel began to move. They watched as several suitcases started coming down and rotating on the oval track. Sam snagged the olive green duffel bag he'd packed and slung it over his shoulder. "Did he send you or did you volunteer?"

Ty glanced at Kelly, then back at Sam. "Volunteered. I hoped we'd have a chance to talk, just the two of us, before the party tomorrow night."

Sam put his free arm around Kelly's shoulders. "Whatever we need to talk about can be done in front of her. She's an aspiring singer herself."

Ty peered at her, and she wanted to squirm under such a harsh perusal. She yanked at the hem of her shirt and shifted her weight to the other leg. She wasn't sure what to say to that. Yes, I am? Have been, since the day I was born? Those words set an expectation in people's minds. And she didn't have an album to show for her efforts.

Her battered purple suitcase came around the carousel, and she moved to grab it, but Sam released his hold on her and grabbed it for her. He nodded to Ty. "Where did you park?"

SAM WANTED TO groan at the sight of his father's driver standing by the car at the curb. Westley hurried forward and took the luggage from Sam and walked behind the vehicle to place the bags in the trunk.

Sam didn't wait for Westley to open his door, but opened the back passenger door himself and swept his arm toward Kelly. She shook her head. "I'll sit up front. That way the two of you can talk with some privacy."

Ty smiled at her and gave a slight nod.

Sam wondered what in the world the kid thought they needed to talk about. Sure, Ty had been hanging around Sam and his band back in the early days, soaking up the atmosphere and any scrap of advice he could get. When Sam had left Nashville, he'd given Ty his cell phone number and heard from the young man often while he prepared his album. Gave input when asked and warnings when he wasn't. He had a stake in the future of Ty's album even if it wasn't financial.

Sam ducked his head as he climbed into the luxury SUV and scooted to the end of the bench seat. Ty came behind him and slammed the door shut. Westley assisted Kelly and got in the car himself, then put the SUV in gear and left the airport.

Once they were on the highway that would lead to Sam's family home, Ty leaned in close to Sam. "I feel like I'm running around without my head attached. What did you do to keep it together before your album came out?"

"Take a deep breath, Ty. Everything that your publicist is telling you is necessary, really isn't. Yes, there are interviews and appearances, but they're not all do or die. Take the time to figure out which ones mean more to you and say yes to those."

"Did your dad tell you that when your first single went platinum on iTunes the day it was released?"

Sam nodded. "Dad's kept me informed about the business side of your career since I left."

"That's a good sign, right?" Ty winced and took off his Stetson. "Unless I'm destined to be a one-hit wonder."

Sam glanced up front where Kelly sat staring out the windshield. Isn't that what she'd called Sam? Said everyone remembered his song, but not who sang or wrote it. "There's nothing wrong with that."

"But I want a long career." He bent forward, and Sam feared that he would be sick. Instead, the young man glanced up, then out the window. "Maybe it's all too much. Maybe everyone will find out I'm a fake once the album is launched."

Sam remembered those feelings of inadequacy. Even before his debut single had been played on air, accusations of nepotism and rumors of tanking sales had swirled around him. He had felt useless and like a fraud. As if Daddy's money and company had been the only reason he'd gotten the album made. Then the first single had hit number one on the charts, and he'd zoomed into superstardom. The problem was he'd still felt like that fraud. He glanced at his friend. "You know you've got the talent, Tyler. What matters is what you do with it."

"What about you? What have you been doing?"

"Not worrying about my next album." Or anything else to do with music. Sam gave him a grin. "I'm leaving the big music career to you. I'm happy fixing up homes and working with my hands."

"But you're the real deal, man." Ty put his arm along the back of the seat. "I never understood why you left when you did. You could have had it all, but you walked away. Dropped out of the whole scene. Might as well have dropped off the face of the earth."

Sam had wanted to most nights, but the promise of a better life had kept him going. He shrugged. "Sometimes the thing you want turns out to be the worst thing for you."

"How? Help me understand. Because after

tomorrow night, I'll be in the middle of it all. What haven't you told me?"

Sam rubbed his forehead. How much to tell? Did he lose the respect of a friend by telling the truth about the train wreck his life had once been? Could his own shortfalls serve as a warning for Ty? "The life that my father is offering you might seem like it's everything that you want. But it comes with a price. And I wasn't willing to pay it after a while. I couldn't keep up with the grueling schedule or the demands on my time. The joy of singing became drudgery. Performing on demand turned out to be the last thing I wanted."

"But you could have been a star."

He had been for a while and it had cost him. A lot. "Maybe. Maybe not. But eventually, that didn't matter to me. I no longer wanted to live the life my father had laid out for me. Finding my own path became my goal."

"And did you find it?"

Sam glanced up front again, but Kelly didn't look back at him. Was she listening? He turned to Ty and said, "It was in Michigan, of all places."

"Are you happy then?"

He considered this. He'd found contentment and peace finally, but happiness? He
thought of the other night holding Kelly while
she'd cried, how she'd gone to him for support
and understanding. The kiss they'd shared.
He smiled. "Yes, I am."

The tight set of Kelly's shoulders seemed to
relax. So she'd been listening for his response,
too. It pleased him more than it should, he
thought. He told Ty, "Figure out what's important now and hang on to that before you
get pulled into the Nashville current."

Ty agreed, but Sam had a feeling that he
hadn't really heard.

THE SUV PULLED up in front of Sam's family
home, and Kelly gave a low whistle. Mansion
was more like it. Three stories with lights
blazing from every window, even though it
was still late afternoon. The driver stopped
the car and got out to open her door before
she had the chance to. He held out a hand to
assist her as she got out of the vehicle. She
politely thanked him.

Sam climbed out of the back of the SUV
and walked to the trunk where he removed
their luggage. Her battered suitcase made her

look out of place among such elegance. She wished that she'd taken up Meg's suggestion to borrow Grammy's vintage garment bag. She tried to take her suitcase from Sam's hand, but he held on to it. "I can take that in for you," he said.

"I can do it myself." She took the case from him and held it behind her as they proceeded up the steps to the grand entrance of the mansion. Sam pressed the doorbell button, then stepped back. Kelly watched him, anxiety making him almost vibrate during their wait. She reached out and put a hand on his arm. He looked up at her and smiled. She returned the look, then saw the woman approaching to open the front door.

"Junior!" the woman exclaimed.

She guessed this was Sam's mom as the woman swept Sam up in a hug until he squawked, "Ma, you're choking me."

Mrs. Etchason laughed but continued to hold on to her son. "Not like I get much of a chance to do anything with you these days."

Sam finally took her hands from his neck and turned her to face Kelly. "Ma, this is Kelly Sweet, the friend I was telling you about."

Mrs. Etchason looked her up and down, and Kelly wished she'd chosen something better than jeans and a T-shirt and jacket to travel in. Sam's mother was dressed in dark wool pants under a cashmere sweater tunic. She was wearing pearls at that. Kelly thrust out her hand. "Nice to meet you, Mrs. Etchason."

Sam's mother pressed forward and engulfed Kelly in a tight hug. "I'm a hugger, sweetie. You might as well get used to that."

Kelly swallowed at the lump in her throat and embraced the woman. The strength and pull of emotion she felt made her think of her grandmother. She took a deep breath, hoping that the tears that threatened at the corners of her eyes would stay where they were.

Mrs. Etchason backed away from her, but still had her hands on Kelly's upper arms. "And call me Joy. The other Mrs. Etchason and I don't see eye to eye."

Kelly glanced at Sam who gave a wry smile. "*Grandma* Etchason." He glanced behind his mother. "Is she here, too?"

"Out with her bridge friends, but she'll be back before we leave for dinner." She glanced behind Sam and nodded at Tyler. "Thank you for getting them from the airport, Ty. We'll see you tomorrow night at the launch."

Ty flicked the edge of his hat. "Yes, ma'am." He nodded to Kelly. "Nice meeting you."

Then he was gone, and Joy ushered them into the foyer. There was a sweeping staircase that reminded Kelly of the one in the movie *Gone with the Wind*. She could picture Scarlett O'Hara swaying down the steps in her petticoats and hoop skirt. This was how Sam had lived, then he'd given it all up for an apartment above Grammy's garage? Was the man mental? She glanced at him as if to reassure herself that he wasn't.

He gestured toward the closed door to the left. "Dad home working?"

Joy sighed. "You know your father. Can't take five minutes to say hello. As if the record label would fold if he wasn't working every minute of every day." She smiled and squeezed Sam's hand. "Just a warning that he's arranged dinner tonight so that a few of his cronies will happen to stop at our table at the restaurant. Please try to be gracious." She hooked her arm through Sam's. "But enough of that. Come into the kitchen. I made your favorite cookie."

Sam's eyes lit up. "Oatmeal raisin?" He let himself be lead into the kitchen, Kelly trailing behind them.

The massive kitchen could have fit the entire floor of Grammy's home inside it and still had room left over. Her mouth dropped open and she touched the beige-flecked granite countertops just to be sure they were real. "You have a beautiful home, Mrs., I mean, Joy."

The woman smiled and held up a plate of cookies to first Sam, then Kelly, clearly establishing the pecking order.

Kelly took one of the cookies and bit into it. The soft crumbly texture melted in her mouth, and she closed her eyes and moaned.

Sam laughed. "Ma may not be much of a cook, but she knows how to bake a mean cookie."

Kelly nodded. "Sounds like me."

"Her family owns a bakery, Ma. You should try her sister Megs's coconut cake. It's to die for."

Joy focused her perusing gaze on Kelly. "Yes, you've told me, son. How are you doing after your grandmother passed, dear? Bless your heart, I think I would be devastated."

Kelly tried not to choke on her bite, but swallowed what remained of the cookie. "It's getting easier, but I miss her every day."

Joy nodded and offered the plate of cookies again. "You always will." She turned to Sam. "Why don't I get you two settled into your rooms and then we can talk some more? I could make some sandwiches if you're hungry."

"Sounds great, Ma, but I could use a nap before we have to leave for tonight." Sam reached over and kissed his mother's cheek. "And maybe a shower."

Joy tweaked his nose and watched him fondly as he took a handful of cookies from the plate, then strolled out of the kitchen, leaving the two women alone.

Kelly nibbled at her lip when she noticed Joy watching her.

His mother looked good. Younger than her age. Soft, but Kelly could sense an edge where her son was concerned. She would have to remember not to cross Sam, or she'd have to face Joy, too.

Finally, Joy smiled. "It's so good to see him. He looks happy. Don't you think?"

"I've only known him like this." Kelly

glanced around the kitchen. "He doesn't talk much about his life here."

A cloud passed over Joy's features, but she kept her faint smile in place. "He's in a better place now. I only wish Frank would see it."

"See what? That our son is wasting his life?" A large, imposing man entered the kitchen. He glanced at the plate of cookies and frowned. "Oatmeal?"

"They're Junior's favorite."

"Of course." Sam's father scoffed, then turned to look at Kelly. "And you're Miss Sweet?"

"Kelly." He narrowed his eyes at her, but she kept her ground. Wouldn't cower or let her nerves portray on her face. "I've heard a lot about you, Mr. Etchason."

She waited to see if he'd insist on his first name like his wife had, but he stayed silent, eyes on her as if measuring her. She had the feeling that she didn't meet whatever standard he had in mind for his son. She glanced down at her feet and back up at him. If she couldn't handle his scrutiny, how would she ever be able to prove that she could make it in the music business? She spoke to Joy. "If you could show me where I'm staying, I'll unpack and get ready for dinner and the party later."

"Certainly." Joy led her by the elbow, but then stopped and frowned at Mr. Etchason. "Junior is resting, so you leave him alone."

"Yes, Mama Bear." He gave her a growl, which made her titter, and he patted her behind as she passed him to leave the kitchen.

Joy led Kelly to the foyer where they retrieved her suitcase, then continued up the stairs. Kelly let her free hand trail on the wooden stair rail. She felt like a princess surrounded by such wealth and formality. Actually, she was more like the pauper pretending to be royalty and she worried that she'd failed at even that.

Joy walked down the hall to the right and opened a door on the far end. A large canopy bed dwarfed the space, light lace hanging from the ends of the frame. A red and pink quilt sewn with hearts decorated the bed, reminding Kelly of the Sweetheart. A rush of homesickness passed through her, but left as soon as it had started. Kelly set her suitcase down on the bed.

Joy pointed to two doors. "Closet on the left, bathroom on the right."

"This is a beautiful room."

Joy gave a smile, but it was tinged with sorrow. "It belonged to Shannon, Sam's sister." The woman touched her lips as if she'd said something wrong. "Let me know if you need anything."

Then she was gone.

Kelly perched on the edge of the bed, as if she were almost afraid to sit down. What in the world was she doing here, anyway? She'd told Sam that she'd come with him, but she wasn't sure why he needed her.

SAM PULLED THE luxury SUV into the parking lot, and Kelly directed him to the back of her apartment building. The dwelling made him want to shudder. It reminded him a lot of his former, darker days. He glanced at Kelly, who clutched her purse to her belly. "So this is home?" he asked.

"Was. Let's just grab my stuff and get out of here. We should have brought someone to watch the car while we're inside. This isn't the best neighborhood."

He'd gotten that hint already. Once she was out of the car, she reached back for several empty boxes and started crossing the parking lot toward an entrance. He grabbed more boxes and double-clicked the lock to set the car alarm. He caught up to her and ushered them inside the building, up the two flights of stairs to her apartment.

She unlocked the door and let him go inside first. He let out a breath as he quickly surveyed the surroundings. The good news was that there wasn't much to pack or get rid of. The bad news was that he couldn't imagine how she'd lived like this for years. A studio apartment, it was one fairly small room with a tiny bathroom attached. A bed, a plastic set of drawers, a metal clothes rack, and a glass patio table with two metal chairs was the extent of her furniture. A vast difference from the heirlooms and antiques that Addy had in her home.

Kelly dumped her boxes on the kitchen counter. She opened the two hanging cabinets and checked what food was there, before putting some of it in a box. He watched her for a moment. "What are you doing?"

"I usually bought things that were on discount, so chances are they've already expired, or are close to it." She waited a beat before dropping the can of tuna in her hand down on the counter. "Go ahead and say it."

"Say what?" he asked.

"That this place isn't what you'd pictured."

No, it wasn't. When he'd pictured Kelly in Nashville, he'd imagined her living in an apartment with several other people striving toward the same dream. He'd thought of a warm, homey atmosphere, much like Addy's house in Michigan. Quilts, shaggy rugs and homemade doilies. Instead, Kelly's studio was sparse and cold.

The place looked as if it, too, had struggled while Kelly tried to pursue her singing career. "Doesn't matter. Where do you want me to start packing?"

She glanced at the bed, but then jerked her attention elsewhere. He appreciated avoiding that particular intimacy of having to remove her sheets and blankets that she'd once slept in. "The bathroom, maybe? I think I left some things in there. Towels and such."

He set the remainder of his boxes on the floor in the dining area and then went into the bathroom. The place may have been tiny, but he could see that Kelly had kept it sparkling clean. He opened the cabinets under the sink and found a few toiletries and several towels and washcloths. He packed them in an empty box, taking only a few seconds. He put his hand on the vinyl shower curtain and shouted to the other room, "Is this curtain coming with us?"

Kelly appeared in the doorway, squeezing into the space with him. He tried to ignore the feelings she stirred inside him by standing so close. She bit her lip, considering…what, he wasn't sure. He tore his gaze away from her mouth and stared at the shower curtain.

She suggested, "Maybe we can make up a box of donations with that and the towels. And I have some mismatched dishes that I won't be using. I can check with my next-door neighbor Sal to see if she wants them or any of the furniture."

He agreed, though still he couldn't look at her. "Good," he said. "I'll bring everything out, and you can sort it."

She left the bathroom then, and he let out a breath of relief. Too close.

KELLY RIPPED THE sheets and blanket off the bed and threw them on the floor. Sam had probably figured out her dire financial circumstances before they'd even set foot in the apartment.

But now, there was no illusion. Her life had been stripped bare before him just like the bed. And no doubt he'd make judgments about her.

She stacked the pillows against one wall. She'd paid good money for those pillows, so she'd take them with her. The threadbare sheets and blanket had been purchased secondhand, and she wouldn't need them in Michigan, since Grammy had left behind plenty. And she'd bring things from Like Mildred once she came back to Nashville. No trying to recreate herself from scratch a second time.

Sam brought out the box from the bathroom and placed it on the floor next to the one that had dishes from the kitchen. "Want me to load these in the truck?"

She hated seeing the pity in his eyes, knowing that it was for her. She needed to keep him so busy he wouldn't think about all this. "Not yet. I still want to go through them and decide what to take." She nodded at the sheets and blanket on the floor. "I'm afraid these are too ruined to even donate. If you could get me a trash bag from under the kitchen sink, I'll throw them away."

He walked around the counter and returned with a large plastic bag in his outstretched hand. She took it from him without looking into his eyes. "The bathroom is empty?" she asked.

"Didn't take long to pack up." He glanced to his left. "The kitchen?"

"Also done. I have to go through the drawers but I should be done in ten minutes."

Sam took a seat at the kitchen table. "This is some place."

"Don't say it." She yanked open a dresser drawer and stuffed socks and under things into an empty box. "We can't all live in Nashville like you did here."

"When you said you'd been struggling, I didn't realize how much."

She raised her gaze to him and shot daggers toward his chest. "Everything in here is paid for by the sweat of my brow. I worked to keep food in my belly and the landlord off my back. I never fell behind in my bills or went into exorbitant debt."

Returning to her task, she pushed the first drawer in and pulled out the second. "And any money Grammy sent me was spent on my career. I promised her that."

"If she'd known how you were living..."

"Grammy always said we had to pay our own way. She'd be proud that I was determined to make it on my own." She lifted her chin. Grammy might not have liked her neighborhood or her sparse furnishings, but she would have understood her desire. "Not all of us have a rich daddy to bail us out."

Sam stood and came toward her. "He never did."

"But you certainly had that safety net, just in case." She tugged on the bottom drawer when it stuck, and tugged again. Once she had it open she collected what clothes she found and dumped them in the box. "I had nothing and no one here. I did all of it myself."

"I can see that." He put a hand on top of his head. "I wish I'd met you then, when we were both here. We might have been able to save each other."

She stared up at him. "I didn't need saving."

He took the box from her and stacked it on top of the others. "Maybe I did."

ONCE THEY HAD finished sorting the items that she was keeping from those she was donating, she and Sam loaded the unmolested SUV.

He drove her around the building to the rental office and waited in the car while she turned in her keys and signed the lease termination paperwork.

Kelly had to pay a hefty fee for breaking the lease, but it had been cheaper than trying to continue paying for something she wasn't using.

She left the office feeling lighter than she had walking in. She opened the passenger door of the SUV and climbed inside. "Let's get out of here," she told him.

They stayed silent as Sam drove toward the affluent neighborhood where his family lived. Kelly noticed the buildings that they passed by turned from rundown concrete and brick to gleaming glass and wood. Such a difference in their lives here. How would he be able to see her in the same way after this? She felt dirty and naked after the morning's activities, more exposed than if she had actually stripped bare in front of him.

Before they reached his parents' house, Sam pulled into a strip mall with a shipping store. "We can send back to Lake Mildred what you want to keep. My treat."

That's exactly what she'd feared after he

saw her old apartment. That he'd step in and take care of things. "I can afford it, thank you." She clutched her purse and got out of the car and retrieved two of the three boxes from the back. She'd have to come get the larger one containing her pillows. She struggled to hang on to the boxes while she opened the door to the store.

Sam ran up and opened it for her, holding on to the larger box effortlessly. "You don't have to do everything yourself, you know."

She didn't say a word beyond thanking him and strode inside the place. They had to wait for a couple in front of them who appeared as if they were shipping their entire life to the West coast. While she and Sam waited, she fidgeted under the weight of the boxes before finally setting them at her feet. She stole a glimpse at Sam who she discovered was staring at her. She cocked her head to one side. "Stop looking at me like that. I'm not a charity case."

"I wasn't thinking that." He shifted the box to his other hip. "I was thinking you're one of the strongest women I know."

Kelly rolled her eyes, scoffing at the suggestion. Desperate, sure. Strong? Only because she'd had to be. "Then you don't know many women."

He put his hand on her arm. "Don't do that. Don't make all the struggles you've had sound like they were nothing. You're right when you said my experience here was different from yours. I did have doors open for me due to my name, but it was my talent that kept me there. For a while, at least."

"My talent couldn't even do that. Just stubborn will." She looked down at the boxes at her feet, all she had to show for eleven years in Nashville. It seemed so insignificant. Who was she kidding? If she had the talent Grammy had insisted she possessed, she'd have that much more to prove it.

"You opened your own doors. You made your own opportunities and refused to take charity to do it. And I'm sorry that I didn't see it before."

She edged one of the boxes with the toe of her tennis shoe. "Does that mean you support my career now?"

He gave a short bark of laughter. "If anything, it means I need to get you out of here sooner."

Before Kelly could ask what he meant, their turn at the counter arrived.

SAM TUGGED AT the collar of his expensive black button-down shirt as he looked himself over in the foyer mirror. His wet hair still shone from the shower. He smiled crookedly at himself and stepped away. Glancing at the clock on the wall, he realized they needed to make a move and soon.

"We're late," he announced to the empty foyer.

"We have twenty minutes, according to your mom." Kelly was at the top of the stairs, looking down at him.

Sam's breath caught in his throat. She wore a short sleeveless dress the color of the ocean and had her hair pulled up in the front but trailing down her back in waves. She looked like an ocean goddess that he longed to pull into his arms and prevent any other man seeing her, wanting her. The vision of her in that depressing apartment earlier that day evaporated.

She slowly walked down the stairs, her eyes on his until she stood at the bottom. She glanced down at her outfit. "You don't like it."

"No," his voice cracked, and he cleared his throat before continuing. "I mean, you look amazing."

She smiled, shifting her gaze to the mirror. "I wasn't sure if this would be fancy enough for a launch party."

"It's perfect." She was perfect. She glowed like a jewel, catching the light and reflecting it back. He tugged at his collar again. "I'm the one who looks out of place now."

She reached up and smoothed the front of his shirt. "You look like you belong here."

"Outward appearances can be deceiving." She caught his eye again and he wished they didn't have to go to this party. He'd rather keep her here to himself. He glanced up as he heard a bedroom door close. His mother came down wearing a long gown in navy. In some ways, Kelly reminded him of her. They were both strong women with their own opinions and no qualms about sharing them. The fact that his mother hadn't brought up his lack of communication lately made him worry. That was an argument waiting to happen, but she seemed determined to keep it under wraps.

For now.

He smiled at her and held out his arm to

her. "What did I do to deserve escorting two such beautiful women tonight?"

"Hands off, son. She's mine." Frank appeared in the doorway of the study.

Sam stepped back as his father passed him and approached his mother. He held out a long narrow jeweler's box to her. "A gift for you."

Sam and Kelly watched as his mother opened the box then gave a soft sigh of pleasure. "You remembered."

His father took the diamond choker and stood behind his wife to fasten it around her neck. "Every first album, I promised you jewelry."

His mother beamed, but rolled her eyes. "I'm always surprised when he remembers." She looked at his father and put a hand on his cheek. "Thank you, love."

Sam swallowed at the lump in his throat. He felt as if he'd caught his parents in an intimate embrace. But then, they'd always been like this, and he'd never been jealous of not having a similar type of relationship.

He glanced at Kelly. Until now.

He offered his arm to Kelly. "We should get going."

She linked her arm through his and together they walked out the front door to the waiting limousine.

When they arrived at the party, the driver pulled up in front of the music hall to let out his passengers. Kelly was staring at her strappy silver sandals and hoping that the hot pink toenail polish wouldn't clash with the bright crimson carpet that would be under her feet. She looked at Sam who watched her with a furrowed brow. "I didn't expect a real red carpet."

"My dad produced the album, so they're expecting him. But I can ask Westley to drop us off up ahead if you'd rather skip this part."

She shook her head. Who knew if she'd ever have this experience again? She took several deep breaths and closed her eyes. *You can do this, Kelly. You've dreamed all your life about a night like this. Even if it's for someone else, you can imagine what it could have been like if you'd—*

If she'd what? She'd done all she could. She'd tried out at auditions. Taken the advice they'd given her and used it to make her voice better. She'd sung back-up to country artists who told her she had real talent. She'd networked and schmoozed and used all the connections she'd made to get her foot in the door. But it had slammed shut in her face. Every time.

Sam put his arm around her bare shoulders. "It's just a party. We can leave early if you want."

"No. Your friend wants you to be a part of this." She put her hand on his arm. "I'm feeling a little jealous, I guess."

He pushed a strand of her hair behind her ears. "Don't be. You're amazing the way you are."

She swallowed, then moved along to find Westley holding out his hand to her. She took another deep breath, accepting his hand, and she stepped cautiously from the limousine.

Bright flashes of light blinded her, and she winced. Then there was a hand on the small of her back and a whisper in her ear, "Don't look directly at the flashes or you won't be able to see all night. Smile as if you know the funniest joke. And try not to trip over your own feet."

She pasted on a smile and stayed right next to Sam.

"Junior, who's the lovely lady with you?"

"Over here, Junior. Are you coming back to Nashville?"

"Why did you leave, Junior?"

The reporters' questions got thrown at them so fast they made her head spin. But she smiled and kept focused on putting one foot in front of the other without falling flat on her face. Sam never answered the questions thrown at him, but led her forward until they had reached the large glass doors that someone pulled open for them.

Once inside the music hall, Sam let out a breath that he seemed to have been holding ever since they'd left the limo. He shrugged as if to get the Junior moniker off of him. "I'm glad that's over."

She noticed a fine sheen of sweat at his hairline. His pale face seemed more so above his dark clothes. "Did you do this a lot?"

He shrugged. "Some."

But he wouldn't go any further. She decided not to push it, but glanced around the large entryway. Loud music played from the ballroom ahead of them. People talked and laughed, adding to the noise. Sam took her hand in his, interlacing his fingers with hers. "Stay by me, and I'll introduce you around."

She nodded, liking the feel of his hand as well as the words he offered. He led her to a small group of people gathered by the stage. He shook hands with a tall guy with long, scraggly hair. "Ol' Jimmy Feeney, you're a sight for sore eyes."

The man grinned, doffing a well-kept, but worn fedora. "I'd say the same, but you look like a horse dragged you through a field."

Sam laughed, and the two men hugged, pounding each other on the back. Sam told Kelly, "Jim was the engineer on my album. Never liked me much though."

Jim held out his hand. "Afraid it's true, miss. He was the worst singer I ever worked with."

Kelly grinned, but wondered why Sam beamed at this description. It didn't sound like something he should be proud of. Sam introduced the other people who were standing there, but his attention returned to Jim. "Ty told me you looked out for him, Jimmy."

The man instantly sobered, nodding. "You talk to him?"

"Some. Do I need to be worried?"

"Reminds me a lot of you on your first

album, especially his friends who hang around."

Sam's grin left his face, and he shook his head. "Thanks for letting me know."

He said his goodbyes and then pulled Kelly away towards the bar area. He ordered himself a soda water with lime, then turned to her. She glanced at the bar's offerings. "I'll take a white wine."

The bartender poured it for her and placed it on the bar. Sam gulped at his soda water, leaving his empty glass next to her still full one. He held up a finger to the bartender and pointed it at the empty glass. He drank the second just as quickly as the first. Kelly took her glass and held it in her hand. "Are you okay?"

He scanned the room, which seemed to be filling quickly. But the atmosphere was subdued as if they were waiting for something dramatic or explosive to happen. He nodded, but didn't look at her.

Pushing off the bar, he tugged her across the ballroom to a table. He sat in one chair, directing her to the other, his toes tapping and his fingers thrumming on the table.

She reached out and put her hand over his. "What's wrong?"

He surveyed the room again. "Nothing."

She wasn't convinced. "If this is nothing, then I'd hate to see you when you're really upset about something."

He gazed at her, his eyes troubled. "Parties like this make me nervous."

"You were fine until you talked to Jimmy."

He shrugged. "It's nothing." He stopped his feet from tapping. "You want to dance?"

No one else was on the dance floor. "No. Talk to me. What's going on?"

He reached up and ran a hand over his jaw. "I hate the waiting part. Don't you?"

"Maybe a little wine would take the edge off." She held out her glass to him. It's not like she needed it, and he looked like he certainly did.

He stared at it but ultimately shook his head. "I don't drink anymore."

Oh. She set her glass aside then took her hands in his. "Is that what this is about? You want to drink?"

"There's a lot of things I want to do right now. None of them good." The tapping foot started again. "I need some air. Want to step outside with me?"

"I'll freshen up in the restroom first, then meet you out there."

He stood and practically ran from the room. She briefly watched him on the patio. On her way to the restroom, she was stopped by Frank. "Where's Junior? I have someone here who wants to meet him."

She pointed to the patio. "He's outside."

Frank looked in that direction, frowning. Not that she'd seen many expressions on his face besides that one. "Alone?" he asked.

"Said he needed some air." She assumed that he needed a lot more than air, but she wasn't in a sharing mood.

Frank replaced his frown with a smile when a second man joined them. "George, have you met Kelly Sweet? She's a friend of my son's. He claims she's got real talent."

The man, impeccably dressed in a tux, looked Kelly over from head to toe. "You could have the pipes, but you'd need to lose at least twenty pounds and about fifteen years if you want to make it in this town."

Kelly opened her mouth to protest, but shut

it. "Thank you for your advice." To Frank she said, "I'll tell Sam you're looking for him."

Frank nodded and turned away from her, about to start a conversation with George concerning his latest talent acquisition. Dismissed, she glanced over at the patio then started to head there. She'd only made it halfway across the room when the deejay announced Tyler's entrance. Everyone standing crowded around the doorway.

Tyler wore the same Stetson she'd seen him in the day before. But he'd changed into tight black jeans and a black shirt with an open collar that had a sheen to it which made him seem to sparkle. He held up his hands and smiled. Everyone parted to let him get to the stage. He'd stop every once in a while to shake hands or to shout out a greeting.

Once he reached the stage, he leapt onto it and held up his hands to quiet the applause of the crowd. Someone handed him a microphone, and he clutched it tightly. "Hey, I'm Ty Wilson, and I'm happy to have you all here to celebrate the launch of my first album 'River Dreams.'" He shadowed his eyes with his hand and scanned the crowd. "Where is Junior? There he is."

The crowd seemed to all turn their heads towards the doors that led to the patio. Kelly straightened and tried to see past those folks standing around her. If only she were taller or had on higher heels. She peered between several bodies and caught a glimpse of Sam standing back by the wall.

"I want to thank you, Junior. This album wouldn't have happened without you." Sam shook his head, but Ty laughed. "He's being modest. He was my mentor throughout this whole process. And my album is better for it."

Several people clapped at this, but Sam ducked his head and pointed to Tyler as if to get the attention off of himself. Kelly made her excuses as she tried to get to where he held up the wall.

Ty hooted as the band started to play behind him. "I'd like to sing a little something you might have heard on the radio recently. This is *Life Lesson Number One*."

Kelly reached Sam just as the young man began to sing. Sam glanced down at her, putting his arm around her shoulders. "I didn't know where you'd gone," he said.

She leaned up on tiptoe and shouted in his ear. "Your father is looking for you."

He noted the crowd and gave a bitter laugh. "I bet he is. Probably has a bunch of friends he wants me to meet."

"He's proud of you."

"He's proud of who I used to be." He looked down at himself and grimaced. "Not the man I've become. Too bad, because I happen to like him a lot better."

Kelly put her hand in his. "Me, too."

He squeezed her hand and pulled her closer to him. "Dance with me."

"No one else is."

"I don't care."

He held her in his arms and rested his chin on top of her head. She closed her eyes and swayed with him. When the song ended, she hated to let him go. But she did and clapped along with the folks around her. Sam whispered in her ear, "I'm going to talk to Ty. We'll dance some more?"

She nodded and then he was gone.

SAM WALKED TOWARD the stage where people crowded around Ty. He nodded at several who called his name and eventually found Ty waiting behind a young woman with white blond hair teased high. She asked for Ty's autograph, and he laughingly signed her T-shirt when she handed him a marker. Sam put his arm around Ty's shoulders then leaned close to his ear. "Can we talk alone for a minute?"

"The crowd loves me."

"Then they can wait five minutes for you to come back. Always leave them wanting more, rule number thirty-two of show business."

Ty smiled and they moved behind the thick stage curtains. People raced around, mostly members of the band setting up for the next song. Ty stopped, faced Sam and gathered him in a great big bear hug.

"I'm so glad you made it to the party. It's like the perfect way to end the night." Ty pulled out a small flask. "Well, you and this," he said.

He then offered the flask to Sam. Sam took it and sniffed the contents. *Bourbon.* He winced. "You know I gave that up."

"A little won't hurt. Takes the edge off."

Sam clutched the flask and held it up to his friend. "You need to stay focused and sober, Tyler. Tonight is only the beginning of your career, and you don't want to have to rely on this to help you get through it."

Ty snatched the flask, sealed it and put it

in his rear pocket. "I'm fine. Really. I haven't had that much."

Sam raised one eyebrow. "Jimmy tells me you have a new friend."

"She's not really new, as you know. But yeah, we've been hanging out quite a bit." Ty took a step back. "It's no big deal."

The kid didn't get it. Sam feared that he never would. "She's no good for you."

"You never gave her a chance. She's changed."

"Really? Is she still dealing?" But Sam didn't need to hear the answer to know. She couldn't leave that world, no matter how much he'd tried to get her out. He'd lost himself in the process until eventually he'd succumbed to the temptations of drugs.

Ty paled and acted the innocent. "I don't know. We don't talk about that part of her life."

"That's why she's not a part of mine anymore."

The curtains parted and a young woman in tight blue jeans, western shirt and a long red leather jacket appeared. She glanced at Ty before turning to Sam. "Hey," she said.

He acknowledged her, but spoke to Ty, telling him, "You are on the edge of something big, but she's only going to ruin it for you. Don't believe anything she says because she's in this for her, not you."

"Ty isn't as judgmental as you, Junior." Shannon put her hands on her tiny hips. "He's willing to give me a chance."

Sam glared at her. "You clean?" The glassy eyes told him he was right.

She narrowed her gaze at him and lifted her chin. "Are you?"

The curtains parted once more, and he spotted Kelly searching the backstage area. Soon, her eyes found his. She smiled and came forward. "Ty, you were great." She glanced at Shannon and held out her hand. "Hi, I'm Kelly Sweet."

Shannon ignored Kelly's offered hand and sneered at Sam. "Trying to change your act with Miss Goody Two-Shoes here? Best of luck with that. Because you all come back to me one way or another."

She sauntered off.

Sam turned to Ty. "Stay away from her. She's bad news."

"You don't know what you're talking about." Ty glanced toward the crowd and took another step back. The band had started to warm up. "I've gotta go out there." He walked past Sam, but paused and put a hand on his shoulder. "You don't have to worry about me. I know what I'm doing."

Sam shook his head. He'd thought that once, too, on a night just like this. That he could handle all of it: the fame, the celebrity, the bright lights. He focused on Kelly instead. "I apologize for what she said about you. She doesn't know what she's talking about."

"Who was that?"

Sam sighed. "My sister Shannon. And my old drug dealer."

CHAPTER ELEVEN

KELLY HAD TO HAVE heard him wrong. Not the part about Shannon being his sister since the resemblance was obvious. *But drug dealer?* "I think the loud music is doing something with my hearing. What did you call her?"

Sam's mouth tightened in a grim line. "Besides my sister, she became my drug dealer. Anything I wanted, she could get. And we'd get high together. Called it family bonding." He shook his head and glanced away from her. "I'm not proud of it."

Kelly glanced in the direction where Shannon had gone. "The way your mom talked, I thought she had died."

"Might as well have, according to my parents. And to me."

Out on stage, Ty began singing. Kelly stepped closer to hear Sam. He leaned down and whispered in her ear to be heard, "I gotta go." He started for the back of the stage. He turned and held out his hand to her. "Are you coming with me?"

She nodded and ran to catch up with him. He opened a door, and they stepped outside into the night air. The temperature had dropped since they'd arrived, and Kelly put her arms around herself as she followed Sam around the side of the building. He pulled his cell phone from his pocket and made a call. "Westley, can you come and pick us up? I'm leaving early. We're waiting by the west entrance."

He had chosen to wait where the paparazzi couldn't find them. Noticing that she shivered, he took off his suit jacket and put it around her shoulders. "If you want to stay..."

"No." This was more important. He was more important. "Is that why you left Nashville? The drugs?"

He looked out across the parking lot. "I could never get enough. Not alcohol. Not sex. Not drugs. Nothing could fill this deep hole I felt inside of me." He laughed, but it came out acidic. "I thought that a singing career was everything I needed. That it would save me from all the demons everywhere." He reached out and held her by her arms. "But that's the lie they tell you. The music couldn't fill that hole inside me, no matter how hard I tried. It wasn't the answer to all my problems. And it's not the answer to yours."

He crushed her to him. "That's why I wish you could have saved me back then."

The limousine arrived. Westley slid out of the driver's seat, but Sam had already opened the rear door and was motioning for her to get inside. He hopped in after her.

What was Sam thinking? She couldn't save anyone. Not then, not now. Did he really think she could save him now? She took his hand in hers, but he kept his gaze front and center.

"I'm glad you told me." And she was. She could tell that he'd let her inside some secret circle that very few had joined. The fact that he included her meant more than him bringing her to some glitzy Nashville party.

Sam scoffed at this. "I'm not glad. I never wanted to tell you." He turned his gaze to her. "Unless it convinces you to leave Nashville and never look back."

"Not everyone has the same experience that you did."

His expression became sour. "More do than you know." He shifted away from her, rubbing his finger over his top lip. "And you're the kind of girl this town will chew up and spit out without thinking twice."

She knew he was wrong. There were plenty of people in this business that didn't succumb to the temptations of drugs and alcohol. There were many that had a successful career and didn't cave in to the pressures of the business. She wouldn't be a statistic like he thought. She wouldn't allow herself to be.

Right?

They remained quiet for the rest of the ride to the house. When they'd gotten to the mansion, Sam spoke to her finally. "If I can make it work…do you mind if we fly back to Michigan tomorrow? I can't be in this town a minute longer."

She nodded slowly. What choice did she have? She couldn't stay here and try to make another go of it until Grammy's house was sold. She had to return to Lake Mildred to keep working and painting, and trying to forget a taste of her future that she'd had. "Sure. Whatever you want."

They exited the SUV. "What I want is to forget this weekend ever happened. I don't like looking back. It only reminds me of how much of a fool I've been."

She put a hand on his bicep. "But you're more resilient now. You don't have to be who you were."

"You don't know how bad I want to find Shannon and buy some of whatever she's selling. To shoot it in my veins so I can forget for a little while. Or to raid my dad's liquor cabinet and drink myself into oblivion. That's not being strong."

"It is if you don't give in to it."

His withering look knocked her over and he strode into the house, leaving her standing in the driveway wondering why he couldn't see how strong he was. He'd beaten the demons before. He would again.

She took a deep breath then stepped inside the foyer. She didn't feel much like going up to her room to change or sleep. It was early still.

Instead, she roamed the lower floor until she found the entertainment room. Frank Sr. had an impressive collection of music. She put in one CD of a country newcomer and listened to it for a while. It was good, but it wasn't what she wanted to hear. She searched until she found Sam's own album amidst the rest.

He looked younger on the cover, but still so handsome. She put the CD on the stereo, then sat on a leather recliner, letting the notes play over her skin, making her heart beat in rhythm to the song. She closed her eyes and drifted off to sleep.

A FEW HOURS LATER, Kelly stirred, recognizing when the fourth song on the CD repeated, her favorite.

"That's my favorite, too."

Kelly opened her eyes and found Mr. Etchason standing in the doorway of the media room. He took a seat next to her in the twin to her recliner. He let the song play, nodding his head to the rhythm. "Such a voice. And he didn't have to work at his talent like some did. It came natural." He shook his head. "What a waste."

She didn't want to argue. The honeyed tones coming from the stereo proved that Sam was a talented singer. But his life hadn't been wasted.

The song ended, and the next began. Frank steepled his fingers in front of his mouth, his gaze intent on hers. "I want my son back, and I'm willing to do whatever I have to to get him." He looked at her assessingly. "Junior mentioned you wanted a singing career. I can make that happen, but in return I want something from you."

She frowned and waited for his proposal. She feared his next words, but couldn't stop them. He leaned towards her and said in a soft voice, "I'll get you a recording deal in exchange for you working with Junior on the album. You bring him back to Nashville, and it can all be yours. An album. A tour. And you can have my son with you in the bargain."

She gasped. All she'd dreamed of held dangling out in front of her. So tempting. But at what expense? "Sam won't agree to it."

"He will if you ask him to." Mr. Etchason gave a wry smile. "I've seen the way he looks at you. He'd give you the world if you asked him."

"So you'd give me my dream, but at what cost to your son? Every minute he's here, he is slowly dying. Do you understand what it does to him to be in this town for even a couple of days? Do you care?" She studied him, wondering if he'd been clueless to Sam's drug abuse. The fact that it had been kept out of the tabloids meant that it had been well hidden.

"You want to know if I knew of my son's weakness." Frank waved the concern away. "I can buy him the best help and whatever program he needs. He'll be fine. You can see to it."

"But this isn't his dream. It's yours." She stood and for the first time saw a desperate father, rather than a powerful record executive. "You think that the work he does is beneath him. Because he fixes doors and shores up sagging foundations. But he does it all with a smile. When was the last time you saw that on his face in Nashville?"

When Mr. Etchason didn't answer, she planted her hands on her hips and continued. "He's changing our plane tickets. We're out of here as we speak because he can't stay in this town." Again, there was no response. "I don't understand how you could sacrifice your son's own dreams and wishes to guarantee yours?"

"And yours, Ms. Sweet. Everything you've always wanted."

"That's a price I'm not willing to pay." She tugged at the hem of her dress to bring it back down to her knees. "I'm sorry, Mr. Etchason, but my answer is no."

He rose, his gaze locked on hers. "Everyone has a price tag. It may take me a while to figure out yours, but I'll get what I want from you and my son."

"I don't think so."

SAM SAT IN the bay window in his old bedroom and looked out to the backyard swathed in moonlight. His fingers itched, his toes tapped. Restless, he stood and paced the length of his bedroom. The desire to feel better by getting high was getting stronger.

He still had Shannon's number on his cell phone. He'd hoped that one day he could help her get clean like he had. That she could work to restore the relationship she'd once had with their parents. That she would turn her back on the lifestyle that had claimed them and ruined everything for them both.

But how could he ask Shannon to turn away from indulging in drugs, when he was still so weak? When, at that moment, he would have agreed to do anything to get high. Just one more time. And then he'd return to being sober.

He shook his head and pounded his fist on the door of his closet. That was a lie. There was never one more time. It would be once, then twice. Then he'd wake up in the back of a car, confused about where he was and how he'd gotten there.

It's how he'd ended up in Lake Mildred. He'd been on a bender in Chicago with so-called friends that used him and his money to get what they wanted. He'd stumbled from a house party, to sleep it off in the backseat of a car, then woken up two days later in Michigan.

He'd fought hard to get sober and find a meaningful life. And he succeeded, for the most part. Sure, he felt the hole inside him aching to be filled every once in a while, but he'd been able to refuse it. That control was now starting to slip.

There was a light knock on his door, and Kelly popped her head inside the room. "Your parents are back from the party. Are you okay?"

"I got us on a flight tomorrow morning at ten. We'll need to leave here a little before eight, so be sure you're ready." He took out his suitcase from under the bed and started to put his clothes inside. He turned to find her watching him.

"I'll be ready when you are." She entered the room and came to sit on the bed next to the suitcase. "What worries me is what can I do to help you?"

He shrugged and folded the T-shirts he'd unpacked only the day before. "Don't, okay? Don't try to make it easier or better because you can't."

"I thought we were friends."

He stopped folding the T-shirt and looked at her. Oh, how he wished she could save him. For a while, he'd even thought it was possible. "We're friends. But I didn't mean it when I said that you could save me…because you can't. Only I can do that."

"And running away will help?"

He closed his eyes. That's what he'd been doing for the last two years, running away from his temptations, his weaknesses. "Yes. I can't stay here a day longer. I can feel the pull of my old life starting to win." He opened his eyes and looked at her again. "I can't let it win. The hole inside me is opening wider every second I'm here."

She got off the bed and put her arms around

his middle. She rested her cheek on his chest and held him. He didn't touch her. Couldn't. But he let her hold him until the shakes disappeared. Until his thirst went away.

She tilted her head to look up at him. "Better?"

Yes. He put his hands on either side of her face and kissed her deeply. She clung to his shoulders, kissing him back. He breathed her in, wanting her to be the slayer of his demons. But he knew that as soon as he let go of her, they'd return. And they'd keep coming until he left Nashville.

He let her go and pushed her toward the door. "You're a nice distraction, but you can't heal me."

She frowned, the nice moment they'd shared suddenly tarnished. "I never claimed I could. Like you said, only you can do that."

She made to leave. "I'll be ready by eight," she called over her shoulder. Then she opened the door and was gone.

But his demons remained.

KELLY PLACED HER battered purple suitcase in the foyer, glancing up at the top of the stairs. Sam's bedroom door remained closed.

Joy walked out from the kitchen in a long, silky red bathrobe. She gave a smile, but Kelly had the feeling she didn't feel it. "Junior said you're leaving early this morning. I've got muffins in the kitchen if you'd like one before you head off for the airport."

Kelly nodded and followed Joy to the kitchen. "Thank you for opening your home to me."

"Anytime. He thinks I don't know why he can't stay, but I'm his mother. I know what troubles my son." She handed Kelly a blueberry muffin still warm from the oven. "I only wish he could see how tough he truly is."

Kelly picked at her muffin. "I met Shannon last night."

Joy chose a muffin for herself, but played with the edges of the wrapper. "Frank won't talk about her anymore. And, obviously we don't normally see her." She lifted her eyes to Kelly. "Did she look okay?"

"She looked tired. Sad." Kelly shrugged and had a small bit of muffin. "But determined."

"Gets that from her father. That and her stubborn refusal to see any logic except her own. Junior thinks that by staying away he can escape the life she chose. Maybe he's right." She reached for Kelly's hand. "Is he happy in Michigan?"

Kelly smiled. "I think so. You should see the work he's planning on doing to my grandmother's house. He is so gifted."

Joy smiled. "Then take him back there and help him find his way again." She let go of Kelly's hand and grabbed her cup of coffee. "As much as I wish he could find it here, this Michigan town and you have been good for him."

Kelly considered Joy's kind words. "All I seem to do is argue with him. And point out that he's not always right. But if that's helping, I'll take it. He's been good for me." She had another bite of muffin.

They ate and drank in silence until Sam showed up. "Westley is here to take us to the airport," he told them.

Joy got off the stool and took a few steps toward her son. She pulled him close, clinging to him as if afraid to let go. Then she did. "I'm only a phone call away if you ever need me."

"Love you, Ma."

Kelly hugged Joy. "Thank you again."

"Remember what I said. You're good for him."

The two women paused and looked at each other before Sam pulled Kelly away and out the door. Her luggage and Sam's was already in the car, so they got in. Sam in the front passenger seat, Kelly in back. Joy stood on the porch as the SUV drove away. She kept her gaze on Sam's mother until she disappeared from view.

THE WORST FLIGHT EVER. Had to be if the extent of Sam's experience meant anything. He and Kelly had been delayed for an hour in Nashville while a mechanical problem got checked. Then they'd been diverted to Louisville when snowy conditions at the airfield in Michigan kept them from getting home.

He shifted in the uncomfortable plastic chair and glanced over at Kelly who slept in the seat next to him. She looked so innocent, so untouched that way. He stroked her cheek gently. She'd be better off staying away from him if she knew any better.

An announcement came over the PA system stating that their flight would be reboarding in fifteen minutes. Sam squeezed

Kelly's shoulder to rouse her. She groaned and stretched, but opened her eyes. "Are we there yet?"

"They're boarding our ride home." He got up and hoisted his duffel bag over his shoulder. "And none too soon."

She jumped then grabbed her purse next to her chair. They joined the line to get on to the plane, tickets in hand. "The first thing I do when I get home is take a long, hot shower. Then I'm going to take a nap. Then I'll order in Chinese and eat it with my fingers while I watch reruns of old TV shows."

"You've got it all figured out." He didn't look at her, but kept his gaze on the people in front of him. Ever since their conversation last night, he hadn't been able to look her directly in the eye. Afraid to see judgment staring back at him. That and disappointment. "What about Megs?"

"She can join me if she wants." Kelly yawned again then stretched her neck, rotating her head from side to side. "Maybe we'll make it like a slumber party." She reached into her jeans front pocket and brought out her phone and started texting. "I'll see if she's free."

Sam smiled gladly, he was happy about the progress made between the sisters, even if he hadn't made any with Kelly. The clerk at the head of the line asked for their boarding passes and scanned them before letting them pass. Sam strode down the hall toward the jet, hearing Kelly behind him. Probably trying to text and walk at the same time.

They found their seats near the middle of the plane. Sam took Kelly's purse from her and stored it next to his duffel bag in the bin above their seats then offered her the window seat. She settled in, put on her seat belt, while he helped an older man get his carry-on stored above as well.

Finally, Sam sat in the seat next to hers. She turned to him. "Just so I'm clear, are we going to avoid the subject of what happened last night for the rest of our lives, or what?"

He kept his gaze on the seat in front of him and pulled out the in-flight catalog. He flipped through several pages. "Do you need a mini staircase for your dog so he can sleep on your bed with you?"

"I don't have a dog." She put her hand on his wrist. "I've waited for you to say something, but I can't take this anymore. Talk to me."

"We are talking." Why wouldn't she let it go? He'd made mistakes. Knew she had, too. But did that mean they had to dissect them to death? He put the catalog back in its pocket and tried to recline his seat. Turned to apologize to the passenger behind him and shifted in his spot. "There's nothing more to say."

She wouldn't let go of his arm, and the heat of her touch seared him. She ran her thumb over his skin. "We've only just started to talk about your past. Don't you find that strange? You know all about mine, but you're a mystery to me."

"That was my choice, to keep it to myself."

"You've invited me in, now it's too late to go back to shutting me out." She put her hand on his cheek and turned his face toward her. "My feelings for you haven't changed because you've let me glimpse your dark side. Now tell me about the hole."

She definitely wasn't going to let this go. As he stared into her deep blue eyes, he admitted he wanted to open up and let her in all the way. Wanted to tell her everything. Because he didn't see anything in those eyes but acceptance. "When I sing, I feel as if I'm giving myself away to the audience. That they are taking parts of me with them." He closed his eyes. "I don't feel that when I'm working with my hands. Holding a hammer or running a chain saw, I feel whole. Complete."

She skimmed his cheekbone. "Then that's what you're meant to be doing."

He opened his eyes and kissed the palm of her hand. "You make me feel whole too, Kel. Like no one ever has." He stared at her, anxious to see how she would take those words. The closest he'd ever come to telling her how he felt.

When she didn't say anything, he took her hand from his face and held it. "You've come to mean a great deal to me."

She took her hand from his. "Don't. I'm not staying in Lake Mildred."

It was his turn to frown. "Even after this weekend, you still want to pursue a music career in Nashville? Haven't you understood a thing about what I've been telling you?"

"That's you and your experience. I'm not like you." She put her hands in her lap. "If anything, my time in Nashville has shown me how much I miss it. I need to go back and find out if I can do this."

"Then you do it without me."

She nodded. "I know."

The captain announced that they were preparing to take off. Sam focused on the flight attendant who walked through the emergency procedures. Kelly turned to look out the window.

IT WASN'T UNTIL midnight that she and Sam pulled into the driveway of Grammy's home. So much for her Chinese takeout. Kelly didn't say a word to Sam, hadn't since she'd told him that she would be returning to Nashville. But then, he hadn't tried to talk to her, either.

The truck stopped, and they got out. Kelly lifted her suitcase from the back of the truck, then said to him, "See you Monday."

He grunted in reply and disappeared up the stairs to his apartment. Kelly let herself inside the side door and found Megs in bathrobe and pajamas at the kitchen island. Her sister looked up, then rushed forward and hugged her. "I never thought you'd get home."

"That makes two of us." Kelly put her suitcase down and hugged her sister back. "Sorry we couldn't have our slumber party."

Megs quickly forgave her. "Another night." She walked to the refrigerator and pulled out a white carton with a silver handle. "I saved you some lo mein."

"You're my favorite sister in the whole wide world," Kelly told her.

"I'm your only sister." Megs smiled and found a plate and dumped the cold noodles on it. "Want them like this or warmed up?"

"I'll take them as is. I'm starving." She accepted the plate and used her fingers to pull out a long strand. She dropped it into her mouth and chewed, eyes closed. "Now this is what I'm talking about."

Megs watched her eat for a few minutes, taking the stool next to hers. "It was really quiet here without you. How was Nashville?"

Kelly paused in her chewing and then looked at the refrigerator. "Do we have any of that tea left?"

Megs started to get up, but Kelly waved her back down. "I can get it. I'm not an invalid."

She took down a tall glass from the cupboard and walked to the fridge. A half full pitcher of sweet tea waited for her. It was probably nothing like Joy's authentic Southern iced tea, but she'd enjoy it. She poured a full glass, having a long draw from it before putting the pitcher back into the refrigerator. She turned and found Megs watching her with a frown. "Was it that bad? Why did you come home early?"

Kelly kept her head down. "You need to ask Sam about that." She pushed her plate away, then sighed. "Is it so wrong that I want what I want? That I don't want to give up on my dreams?"

"You mean Nashville."

"I mean my music. And yes, for me that means Nashville." She picked up a noodle but left it. "I caught a glimpse of the life I want, and it made me even more determined."

Megs nodded and put her hand on Kelly's arm. "Then don't let anyone get in your way. Not Sam. Not even me. If that's what you want, then go after it."

"Easier said than done."

"Maybe." Megs got up and poured herself a glass of sweet tea. "Grammy believed that all you needed was the right opportunity to show everyone the star that you already are. So why not?"

"Even if that means I leave here again?"

Megs agreed slowly. "If that's what you really want, I'd rather have you there and happy, than here and miserable."

Kelly got off her stool and walked over to hug her sister. "Sometimes I think you were given the wise, older sister genes instead of me."

They held each other for a long while, until Kelly yawned. Megs soon did the same and they both laughed. Kelly glanced at the clock on the wall. "I think I'm ready for a shower and then my bed."

"Sounds good to me." Megs wrapped up the plate before placing it in the refrigerator. "Go ahead and sleep in tomorrow, Kel. You deserve it."

Kelly paused, confused. "It's Sunday, isn't it? The Sweetheart's closed."

Megs winked at her. "That's why I said you could sleep in."

SAM HATED HIS BED. And had his pillow always been this lumpy? He leaned on one elbow and tried to fluff the pillow into the proper shape. Laid back down and stared into the darkness.

He flopped onto his side to stare at the wall.

Then onto his other side to stare at his dresser across the room.

This was insanity. He sat up and ran a hand over his face. He'd been restless last night, but he'd still been able to sleep, knowing he was coming home soon. And now that he was here, the demons seemed to have followed him.

He swung his legs over the side of the bed and crossed the room to the picture window. Looking at Addy's home, he noted the lights were all off, and he envied the sisters their sleep. He turned toward the darkness of his apartment, leaning against the windowsill.

One drink couldn't hurt, right? It wasn't yet two a.m., so he could make it to The Penalty Box before last call. Have one beer. Knock the edge off this day so he could sleep.

He ran a hand over his face again. No. It wouldn't work. He'd only wake up tomorrow hating himself. Or worse yet, thinking he could do it again. He walked to the sofa and sat, holding his middle as he rocked back and forth, back and forth.

He stood and walked to the kitchen, switched on the light and grabbed a glass from the cupboard. Twisted the faucet and filled the glass with water. Gulped it down. Refilled it. Then drank that, too, and smacked the glass on the counter.

Demons, go away. I won't let you win. Not tonight. Not again.

He returned to the living room and found his guitar standing there, mocking him. He smacked it and let it fall to the ground, strings groaning in protest. He spotted his tool belt lying nearby. His toolbox next to it by the front door. He slid out his hammer then strode back across the room to take the guitar by the neck, holding the hammer above it. Wanting to bring it down and smash the thing to pieces. To tear it apart until it was only a pile of wood and strings. To take away its power. To remove the temptations that still held him in their clutches.

Instead, he kneeled on the carpet and clutched the hammer tightly in his hands. Let the hot tears gather in his eyes and slip past, onto his cheeks.

He cried for the loss of the sister he'd once known and loved. For the weak woman she'd become. For his own descent into hell and his fight to come back. For Kelly's dream that would take her away from him. And finally, for Addy and the new life she'd helped him find. He'd once been lost, but now was found. And he could hold on to that.

He wiped his face with one hand. The demons were still there, not dependent on his career or geography. But he was stronger than they were. And they wouldn't win.

Not tonight.

He put the hammer down beside him and picked up the guitar. Plucked a few chords and started to sing Addy's favorite song. And sweet the sound it was.

CHAPTER TWELVE

GRAMMY HAD LEFT too many things behind, not including her granddaughters. Kelly groaned as she opened the closet door and looked inside at the packed floor-to-ceiling space. Too many clothes. Too many shoes. And this from a woman who wore T-shirts and jeans with sneakers most days of her life. Kelly stumbled backward and sat roughly on the bed.

At least Megs had let her go early this afternoon so that she could work on the house. Part of the new bakery plans meant Kelly would do the mornings except for Wednesday and Thursday when she worked all day in order to give Megs a break.

Kelly glanced at the cardboard boxes that she'd brought over from the bakery and figured she'd need to bring more if they wanted to donate Grammy's stuff. She took a deep breath and started pulling items out of the closet, dividing them into three piles: keep, toss and donate.

She'd only made a dent when she heard her name being shouted from the basement. She paused to make sure she'd really heard it. Yep, that was her name. She ran along the hallway, around the corner and down the basement steps to find Sam pressed against one wall. "I need your help."

Okay, but she didn't have a clue about hanging drywall. He stared at her, holding the piece of drywall in place, and sighed. "I can't get the nail gun and hold this at the same time."

She nodded, snatching up the nail gun she'd seen him using before. "I'm not sure how to operate this thing."

"You don't need to. Just carefully put it in my right hand and hold the end of this where it is now." He spoke slowly, with purpose, as if she couldn't follow his instructions.

She did as he'd told her while he nailed his side of the wall into the framing. She noticed that his jeans hung low on his hips with the weight of his tool belt tugging them lower. She thought about saying something, but he'd been avoiding her ever since they'd returned from Nashville. Let his pants fall if his pride couldn't get him to talk to her.

He edged closer to where she was standing, still holding her end of the drywall, nailing it into place. She glanced down and noticed that an inch of his underwear waistband now showed. Biting back a giggle, she glanced away. The closer he got, the more his jeans sagged. By the time he reached her, one good tug would bring them to the floor. Which wouldn't be so bad…if he wasn't wearing black boxers with bright neon orange pumpkins on them. She put her head on her arm and gave in to the laughter.

"Don't say it, Kel."

She couldn't say much of anything she was laughing so hard. By the time he finished hanging the piece of drywall, he dumped the gun on the ground and tugged up his pants. Kelly collapsed on the floor and tried to stop giggling. "Pumpkins?" She wiped her eyes. "I never figured you for those."

"I haven't done laundry in a while." He tightened the tool belt around his hips. "It's not funny."

She bit her lip and nodded. "You're right. It's more like hilarious." She stood and started to walk up the stairs. "I gotta tell Megs about this." She pulled her phone from the front pocket of her jeans.

"Don't you dare." He went over and took the phone from her. "She doesn't need to know anything about it."

"Oh yes, she does." She tried to get the phone back, but he was taller than her and could keep it out of her reach without much effort. "Give me my phone back."

"Not til you promise not to tell Megs." He dangled the phone in front of her. "Promise or you don't get it back."

"Fine. I promise." He handed over the phone. "I should have taken a picture though, when I had the chance, Pumpkin." He smirked at this, and they both started to laugh. Kelly wiped at her eyes again. "I've missed this. Being with you like this."

His laughter stopped, and his expression became stony. "I have to get back to work."

She reached out and touched his upper arm. "Wait. What did I do to make you shut me out like this?"

He turned away from her, answering in a low voice, "I can't be around anyone right now, Kel. Nashville brought back too many bad memories."

"But that's just it. They're memories." She took a few steps toward him. "You left that life behind, but that doesn't mean you're going to fall back into it. You've proven that you can beat it."

He stared at her, his eyes sad. "I wake up every morning feeling that hole inside me. And since Addy died, I'm afraid that it's growing. Work isn't making it disappear like it used to."

"Does it make it worse?"

He shook his head. "But it's still there. I can feel it."

"So what can I do to help you?" She moved her hand to his chest. "You're bigger than that hole inside you. Why are you so afraid of it now?"

He put his hand on hers. "You don't really know me. So why do you believe in me?"

"Because Grammy did."

SAM FINISHED HIS sandwich and took a swig of his soda. He'd been in Michigan for almost two years, and he still couldn't think of it as "pop." He stood and wiped his mouth with a napkin. On his way to the sofa he glanced out the window at Addy's house. He could spy Kelly through the window of Addy's bedroom. She was supposed to be cleaning out the closets, but it looked more like she was sitting on the bed and writing in her journal.

He hoped she wasn't writing about seeing his pumpkin boxers. He still smiled at the memory. Sure, he could laugh about it now, but it hadn't been so funny when it was happening.

Once lunch was over it was time to get back to work. If he kept up this pace, and with Kelly's help, he could finish the basement this week and start on the kitchen the following one. It was almost November and that meant he'd need to keep the momentum to complete the kitchen and living room in time for the upcoming holidays. He paused. Their first Thanksgiving and Christmas without Addy. What would that look like?

He left his place and crossed the driveway to enter Addy's by the side door. He hesitated at the top of the basement stairs. Maybe he should check in on Kelly? He walked down the hall and knocked on Addy's bedroom door before letting it swing wide open. "How's it going in here?"

Kelly stood up and tucked the journal under a pillow. "Oh, you know."

"I don't. That's why I asked."

She put her hand on a stack of clothes. "I figured I'd get Megs's opinion before I donate these. There might be something she wants, though I don't know why."

He pointed toward the pillow and hidden journal. "What were you working on?"

"Nothing." He stepped toward her then tried to reach under the pillow. She snatched the journal from him before he could get a grip on it. "These are my private thoughts. Sort of."

"They're sort of private or sort of your thoughts?"

She took a deep breath then released it slowly, as if she were trying to keep her cool. "Both." She clutched the journal to her chest. "Sometimes I get lines that come to mind that sound like a song, so I write them down." She brought out the journal and flipped open to a page, but she then shook her head and snapped the book shut. "It's nothing."

"Why don't you read some of it to me?"

"No, it's not good."

"How do you know unless you share it?"

"I'm not ready." She scowled at him, but he refused to back down.

He held his hand out for the journal. "I promise not to laugh."

"Or judge?" she asked.

"Definitely. Or judge." He continued to hold out his hand and eventually she gave him the slim volume. He opened the bright turquoise cover and started to read while she watched him, biting her thumb nail. She was right about it being lines that sounded like songs. He jumped to the last page she'd been writing on and froze.

He glanced up at her as she winced. "It was just this line that kept playing in my head."

He nodded. "How does it sound when you sing it?"

Her eyebrows furrowed, and she shrugged. "I don't know."

"Sure you do." He turned the journal toward her so that she could read it. "Sing this line."

"I can't sing."

"Yes, you can. You've been choosing not to.

That's a misuse of your talent." He dangled the journal in front of her. "Sing it to me."

She took a deep breath and hummed, then sang, "The hole inside is deep and wide but your love is even bigger." She shrugged again. "I don't know. That sounded stupid."

"It sounded like a song." He flipped through a few more pages. "I haven't heard much of your singing, but you've got a real talent for songwriting."

She took the book back from him and scanned what she'd written. "Do you really think so?"

"The words more than the tune." He watched her as the tips of her ears burned red. "Why didn't you tell me you were a songwriter?"

"Because I'm not." She tossed the book to him. "These are just ideas. There's nothing really here to make a song out of."

Did she really not see it? She had the start of an album full of songs, more than he'd ever been able to come up with on his own. With some hard work, some collaboration she could have a future. "It's a start though," he told her. "If you want, we could work together in the evening so that when you go back to Nashville, you'll have a strong calling card."

She frowned up at him. "But you hate the idea of me going back there."

"I do, but it's your decision."

She glanced at the book and smiled. "Hey, maybe we could even write one for the library benefit. The mayor asked me to sing, but maybe we could sing it together."

This time, he was the one to balk. "I don't perform anymore."

"Then that's a misuse of your talent."

AFTER DINNER, SAM and Kelly gathered at the dining room table. Kelly had her journal while Sam brought his guitar. Megs had the television on low in the living room so they could collaborate. Sam tuned the guitar as she paged through the journal. "Where do you want to start?"

"The hole song," he replied.

"No, I shouldn't have written that. It's too personal."

He stopped and looked at her. "Making it the perfect one to work on. Read me some of what you have."

"The hole inside is deep and wide but your

love is even bigger." She slapped the journal down on the table. "This sucks."

"First rule of songwriting, nothing sucks. It's raw material waiting to be edited and polished." He plucked a few of the strings, and she found herself humming along. He looked at her again and winked. "What else do you have about the hole?"

"It threatens to take over, but your love gives me the strength to hold on." She shook her head. "It's too long. And it pretty much repeats what I already wrote. And I like the first one better."

"We could keep that line as part of the chorus. How do you think this song should start?" He played around with chords on the guitar, giving her space to think. "What about something like the sunshine of your love found me in my pain?"

"Your hand in mine, we walked out of the rain." She made notes in the journal. It sounded cheesy right now instead of reflecting the redemption she'd been trying for. She wrote another line before glancing up at him. "I've been walking around acting like I knew what I was doing, but I was pretending, hoping you didn't see the hole inside. The hole I sleep with, eat with, work with. The hole that kept me from you."

He grinned. "I like that better. Has a darker edge to it. Sets us up for a bigger payoff."

She shifted the journal closer to him so that he could figure out the chords for the lines. He started and stopped several times, shaking his head, making his own notes in the journal.

Megs joined them. "How's the song coming?" she asked.

Sam sang the first lines. Megs nodded and skimmed the page of the journal. "I like it, but I'd change the sleep and eat part to past tense. Cause that part of his life is over, right?"

Kelly agreed and made the changes. "Thanks, Megs."

"No problem. Just make sure you guys give me credit when it becomes a big hit." Megs leaned against the counter. "Who would have figured the two of you fixing up this house and now writing a song together?"

"Your grandmother," Sam answered. He kept strumming, but said, "Why do you think she left the house to us both?"

Kelly wasn't so sure. "You think she was matchmaking?" He gave her a look. Kelly shrugged. "Okay, maybe she was trying to do that. But why would she do that?"

Megs smirked at them. "Because she loved the both of you so much, she thought you'd be perfect together." Her sister pushed off the counter. "I wouldn't rule out a relationship between you two, either. I've seen how good a team you are."

Sam seemed skeptical. He leaned in to Kelly and whispered, "She thinks we're a good team? That we might have a relationship together?"

Kelly and Sam laughed until Megs left the room.

DRIVING TO TOWN to get supplies to finish the basement, Ty's debut song came on the radio. Sam reached over and turned up the volume. Man, that kid had talent. He only hoped Ty wouldn't squander it or throw it away like Sam himself had.

He pulled the truck into the parking lot of the hardware store and found a spot that straddled the store and the bakery. He'd been working hard enough to deserve a treat from the Sweet sisters. If things hadn't been tense between him and Kelly before, their discussion about Addy's matchmaking had made things worse. Though Kelly pretended as if it was one big joke. Unfortunately, he didn't think it was funny.

The problem was that Sam couldn't stop thinking about Kelly. He worked with her on the house during the day, on their song at night, then dreamed of her when he lay in bed by himself. Maybe he'd skip the bakery. He saw a lot of her as it was whether awake or asleep.

He entered the hardware store and found what he needed, paid for his purchase, then walked to the truck and put the sander in the truck bed. Noting the back door of the bakery, he sighed and locked the truck before walking around to the front door of the Sweetheart.

Kelly was manning the register when he went inside, looking up at him, a smile on her face. "Welcome to the Sweetheart. Would you like to sample one of our tasty treats?"

"You say that to all the customers."

She laughed and held up a small white cup with a portion inside that smelled spicy. "Try this. I think you'll like it especially."

He took the cup from her, smelled the cake then used his fingers to take it out and pop it into his mouth. She watched him chew it until he swallowed and nodded. "It's good." He ate another piece.

"I figured you'd like it. It's pumpkin." He almost choked. She frowned and immediately started to pound him on the back. "Breathe," she told him.

Megs came out of the kitchen with a glass of water. "Here, drink." She grimaced. "So the pumpkin cake wasn't a good choice?"

Sam downed the glass of water. "No, it's good. Just a surprise." He gave Kelly what he hoped was a searing look even as her cheeks became pink. "But then anything you make is good."

"Well, the jury is out on that one so far." Megs stared at the empty bakery. "I've lost a few customers already."

Kelly put her arm around Megs's shoulders. "They'll be back when they realize that you make the best bread and pastries in the county."

Megs returned to the kitchen, seemingly unconvinced. It was mid-morning which could account for the empty bakery, but then Sam didn't know the ins and outs of the business. Kelly merely shrugged.

His phone buzzed, and he stepped away to answer it. "Hi, Dad."

"Junior. Did you hear the good news about Ty's album? Number three and still rising on the charts."

Sam could imagine the buttons popping off his dad's shirt. "That's great. I'm sure you must be proud."

"You should be, too. You discovered the kid, after all." There was a pause. "And it looks like you discovered that girl you brought home."

Sam stepped closer to the front window, but glanced over at Kelly. "What do you know about Kelly?"

"I offered her a contract." Another pause. "Didn't she tell you?"

Sam turned to stare at Kelly. "No, she didn't share that with me."

"Turned me down, too. Can you believe that?"

Sam watched her as she busily cleaned the display cases with a cloth. If she'd shot his dad down, that probably meant the offer had come with strings attached. "She must have her reasons, Dad."

"I want her to sign, Junior. I'm depending on you to ensure that."

Like he could force her? The woman had her own mind and will, something he'd learned the hard way. "I'll talk to her."

His dad chortled and said, "I knew I could count on you. Here's your mother."

Sam made small talk with his mom and promised to call later in the week, but his mind was on Kelly and the news he'd learned from his dad. Kelly hadn't breathed a word to him about a contract, and he was sure she would have if it had been a bona fide offer. He ended the call and put his phone away. When he strolled up to the display cases, Kelly stopped wiping. "How's your mom?"

He frowned. "You were listening in on my conversation?"

"You said you loved her and promised to call later. It's a mom thing." She reached over to a tray and slid it under his nose. "We have another sample for you to try as long as you promise not to choke."

He took the small white cup and sniffed at what looked like bread.

She rolled her eyes. "It's a peasant bread Megs is experimenting with."

He tossed the contents of the cup into his mouth and chewed, moaning appreciatively. "Good."

"Make sure you tell her before you leave." She pointed to the display cases. "And you should probably buy something rather than eating all of our samples."

He quickly pulled out his wallet. "Oh, right. I'll have a cinnamon roll and coffee to go."

She nodded and took the pink tissue paper to grasp the pastry and put it in a paper bag for him. She handed him an empty paper cup and pointed at the coffee station. "It's still a help-yourself kind of operation here. At least for now, although Megs is talking about getting an espresso machine."

Sam hadn't heard that, but he figured it made good business sense to have fancy drinks accompany the pastries. "The diner already has one of those machines. And I don't think they sell many of those designer coffees."

"Which is why Rick is giving her a great price to buy it off of him. They would sell better over here." Kelly rang up his purchase on the old-fashioned register, and he handed her a few bills. "Thank you for the business," she said, a warm smile lighting up her face.

He glanced around the bakery. "What time do you get out today?"

"Anxious to work with me this afternoon?" She put a hand to her chest. "I'm flattered. I didn't think my construction skills were all that great."

"We need to talk."

Her face paled, and she glanced behind her at the swinging doors. "We can't talk about it here?"

He shook his head. "I'll see you at the house later?"

"You won't even give me a clue what this is about?"

"Not here."

"Oh." She fiddled with her sleeve. "I'll be home about one. Is that soon enough?"

It would have to be.

A HOT FEELING in the pit of her belly increased as Kelly got closer to home. She still believed that no good conversation ever came after hearing that someone thought they needed to talk to you. She pulled into the driveway and parked next to Sam's truck. She turned off the engine and sat for a moment. Anything to distract from whatever discussion Sam had in mind.

No use putting this off any longer, she thought, and got out of the vehicle.

Guilt dogged her steps. She slowed walking up the stone driveway. Why should she feel like this? She hadn't done anything wrong. Feeling a little better, she strode confidently toward the side door, opened it and walked into the kitchen.

Boxes were stacked on the counters so that she and Megs could finally go through the kitchen cupboards and pack them before Sam started the renovations the following week. She couldn't imagine what she and her sister would do without a kitchen, but Megs promised they'd be okay even if they ate at the diner for the length of time it would take Sam to finish.

The kitchen was also empty of Sam. She paused, trying to hear the whine of a drill or the bang of a hammer coming up from the basement. Nothing. "Sam? You here?"

Maybe he'd changed his mind. Maybe he'd forgotten.

The side door swung open. Or maybe he'd

been at his apartment watching and waiting for her to arrive.

She faced him, and the ache in her belly worsened. "What do you have to say?" he asked without preamble.

He hustled past her, past the dining room table where they'd been writing their song together. In the living room he turned and opened his mouth, but then shook his head and sunk onto the sofa. She took a seat in the recliner across from him, folding her hands in her lap, waiting.

Finally, he said, "Why didn't you tell me about my dad's offer?"

That's what this was about? The contract Frank had tossed at her, hoping she'd betray his son? "I told him no. Didn't seem worth talking about."

"Why did you turn it down? He's handing you your dream on a platter and you refuse?" He stood and paced to the front window, then turned back toward her. "Explain it to me, please, because it doesn't sound like the woman I know who's desperate for this. For success."

She stood. "What doesn't make sense is that your dad would offer me a contract without ever hearing me sing a single note." She folded her arms across her chest. "I might be naïve, Sam. And I might not understand the ins and outs of the music business as well as I probably should. But even I know that no one gets something for nothing."

His expression softened a bit. "What did he ask from you?"

"Something I couldn't give." She eyed him, willing him not to ask. She didn't want to cause more problems between Sam and his dad. Didn't want to be another reason that he would avoid Nashville and his family.

He walked toward her and put his hands on her shoulders, facing her. "What did he ask for?"

Hot tears pricked at her eyes, she looked up at him. "Don't."

His fingers tightened, and he pulled her closer. "I won't be angry. Just tell me."

"No." The tears spilled down her cheeks. She couldn't do that to him. Couldn't tell him. "It doesn't matter."

"It does to me." He reached up and wiped her tears with his thumbs. "Please be honest with me."

She put her head down, unable to face him

and that imploring expression of his. If he wasn't so earnest, so determined to find out... She forced herself to raise her head. "I don't want to hurt you."

"You can't. He already did by offering what you want but making me a part of the deal."

Sam chuckled when her mouth dropped open, but his laugh lacked any warmth or humor. Had he known all along? "But I didn't tell you."

"I know my father and how he works." He let go of her and took a few steps back. "Let me guess. He would give you the contract if you brought me in on the project."

She nodded, hating how his eyes showed a flash of pain despite his previous bravado. She hated how she'd been partly responsible for putting it there. "I'm sorry."

"Don't apologize for him."

She put her hand on his arm. "Do you want to talk about it?"

"Nah." He took a deep breath and looked past her. "I think I'll go for a drive. Clear my head, you know?" He walked away, but then turned back. "Are you coming?"

For the second time, she hurried after him, pulling her jacket from the hook by the door.

SAM DROVE THEM AROUND for a while, eventually heading toward nearby Traverse City to a design showroom that he'd heard of. He thought that since they had a moment together, they could get some ideas for Addy's kitchen. He parked the truck then came around to help Kelly down to the pavement.

When they entered the store, Kelly gasped as she took in the sights. He pointed to the right, and they walked through the bathroom design section to get to the kitchens.

There were several mock kitchens set up to give a sense of the direction they could take. Kelly ran a hand along a shiny black granite countertop, but wrinkled her nose. "It's the in thing right now, but I don't like this one."

He nodded and led her toward what he'd been considering. The blue-gray soapstone counter had more character and cost about the same as granite. He'd been in a house in Nashville once that had it and remembered admiring it. "What do you think of this?"

She put her hand on the countertop and ran her fingers down it slowly, caressing. "I like how you can see the veins running through it. Gives it a natural look. This paired with a light colored cabinet would look amazing."

"Not white?"

She shuddered. "No, too stark. But a blond wood with glass doors? It would keep it warm and inviting." She glanced around and pointed to a type of drawer pulls. "We could use copper accents to keep things warm rather than cold."

"You have a real eye for color."

She shrugged. "Music and art were my favorite classes. Just don't ask what kind of grades I got in the rest."

"Not an A student?"

"That was Megs. She couldn't do anything wrong when we were growing up, and that included school."

He put his arm around her and led her to the bathroom fixtures. He stopped in front of a claw-foot tub. "What about this for the upstairs bath? It would give it a vintage feel."

She walked around the tub, trailing her fingers along the edge. "It would take up too much space and would make it look dated rather than a true rustic feel, not to mention crowded. I'd go with a glass shower enclosure with stone tiles. Maybe a soapstone countertop like the kitchen for the bath, and a green glass tile for an accent."

He liked her ideas. He knew there was a good reason he'd brought her in on the project. Maybe they did work well together...

SEVERAL DAYS LATER, Rick stopped by the bakery, bringing with him two tickets for the library fund-raiser and a sample program for the evening. He pointed to where Kelly's name was listed. "I wasn't sure what you were going to be singing so I left that part blank."

A flutter started in her belly. "Right. I haven't decided yet," she told him.

"Let me know if you need a piano or whatever. We'll make sure to have it set up for you." He looked past Kelly to the kitchen. "Is Megs here? I was hoping to discuss the dessert selections for the benefit."

"I'll go get her." Grateful for the chance to escape, she disappeared into the kitchen and pressed a hand against her chest.

He wanted her to sing, and she still didn't have her voice back. What had she been thinking when she agreed? She took a few deep breaths, then opened her eyes. "Megs, Rick needs to see you about the desserts for the fund-raiser."

She wiped her hands on a towel. She gestured toward the ovens. "Can you take those trays out when the timer goes off in about three minutes?"

Kelly nodded and walked to the work island and sat heavily on a stool. She glanced at the tickets and noted the date. Ten days left to find her voice. She tried to calm her breathing before she hyperventilated and passed out.

The timer went off, and thankful for the distraction, she took the cookie trays out of the ovens and put them on the cooling rack. She sniffed them. Lemon. She glanced behind her and took one of the cookies, but then dropped it, blowing on her fingers to prevent them from burning. Finally, she lifted the cookie to her mouth and took a tiny bite.

Her sister definitely knew how to bake.

The swinging doors opened, and Kelly grimaced. "I had to try one. Quality control, you know."

Megs laughed. "Call it what you want, I know what stealing one of my cookies looks like. Gina is going to stay on the floor if you want to give me a hand here."

"Instead of a hand, it'd be more like two left feet. I still have no clue what I'm doing."

"You know how to follow a recipe." She

pushed the open binder toward her. "Rick liked my suggestions for the desserts, but I need a couple more ideas for variety. Why don't you look through there and find something?"

Megs took her dirty bowls and utensils to the sink and plunged them into the soapy water. When she returned, Kelly knew she had something on her mind. "What?" she asked.

Megs shrugged. "Just thinking. Have you decided what to sing for the benefit?"

"No," she replied, and kept her gaze on the recipe binder. "But I'm sure I'll think of something."

"Have you been able to sing yet?"

Kelly pushed the binder at Megs. "This one looks good. It has lots of chocolate, so it's gotta be good, right?"

Megs narrowed her eyes. "You don't have your voice back? And you didn't tell Rick that either, did you?"

"What was I going to say? Grammy died and took my voice with her? It sounds crazy, even if it is true."

"What's crazy is that it isn't true. You still have your voice," Megs insisted.

"I've tried, Megs. I really have. But it comes out strained and forced." Kelly stood and paced. "You're right. I should have told him that I can't sing. Maybe he still has time to find someone else."

Kelly reached into her pocket to get her cell phone, but Megs stayed her arm. "You can't back out. And you can sing. You're choosing not to."

"That's ridiculous. Why would I do that?"

Megs took the cell phone from her and put it on the counter. "Because Grammy isn't here anymore to make you."

That was a joke, but Kelly didn't feel like laughing. "Make me as in force me? She didn't do that. I chose to because I love to sing."

"So choose now."

If only it were that easy. As if only the wanting of something could make it happen. She opened her mouth, but couldn't find the words at first. She stared at the floor, refusing to watch Megs's reaction. "I can't sing because without Grammy, it doesn't seem right." She let the tears seep from the corners of her eyes. "I can't sing because she's not around to hear it."

Megs ran to her and her sister put her arms around her. Megs rested her head on her shoulder and said, "She can still hear you, Little. I know she can."

CHAPTER THIRTEEN

LOOKING GOOD. SAM surveyed the basement with more than a little satisfaction. The floor joists had been reinforced. He'd finished the walls and updated the plumbing for the laundry area. The furnace and hot water tank had been replaced, and as soon as Kelly made a choice on the carpet color, he would lay that as well.

On to the kitchen.

His phone beeped, and he glanced at it before he finished packing up his tools. His dad. Great. The last person he wanted to talk to.

Call me. Fat chance.

He put his cell phone back in his jeans pocket and walked up the stairs, closing the door on the basement. One job done. Only about a dozen more to go to get the house ready to put on the market.

He walked through the kitchen and noticed the Sweet sisters had been busy packing things up. Good. It would make his job easier the more they could pack and get out of the way of his sledgehammer.

He put a hand on the oak cabinets. They looked good on the outside, but they were worn and sagging inside from years of use and heavy china. And they didn't serve the floor plan he and Kelly had finally agreed on. He opened one and put his hand on the smooth wood. Shame to lose such workmanship. Unless he could repurpose them in another way.

He removed his phone from his pocket and took several pictures. Maybe he could salvage the doors. They were solid and could still fit into the overall design. Or he could repurpose them in the bathrooms or elsewhere. Even another project later on down the road. He'd have to remove and store them carefully, but it could work. The fact that it also saved them some money didn't hurt, either.

He took the last picture as another text came through. I have a proposal for you.

Sam was sure he did. If he didn't call his dad, he wouldn't stop with these relentless texts. He pressed his dad's name on his contacts list.

"Junior, I knew that would get your attention."

Sam rolled his eyes, knowing his dad wouldn't see it, but still he felt justified anyway. "I'm in the middle of a renovation job. What do you want?"

"I want you and that Kelly girl to sign a contract with me. What do I have to do to get that?"

Yep, relentless. The truth was that there was nothing his dad could offer that would get him to sign a deal with the devil. Never again. "It's not going to happen. Accept that and move on."

"I can tell you care for her. Wouldn't you like to be the one who hands her her dream? To take her talent and nurture her into the superstar she could be?"

Sam laughed though it wasn't funny. "You've never heard her sing. How do you know she's got talent?"

His dad cleared his throat. "Actually, she auditioned for my label about two years ago. Shortly after you disappeared, she came in and recorded backup vocals for one of my albums. I knew her name sounded familiar, so I went into the archives and found the tape.

She's got the voice of an angel, Junior. And I know talent when I hear it."

"So why didn't you offer her a contract then?" Sam sighed and rubbed the back of his neck. "It's because of her relationship with me that you're interested all of a sudden. You think you can get me by using her."

"That's merely a bonus. I'll send you a clip of her audition. You'll see. And then you'll take my offer, and we'll all win."

Everyone but me. "I'm never going back to your label, Dad. Ever."

His dad chuckled. "Never say never, Junior." And then he was gone.

Sam waited for the text to come. Sure enough, his dad hadn't waited to send him the audition clip. It wouldn't change Sam's mind, but it wouldn't hurt to listen to it. Addy had been convinced that Kelly was one audition away from being a star. Time to see if she'd been right.

He pressed play, and a producer identified Kelly and asked her to sing a portion of a song. Sam steeled himself. He wouldn't let her voice get to him. Wouldn't let it drag him back to Nashville.

When the clip ended, he played it one more

time, closing his eyes to fully experience the rich melody.

His dad had said never say never. And damn, if he hadn't been right.

KELLY FLIPPED THE bakery's sign to Closed and locked the front door. She liked this time of day, when Megs and the other employees had gone home already and it was just her and Grammy's ghost.

Kelly twisted the knob on the radio to raise the volume to a wall shaking level and pulled out the broom from the cleaning supply closet. The song ended, and another started. Her latest favorite with a fast beat and a sultry singer. She wiggled her hips as she pushed the broom around the room, pausing every once in a while to use the long handle as her microphone. She let the song take over, using her body and voice to pay homage to it. The song ended, and she heard applause.

Sam watched her from the open swinging doors to the kitchen. Kelly blushed, but took a bow. "Thank you. I'll be at the Sweetheart all week."

"You got your voice back."

She shrugged. Maybe she had. It had been

fun to sing along with the radio with no expectations. It felt good and natural. But that didn't mean anything.

He grinned and came toward her. "Megs said I'd find you here."

"It's my afternoon to close. What's up?" Kelly returned to her sweeping, moving the chairs away from the tables to get the crumbs and debris underneath. When Sam didn't say anything, she paused from her task and looked up. "Something wrong?"

"I'm going to ask you a question, and I want you to be completely honest with me." He was clearly trying to appear casual, but the tense line of his shoulders told her he was faking it. "How much do you want a singing career?"

She tilted her head to one side. "What kind of question is that? You already know the answer."

He held up his hand. "Okay. What are you willing to do to get it?"

A month ago, she wouldn't have had to think about it. She would have jumped at saying whatever she had to. But now? Confusion clouded her thoughts, and she didn't know what to say to him. She loved to sing and hoped for a career, but she no longer had the single-minded ambition to pursue it. She'd found family and friends when she'd returned to Lake Mildred, and they had added to her life, bringing balance.

If she returned to Nashville, she'd be alone again. And she didn't think she could go back to that. She watched him, curious.

He took a few more steps, and she put the broom in front of her, protecting her from him. He stopped and stared at her. "I need to know if it's something you really want."

"Why?"

He took a deep breath and paused before he replied. She could see the conflict of emotions running over his face like pixels on a computer screen. Together they only added to the confusion she already felt. He pulled out a folded piece of paper from his back pocket and handed it to her. She opened it and read the first few words, stopped and glanced up at him. "I don't understand."

"It's a contract for your first album on my dad's label and produced by me. But only if you really want it."

"You can't go back to Nashville. It will kill you."

He reached out and touched her cheek. "Someone told me I was stronger than the demons. And if this is what you really want, maybe we could do it together. We're partners, after all."

He stood before her, offering her everything she had ever wanted. So why did she hesitate? Why wasn't she jumping at this chance and moving forward? "I, I don't know."

"Not the answer I was expecting."

And not the answer she'd meant to give.

SAM DROVE AWAY from the bakery, tempted to turn back and find out what was really happening with Kelly. She didn't seem like the same confident and independent woman who had blown into town for her grandmother's funeral. Nor was she really the unsure wanderer he'd just left.

He pulled out his cell phone and called his dad. "I guess it's a no go with Kelly. She's not on board with the album yet."

"You listened to the clip then."

Yes, he'd listened to it seven times to be sure that he could willingly return to Nashville to help her career. And with each listen, he'd become more convinced that Addy had been right about Kelly. She was destined for great things with that voice. "I'll talk to her some more. She's too good to let this go."

"We finally agree on something, Junior."

Sam tightened his grip on the steering wheel. "But if I get her to sign with you, I'm the one in charge of her album. Otherwise, we both walk."

A moment of silence passed. "I wouldn't expect less from you."

"Good."

He could hear the smile in his dad's voice. "Great."

KELLY ARRIVED BACK at the farmhouse and hung her coat up on the hook by the side door. She walked through the kitchen and saw Megs standing on a step stool, reaching for the large platters Grammy had used for holidays. Kelly rushed forward and put her hands on her sister's legs to keep her steady. "Why are you doing this when I'm not here?"

"You're late, and this needs to get done." Megs handed the turkey platter to her and pointed to a box on the counter. "I've been packing this stuff in that one."

Kelly wrapped the platter in old newspaper before placing it gently in the box, then walked back and took another dish from her sister. "How many of these does she have?"

"Too many. That's why I'm donating most of them."

Kelly glanced down at the one in her hands. "How are you going to decide which ones to keep? They look the same."

"If you see one you like, put it aside." Megs waited as Kelly put the last one carefully into the box. "And we haven't even gotten to the fancy china cabinet."

Kelly groaned and leaned on the counter. "Sam said he'll start in here tomorrow. We've got to get this stuff packed up."

Megs came down from the step stool and nodded, scanning the kitchen. "It will be done, even if we have to work late tonight." She grabbed an empty box. "I thought I'd work on the coffee mug cupboard next."

Kelly debated telling her sister about Sam's offer. Megs wouldn't be happy, but then maybe she would. "I got offered a recording contract," Kelly told her.

Megs stopped wrapping a Michigan State mug and turned toward Kelly to stare, open-mouthed. "You've been home ten minutes and this is the first you've mentioned it? When? How?"

Kelly shrugged and stood next to Megs and wrapped a Snoopy mug before putting it in the box with the others. "Sam's dad runs Jesse James Records, and he gave the offer to Sam to give to me."

"That's great news. When do you leave for Nashville?"

Maybe she'd made the wrong choice. Maybe she could call Sam and tell him she'd changed her mind. And maybe she was a fool for thinking that it could really happen for her without hurting him in the process. "I'm not leaving. I didn't take it."

Megs took a deep breath and closed her eyes. She put her fingers on the bridge of her nose. "Please explain this to me. You just got offered your dream, and you said no?"

"It was my dream."

"Was?"

The packing forgotten, Kelly continued. "I need to make sure it's right for me now. I don't know about doing this when you're in the middle of taking over the bakery, and Sam and I are neck deep in fixing up the house. And then...I don't want to leave you or Sam."

"Aren't they paying you enough money for it?"

More than enough. She nodded and sighed at the thought of being able to pay off all her debts at once. "It's a good offer."

"Then tell them yes."

"It's bad timing. Maybe Mr. Etchason would wait six months for us to get everything finished here. Then I could go. I still want to be a singer."

Megs pursed her mouth and resumed wrapping the mugs and packing them in the box.

Kelly couldn't understand her sister. "Why are you upset? I figured you'd be happy I'm not ready to leave here. That's what you want, right?"

Megs put her arms on either side of the counter so that she blocked Kelly's retreat. "But what do you want?" her sister pressed.

"You know what I want. A singing career." But she couldn't look Megs in the eye. It's all Kelly had dreamed about for so long, but now that it was within her grasp she found that she wanted something else. Something more.

"No, Grammy wanted you to be a singer," Megs said.

"She supported my dream."

"But who gave it to you?"

This talk was making her head ache. "Megs. Stop."

Megs took a hold of Kelly's arm. "I loved Grammy, and I miss her every day, but she was no saint. She was a strong woman who often pushed her own dreams onto other people."

Kelly shook her head, but Megs insisted, saying, "When Daddy died, her dream of keeping the bakery in the family got transferred to me. She never asked if I wanted it or liked it. But she groomed me to take over since I was twelve." Megs released Kelly. "What preteen do you know that dreams of running a bakery?"

"You're wrong."

"Am I? Then why are you shaking? Because you know I'm right."

Megs had to be wrong. Because the woman Kelly loved wouldn't do that, right? "I always loved to sing."

Megs offered a weak smile. "Yes, I don't deny that. But Grammy wanted you to be a famous country singer. She dreamed of hearing you on the radio on her favorite music station. She talked about Nashville so much, what choice did you have, but to go?"

Kelly bit her lip. Had she been living her life according to Grammy's dreams and not her own? "You shouldn't say this."

"How many times did you call begging to come back home, Kel? And how many times did she tell you that you had to stay and keep at it?"

At least a dozen times in almost as many years. Kelly touched her forehead and wondered what might have happened if she'd come home when she'd wanted to? She opened her eyes and looked up at Megs. "So what do I do? Stop dreaming?"

Her sister threw her arms around Kelly's neck and hugged her tight. "No. Don't ever stop. But find your own dream. Maybe that's why you haven't been able to sing since she died. You need to find your own voice." Megs squeezed even tighter. "What do you want to do, Little?"

That was the question, wasn't it?

CHAPTER FOURTEEN

THE NIGHT OF the benefit arrived. Kelly and Megs carted boxes and trays of desserts from the bakery to the Veterans of Foreign Wars hall most of the day. The room had been changed from plain to regal with gold table runners and centerpieces that featured a red rose with a glowing white candle. The wooden folding chairs had been draped with white linen covers held in place with gold trimmed red velvet ribbon. They had even placed a red carpet at the entrance to the hall.

Kelly sighed as she put the box of pastries on one of the large banquet tables. She glanced at her sister, who seemed awestruck. "It's so elegant, isn't it? And I have to sing at this thing." Kelly shuddered and rubbed her arms.

"Have you decided what you're singing?" Megs asked.

"Not yet, and I also don't know what I'm

wearing. And after seeing this place all decked out, I don't think I have anything that will work."

"Grammy had some cocktail dresses."

Kelly wrinkled her nose. No offense to Grammy, but she didn't want to wear an old lady dress. Back in Nashville, she had had a simple black dress with sequins that might have been all right. She'd never thought she might need it here though. And after being packed in a box for so long, it would need to be dry-cleaned, but she was out of time. "I'll figure something out."

"There's my closet, but I don't have anything quite as fancy. Maybe a few old bridesmaid dresses." Megs headed toward the exit. "Come on. We have a couple more boxes."

Kelly took her time walking out of the hall. What had she gotten herself into?

SAM QUIT USING the drill and glanced down at his cell phone. A text from Kelly read, 911. What do I sing tonight?

He paused, his fingers poised over his cell phone. What did she expect from him? He wasn't her manager or agent. Though if he could convince her, he'd be her producer.

Stick to something simple and classic. Over the Rainbow?

Not bad but overdone. Any other ideas?

He had several, but the one that would scare her the most kept turning in his mind. It would be a risk, but it could pay off. Our song.

She didn't reply right away, and there were no messages telling him that she was typing. He waited. Well, he'd tried.

Fine. But we do it together.

Now he was the one to be scared. Could he do it? Sing and play his guitar in front of an audience again? He expected the familiar itch and thirst to begin. He swallowed, but felt nothing. Maybe it was time to face those demons head on.

Deal.

KELLY STOOD TO the side of the stage, pressing her hand against her belly. Breathe in. Breathe out. Remember the lyrics. Think of the audience in their underwear. Though the elegant clothes they wore would make that difficult.

Dinner had been served, and dessert would follow. She glanced out at the crowd and noticed Megs bent in close to Rick's wife, Lizzie, laughing at something Lizzie had said. Kelly looked around some more, but couldn't find Sam. He'd said he'd be there, but what if he'd changed his mind? Wouldn't be the first time she'd have to sing a capella when the pianist didn't show for an audition.

Breathe in. Breathe out.

"Relax, Kelly. You'll be great."

Her eyes snapped open and she peered up at Sam. He wore a dark grey suit that brought out the gray-green of his eyes. She whistled. "You clean up good."

He eyed Kelly's black dress with white piping that Megs had dug out of her closet, and nodded. "You do, too," he said.

Sam touched one curl that had escaped her top knot and cascaded down her cheek. "You're beautiful."

She licked her lips and took a deep breath. "Are you sure about this?" she asked.

"As much as anything else. Aren't you?"

"No." She clutched at her stomach. "The song isn't ready. We're not ready."

"We've been writing and singing it for almost two weeks. It's as ready as it'll ever be." Sam chuckled. "This is a case of stage fright. You're fine."

"I know what stage fright is. Singing at my grandmother's funeral is stage fright. But this is a whole new level, debuting our song."

She turned away from him as Rick took the stage and tapped on the microphone. Someone flipped on the stage lights. "Ladies and gentlemen, I'd like to thank you all for coming out this evening for the library fundraiser. Due to your generous efforts, we've already raised over twenty thousand dollars to upgrade the computer system."

There was applause and Rick smiled. "Before we bring out the desserts supplied by the Sweetheart, I'd like to introduce local favorite Kelly Sweet who will be singing for us." He covered the microphone and asked her, "What are you singing?"

"It's an original song. And Sam is here, too."

Rick's eyebrows went up, but he nodded. "She says she's singing an original song with Sam Etchason. Kelly and Sam?"

Some polite applause followed as they took the stage. Kelly looked out at the audience and concentrated on Megs who was giving her a thumbs up. Kelly waited as someone brought a stool for Sam and a second microphone. She did a sweep of her eyes across the room, then smiled. "Sam and I wrote a song that we hope you'll enjoy. It's called 'The Hole Inside.'"

She glanced at Sam and he began to strum on the guitar. The crowd had gone silent. Softly, she sang, "I've been walking around acting like I knew what I was doing, but I was pretending, hoping you didn't see the hole inside. The hole I slept with, ate with, worked with. The hole that kept me from you."

Sam joined in with her as the lyrics talked about a love that could redeem the darkest night, the bleakest soul. Their voices blended, telling of their pain and their hope of redemption. "The hole inside is deep and wide, but your love is even bigger. Help me to hold on to you when the demons want me to let go. Love me always, leave me never. Fill me and make me whole."

Kelly shut her eyes and let the words take over. Let the beat of the song take over her own heartbeat. Gave herself completely to the music and held her arms out. While she sang with Sam, she felt whole. As if everything that had happened had brought her to this moment, to share it with him. They repeated the chorus, and she lifted her face to the ceiling as the song ended.

Silence. She opened her eyes and looked at Sam who gave her a smile. So what if the crowd hadn't liked the song? It meant the world to her and the man seated next to her. It spoke of the pain they'd faced and the love they sought. She didn't need applause and cheers for that. She reached out her hand, and he took it in his, raising it to his mouth to kiss it.

Then out of the corner of her eye, she saw Megs stand and start to clap, tears streaming down her face. Her sister cupped her hands around her mouth and gave a loud cheer as more and more people applauded. Sam gestured to her. She stepped underneath his arm as he stood, and they bowed to the audience amid the enthusiastic cheers.

"Encore."

Kelly smiled at Sam, and he started to play, "Over the Rainbow."

AFTER EVERYONE HAD their dessert and coffee, people he'd never met before came up to compliment Sam on his singing. He could have told them he'd once been Frank Junior with a number one hit on the country music charts, but the song he'd written with Kelly had more meaning than any of that. She walked up to him, her eyes bright and shining.

Putting her hand in the crook of his elbow, she pulled him to the side of the stage.

Away from prying eyes, Kelly held his face and kissed him soundly on the mouth. He wanted to reciprocate, but needed answers first. "What's that for?" he asked. She tried to kiss him again, but he kept her at arm's length. "Talk first."

"That was incredible, wasn't it?" She glowed even in the shadows of the room. "I've never felt like when I've performed before."

"You were amazing."

"You mean *we* were." She beamed at him and glanced at his mouth. "You're right. We do need to talk." Her smile quickly faded, and her light dimmed slightly. "I can't sign that recording contract."

Was she kidding? They've just given the

performance of their lives and she was stopping her future, theirs together? It didn't make sense. "But it's what you've always wanted, Kel. What about your goal to have a deal before you're thirty?"

"It's enough for now that I got offered one. But I can't let you go back into that world right now. And I can't do any of this without you."

He shook his head and put his hand on her shoulder. "No. Listen to me. You're taking that contract because you have a voice that needs to be heard. I'll be fine."

"No, you won't. And I won't be responsible for you losing your soul."

He stared at her. Why would she ditch her dream for him? "Kel, you don't understand. You need to do this like you need to breathe air or drink water. It's a part of who you are. Why would you give that up?"

"Because you're more important to me than any silly album." She slipped her arms around his waist and pulled him toward her. "You asked me before what I want. I've finally figured it out. I want you." When he didn't say anything, she looked down. "I won't ask you to do something that would hurt you and in the end destroy us both. I still want a music career, but I want you more."

He sighed and glanced up at the ceiling. "Why did I have to fall in love with such a stubborn woman?"

A smile instantly played at the corners of her kissable mouth. "Really? You mean that?" she asked.

"The stubborn part? Definitely." He reached out and pushed a strand of hair from her forehead. "And I do love you, my sweet Kelly Sweet."

She gasped and tears shone in her eyes. "I'll tell you something else I want."

He kissed the tip of her nose. "For you, anything."

"I want to finish the renovation of Grammy's house before we make any other decisions. I've had more fun picking out tiles and paint chips than I thought possible. There will be time for our music career later."

"You do have an eye for color which I lack. And I have the muscles you don't." He smiled at her. "Together, we make a pretty perfect pair."

"Agreed." She reached up on tiptoe and kissed him thoroughly. He threaded his hands through her hair and brought her closer to him.

Someone cleared their throat behind them, and he and Kelly broke apart to find Megs watching them. "People are asking if you two can come back up and sing one more song."

Sam glanced down at Kelly. "What do you think?"

"We do make beautiful music together, Pumpkin."

* * * * *

LARGER-PRINT BOOKS!

GET 2 FREE
LARGER-PRINT NOVELS
PLUS 2 FREE
MYSTERY GIFTS

Love Inspired®

Larger-print novels are now available...

YES! Please send me 2 FREE LARGER-PRINT Love Inspired® novels and my 2 FREE mystery gifts (gifts are worth about $10). After receiving them, if I don't wish to receive any more books, I can return the shipping statement marked "cancel." If I don't cancel, I will receive 6 brand-new novels every month and be billed just $5.49 per book in the U.S. or $5.99 per book in Canada. That's a savings of at least 19% off the cover price. It's quite a bargain! Shipping and handling is just 50¢ per book in the U.S. and 75¢ per book in Canada.* I understand that accepting the 2 free books and gifts places me under no obligation to buy anything. I can always return a shipment and cancel at any time. Even if I never buy another book, the two free books and gifts are mine to keep forever.

122/322 IDN GH6D

Name _____ (PLEASE PRINT) _____

Address _____ Apt. #

City _____ State/Prov. _____ Zip/Postal Code

Signature (if under 18, a parent or guardian must sign)

Mail to the **Reader Service:**
IN U.S.A.: P.O. Box 1867, Buffalo, NY 14240-1867
IN CANADA: P.O. Box 609, Fort Erie, Ontario L2A 5X3

Are you a current subscriber to Love Inspired® books
and want to receive the larger-print edition?
Call 1-800-873-8635 or visit www.ReaderService.com.

* Terms and prices subject to change without notice. Prices do not include applicable taxes. Sales tax applicable in N.Y. Canadian residents will be charged applicable taxes. Offer not valid in Quebec. This offer is limited to one order per household. Not valid to current subscribers to Love Inspired Larger-Print books. All orders subject to credit approval. Credit or debit balances in a customer's account(s) may be offset by any other outstanding balance owed by or to the customer. Please allow 4 to 6 weeks for delivery. Offer available while quantities last.

Your Privacy—The Reader Service is committed to protecting your privacy. Our Privacy Policy is available online at www.ReaderService.com or upon request from the Reader Service.

We make a portion of our mailing list available to reputable third parties that offer products we believe may interest you. If you prefer that we not exchange your name with third parties, or if you wish to clarify or modify your communication preferences, please visit us at www.ReaderService.com/consumerschoice or write to us at Reader Service Preference Service, P.O. Box 9062, Buffalo, NY. 14240-9062. Include your complete name and address.

LILP15

READERSERVICE.COM

Manage your account online!

- Review your order history
- Manage your payments
- Update your address

*We've designed the
Reader Service website
just for you.*

Enjoy all the features!

- Discover new series available to you, and read excerpts from any series.
- Respond to mailings and special monthly offers.
- Connect with favorite authors at the blog.
- Browse the Bonus Bucks catalog and online-only exculsives.
- Share your feedback.

Visit us at:

ReaderService.com